Storm Front

Linda Kay Silva

Publishing
Company

San Diego, California

This is a work of fiction. Any similarity between characters and people, dead or alive, is a coincidence.

Cover Design by Hummingbird Graphics
Book Design and Typesetting by Paradigm Publishing
Copy Editing by Brenda Hines

Printed in the United States on acid-free paper
First Edition

Library of Congress Catalog Card Number: 94-69817
ISBN 1-882587-07-3

Other Books by
Linda Kay Silva

Taken by Storm
Storm Shelter
Weathering the Storm
Tory's Tuesday

Dedication

To all of you who have let Delta, Megan, and Connie into your lives. Without you, they would still be roaming around my attic driving me crazy. They exist because of you, and I hope they've touched you as deeply as they touch me.

Special Thoughts for My Non

You and Papa taught me to be strong, to never give up, and not to be afraid to rock any boat. My feminist ideals are firmly rooted in your history. I love you so very much.

Special Thanks To

Ali—for being my rock, my joy, and my friend. You make my life a better place to be. Thank you, my love, for your incredible support of my work, my eccentricities, and that twelve-year-old boy.

Gina—for knowing me so well, for always laughing with me, and for being my very best friend in the world. Love you, love your show...hoot, hoot, hoot, hoot!

Chloé—for coming back. When your dream comes true, I'll be there to share it just like you did for me.

Ginny—your enthusiasm and laughter light up the world. Let's ride the wind forever.

Chrissy—Twenty years later and we're still playing! You're the best lethal enforcer I know!

Jackie, Carol, Kathi, Ginger—for your contributions to the gay and lesbian community.

Katherine Forrest—for paving the way and being supportive of other writers. You're a class act.

1

The only sound she heard was her leather jumpsuit creaking like a horse's saddle as she hoisted herself up through the second-story window. Leather in motion made a distinct sound that Taylor had loved ever since she was a little girl. She especially enjoyed it when she was wearing this particular outfit. The pitch, the perfect groan the suit made as she squatted on the window sill was exhilarating.

Jumping through the open window and landing nimbly on the balls of her feet, Taylor slowly rose and waited for her eyes to adjust to the darkness of the room.

"Perfect," she murmured, checking her black digital watch with the backlight button. "Right on time."

Swiftly moving through the darkened house, Taylor's mind reeled in and absorbed all the necessary information that would aid in her escape in the unfortunate event the owners arrived home earlier than anticipated. She located three bedrooms upstairs; the last of which was the master bedroom—her ultimate destination. The staircase wound down to the entry hall, and Taylor could only envision the staircase kissing a beautiful marble floor leading to the two huge oak front doors.

Stepping lightly down the hall, Taylor stopped suddenly when she saw movement. She sighed with relief when she realized it was simply her reflection in a floor-to-ceiling mirror. Fully facing the mirror, Taylor smiled. Even in the darkness, she was impressed with the way her black leather jumpsuit glistened like a black cat in the moonlight. She called the suit Emma, after the first real feminist on television; Mrs. Emma Peele of *The Avengers*. Oh, how she, and other young lesbians, had fallen in love with the venerable Mrs.

Peele. How courageous Emma Peele had always been; she was brave and strong, and so very sexy in that black leather jumpsuit. She was exactly what a young Taylor had aspired to be; tough, smart, physically able to protect herself. Emma Peele had been Taylor's first crush, and had remained the epitome of a heroine until another woman leapt from the pages of the media and stole Taylor's heart. And though she knew she'd never have the chance to meet Mrs. Peele, she was sure she'd meet the woman great enough to unseat her fifteen-year crush; but then, it was easy to be sure when she had planned it that way.

Turning from the mirror, Taylor opened the door to the master bedroom. Judging by the shadows and murky images, she could tell this was a spectacular room. After all, she'd seen enough dark rooms to be able to distinguish quality decor from the obviously mundane. Ten years in the business had dramatically sharpened her night vision. If the moon was out, and she tried really hard, she could even distinguish colors. Some nights, when she was bored or just wanting to kill some time, she'd guess colors or patterns before pressing the backlight button on her watch to see if she had been right. Tonight, however, was not one of those nights. No, tonight served a more important purpose.

Tonight, she had a score unlike any she'd ever attempted. Tonight, she was under a very strict time-line. She had to get in, get the prize, and get out before starting the next phase of her plan. And timing was everything. Since she'd orchestrated this for quite some time, Taylor couldn't allow any distractions to prevent her from reaching her goal.

Entering the bedroom, Taylor snuck over to the large chest of drawers protruding from the far wall. Even in the night, she could make out the large jewelry box perched on the corner of the chest. Pulling her black gloves taut, Taylor carefully opened the jewelry box. It was one of those three-tiered monstrosities that her grandmother used to hold her gaudy costume jewelry. Clamping her penlight between her teeth, Taylor lifted the earring holder out and stared down at the collection of rings and pendants sparkling up at her. "Jackpot," she said, grinning. Inside, perched in neat little rows, sat a pear-shaped emerald, an opal, a three-pearled ring, a sapphire with two diamonds, and a large, square ruby, obviously a replica to her trained eye. At another time, Taylor would have cleaned out the contents of the entire jewelry box, but not tonight. Tonight, she had to race against the falling grains of sand in order to set her plan in motion. Tonight, she needed that diamond ring, only it didn't seem to be occupying a space in the box.

"Damn it."

Stepping across the room, careful to avoid the windows, she made her way to the night stand. It was free of any jewels.

"Where'd she put it?" Taylor mumbled as she pushed the silver button on her watch. She was thirty seconds behind schedule. If she lost any more time, she'd have to scratch this house and start all over again.

Moving around the bed, Taylor stepped into the bathroom and felt around for a towel. When her hand landed on one, she tucked it in the curtain rod before turning her tiny penlight on. During her childhood, she'd grown up with more guys who got caught because they couldn't understand that a flashlight in a dark house was like a lighthouse on a cliff; both warned people there was something dangerous ahead. Taylor swore to herself when her best friend was captured and incarcerated for five years that she would never be caught because of stupidity. If she were ever to be arrested, it would have to be by someone with detecting abilities better than her thieving talents. Besides, her claustrophobia guaranteed that she would die in prison, so she vowed to herself long ago that she would rather die in an escape attempt than to spend even a minute behind bars.

Thus far, she had kept that promise.

Double checking the towel on the window, Taylor quickly shined her penlight around the bathroom. When a flash sparkled in her eye, she flicked the light off. Squatting down so her eyes were level to the jewel, Taylor cupped her hand over the penlight and shined it directly at the ring.

Yep.

There it was, sitting next to the soap dispenser. Taylor nearly laughed out loud. People were so predictable, it was scary. Threading the towel back through the towel ring, Taylor reached over and carefully plucked the ring from the sink.

"Come to mama," she whispered, feeling the adrenaline surge through her. Oh, how she loved the taste of victory. After all these years, the thrill, the edge of excitement hadn't dulled. This was her truest high, her vertical orgasm. This was better than anything tactile she had ever encountered. Taking what didn't belong to her was the greatest joy. Nothing she'd ever done had matched the heart-pounding, nerve-wracking stimulation of sneaking around in someone else's house and snatching precious items the owners didn't care enough to adequately protect. This was success, and Taylor was successful because she was so very good at it.

Holding the ring in her left hand and the penlight in her right, Taylor checked her watch before opening the closet door, stepping in, and closing it behind her. Then, she reached into the leather pouch specially sewn into Emma and pulled out a jeweler's loop. Carefully examining the 1.5 carat diamond, Taylor grinned. She'd inspected enough diamonds in her career to know an exquisite cut when she saw one, and this one was a beaut. Assured now that she hadn't stolen a cubic zirconia, Taylor dropped the ring into a different pouch and zipped it closed.

Looking once again at her watch, she made her way out of the closet and back to the window she'd entered. She was slightly behind schedule, but she saw no problem with that. She had the ring and a few minutes leeway to insure the success of her plan.

As Taylor climbed back out the window, she grabbed a rope and quickly rappelled down the side of the house; this was another vital skill she'd learned from her brother and best friend over a lifetime ago. They had taught her that, given a suitable length of rope, Taylor could escape from anywhere, and that's precisely how she wanted it. Her claustrophobia appeared when she was five years old. She had been trapped in a well for nearly two days. Since then, Taylor preferred height to depth, and always made sure she had a rope.

As her feet hit the ground, Taylor gave a quick, sharp yank on the rope, and it fell like a bird shot from a tree. After she'd secured it in Emma, she stood with her hands on her hips and studied the large, colonial-style house. She wondered what it was about colonial architecture that so fascinated Americans. Nothing she'd ever seen in America could outdo incredible Victorian architecture. Ah well, Americans were still trying to prove their independence, weren't they?

Walking around to the front of the house, Taylor searched the ground for a large rock and hefted it in her hands. Looking down at the rock, she grinned slightly before tossing it through the large plate glass window overlooking the front yard. As the window smashed into thousands of shards of glass, an obnoxious alarm began clanging through the night air.

Glancing at her watch one last time, Taylor's grin turned into a smile. Maybe there would still be time to catch another rerun of *The Avengers*.

2

Gina set a steaming cup of coffee in front of Delta before sitting down next to her. "Didn't sleep well last night?"

Delta shrugged, averting her eyes from Gina's penetrating blue eyes.

"You don't need to answer me, Delta Stevens, because I know you well enough to know that missing Megan isn't getting any easier."

Wrapping her hands around the mug, Delta took in the warmth. Since Megan had traveled to Costa Rica for a semester, Delta had found it nearly impossible to stay warm. It wasn't that this California winter was harsh; the chill came from within. It was the kind of cold that sprang from loneliness that distance causes. Like an ice-blanket, she wore her loneliness every night and spent most of the morning trying to shake off the cold.

On the night after Megan left, nearly two months ago, Delta put a second down comforter on her bed. Every night since then, she has worn her flannel pajamas to bed. Night after night, she would lay in bed wondering what Megan was doing or thinking or feeling. Delta questioned if Megan was experiencing the same hollowness she'd been living with since Megan's plane took off. Did Megan wake up at night, like Delta did, and reach for her, only to grasp the emptiness? Delta wondered.

When she wasn't wondering about Megan, Delta worked as many overtime hours as she could just so she would drop when her head finally hit the pillow.

Delta sighed and stared down into her distorted image reflecting off the caramel-colored coffee. "I thought it would get easier, Gene, but it hasn't. I miss her more and more every day."

Gina reached over and laid her tiny hand on Delta's. "I know. The most Connie and I have ever spent apart is the week she took those classes at the FBI. I can't imagine what it must be like after two months."

Delta nodded, but didn't look up. "I never thought I could miss someone so much that it hurt all over. Physically, mentally, emotionally, I ache. Help me if she leaves me after all this."

Suddenly, a short Latina woman walked into the kitchen rubbing sleep from her eyes. "Leave you? You got rocks in your head, Storm?" Wrapping her arms around Delta's neck, she hugged her.

"Good morning, sunshine," Gina said, rising to pour a third cup of coffee.

"Hi, gorgeous. Was that a dream last night, or did you really wake me up at two in the morning and..." smiling, she pulled away from Delta and kissed the back of Gina's head. "I didn't hear you come in, Del. Now what's all this stupid talk about Megan leaving you? You having another bout with the insecures?" Sitting next to Delta, Consuela Rivera laid her hands around Delta's hands, which were still hugging the mug.

Connie and Delta were working on their seventh year as inseparable friends. Connie knew Delta better than any lover Delta had ever had—often being able to reach right into Delta's heart to pull out her true feelings. There was nothing Connie Rivera wouldn't do for her. Nothing. And vice versa. If ever there had been two people truly devoted to one another, it was Connie and Delta. And even though they both had lovers, there was no one capable of coming between them. No one. If there was a woman Delta could not live without, it was Connie.

"Storm? You okay?"

Delta shrugged. "It's just one of those mornings when I wake up after dreaming about Megan, only to remember that she isn't here."

"Must be awful." Connie took her coffee from Gina and puckered so Gina would kiss her. Gina kissed her forehead instead and sat across the table from her.

"When I realize I'm alone," Delta continued, "the bed feels colder and I start feeling sorry for myself. And you know how much I hate pity parties."

Connie grinned slightly at one of her own phrases coming from Delta's mouth. They were so enmeshed, they were beginning to sound alike. "I wouldn't call missing your lover a 'pity party,' Del. You just have to remember that she loves you."

Delta looked up from her coffee and held Connie's gaze. Not only was Connie the most intelligent woman Delta had ever met, she was also the most sensitive. If Delta needed a hug, Connie was there. When Delta needed someone to knock some sense into her, Connie obliged. She was the scale with which Delta balanced nearly everything in her life. Together, they kept each other slightly insane and in as much trouble as they could find. It was a symbiotic relationship where give and take were never measured and score was never kept. And though they had never shared sexual intimacy, Connie and Delta loved each other as much as they loved Megan and Gina. Sometimes, even more.

"That's what I spend my nights doing; remembering. Remembering how she feels, how she looks, how her mouth moves when she talks to me.

"In other words, you're driving yourself crazy."

Delta nodded. "I'm sorry for being such a downer this morning. I didn't sleep very well, that's all."

"Don't apologize for missing Megan, Del. Connie and I would be the same way if we had to spend months apart." Reaching across the table, Gina held Connie's hand. "I'd go out of my head if I had to do it."

Connie nodded. "Me, too. And I'd be needing you just like you need us. That's what we're about. So put your apologies back in your pocket."

Delta finished her coffee and stared blankly at the bottom of the cup. Need wasn't an emotion she was familiar with. It felt awkward and unsettling. The only people she had learned to rely on in her life were other cops. Even though it tended to be more of a life-and-death variety, the need of others wearing a badge was an easier task than needing a lover. Maybe physical vulnerability was simpler than emotional uncertainty; at least, in Delta's eyes. What she had discovered since Megan's departure was that she did, in fact, need Megan.

"When's the last time you two talked?"

"It's been almost a week. She did call the day before yesterday and left a message, but I haven't been able to connect with her. I suppose it's just as well. I haven't figured out how to tell her what happened."

"About the shooting?" Connie's voice was soft and gentle.

Nodding, Delta let out a big sigh. "God, how do I tell her that I killed another suspect? It's hard enough to come to terms with it myself, but I have no idea how it might affect her."

"You think it will change the way she feels for you?"

"That's just it." Pushing her chair back, Delta went into the kitchen and poured herself another cup of coffee. "I don't really know how she feels about me anymore. The distance is killing me."

"You can handle the distance, Del," Connie said, eyeing how much nondairy creamer Delta heaped into her coffee. "And you're only fooling yourself if you think it's Megan's reaction you're afraid of."

"Meaning?"

Gina and Connie exchanged glances, and Delta felt as if there was a pre-rehearsed dialogue going on between them and she'd missed rehearsal.

Leaning towards Delta, Gina brushed one of Delta's wavy hairs away from her forehead. "Honey, I'm living with a woman who watched a man fall ten stories to a very bloody and brutal death. You know how Connie was afterward. She felt that her actions on the job had somehow changed her; changed us. She thought that I loved her less."

Delta suddenly felt very small. Try as she might, she could not release the memory of killing another human being. "And did it?"

"It might have, if Connie didn't trust me enough to talk to me about it."

"But you're a shrink. That's what you do. You're trained to know how to listen objectively."

"And Megan can't?"

"I—"

"Don't underestimate her, Delta, just because she's far away. Megan loves you. She knows how important your job is to you. If you're afraid, try looking a little deeper to determine the cause, because Megan's reaction isn't it."

Lowering her face, Delta laid her hands in her lap and struggled to acknowledge the fear, the dull, throbbing ache inside her. She had tried to bury it, rationalize it, and even attempted to blame it on someone else, but night after night, there it hung, like an anchor around her neck, threatening to choke the very life out of her.

Slowly rising from her chair, Connie moved over and squatted in front of Delta, taking both of Delta's hands in hers. "Come on, Kimo. It's us. You were there for me when Elson fell. Let me be here for you now."

Delta stared down into the chocolate brown eyes of her dearest friend, knowing that she could tell Connie her deepest, darkest fear, and still remain safe. Connie Rivera was the only woman Delta had ever truly felt that way toward.

"Con, for the first time in my life, I'm not afraid *of* anything. I'm afraid *for* it. For *me*. There. I said it. I'm afraid for me."

"How so?"

Delta thought back to the warehouse; back to the fear, the darkness, the moment of decision when she pulled the trigger to end another life. As she stood over the bullet-ridden body of one who had come to kill her, she'd felt no remorse, no guilt, no apologies for her actions. She'd done what she needed to do to survive.

She had proven to herself that she was the fittest in the Darwinian sense of survival, and when she walked away from the corpse, she never looked back. As far as she was concerned, the man who had shot at her, who had intended on leaving her bloody body laying on the cement floor, got exactly what he deserved. Delta walked away, never, not even for a moment, feeling the least bit sorry.

Then came the second death at her hands.

A night as dark and as foreboding as the night Miles, her first partner, had been killed. And one shot, one bullseye to the head, and the night had suddenly become calmer again. In the millisecond it took for Delta to squeeze the trigger, a child pornographer had breathed his last breath. She had taken him out with a single .357 shot to the forehead. And still, Delta never blinked. She never looked back upon the body of a man who hurt children. And again, Delta had simply shrugged it off as part of her duty. Officer Delta Stevens killed another human being in the line of duty, and again, the public applauded its heroine, her superiors beamed, the media blitzed, and her colleagues patted her back. So...what was the problem?

"Del?"

Running her hand through her hair, Delta sighed. "I'm a little scared of how easy killing those men was for me. Do you have any idea what it's like to put a bullet through some guy's brains and not feel the least amount of pity? Their deaths don't even affect me."

"Obviously they do, honey, or we wouldn't be having this conversation."

Delta shook her head. "But that's just it, Con. It isn't their deaths that bother me. It's the fact that their deaths *don't* bother me."

Connie rose. "You're being a little hard on yourself, Del."

"Am I? I've tried and tried to feel sorry, even sad for having snuffed out two lives, but it's all contrived. The bottom line is, I'm not sorry. And that scares the shit out of me. What have I become if I no longer have a conscience?"

Gina looked over at Connie, who understood that it was Gina's turn to have the floor. "Del, when you hit a dog with your car, you feel sad and upset; horrible that you've killed someone's pet. But when you run over a snake, you probably don't even look in the mirror because you know if you didn't run it over, the person behind you would have. In the human jungle, Del, you killed two snakes. Two poisonous snakes who served no purpose but to harm others. Given that, why should there be any remorse?"

Delta fiddled with the class ring she always wore on her right hand. "Because Carducci feels remorseful. He honestly feels sad that he had to kill that guy."

"Honey, Carducci doesn't walk in your shoes. You're being paid to keep the streets and the people on them safe from men like that. You didn't kill either of them because you wanted to. You did it because you had to. Don't you think you're confusing duty with desire? You didn't desire to kill them. It was your duty to stay alive and keep Carducci and that little girl safe as well. You had no choice."

"Besides," Connie interjected, "don't ever apologize for self-preservation. Both times, Del, your own life hung in the balance. You did what any of us would have done in the same situation. It doesn't make you a killer. It makes you a survivor."

Delta nodded and sighed loudly. "I should have come to you two earlier. You always know how to make me see the big picture."

Gina laughed as she rose from the table. "Yes, but sometimes, it's like trying to administer an eye exam to a rhino." Collecting two of the empty coffee cups, Gina tousled Delta's hair. "She'll be back, Storm. In the meantime, stop creating pain in your life in order to have something to do."

Connie nodded, rising from her chair as well. "Right. Start focusing on being a carefree, happy-go-

lucky auntie for a precious bundle of Native American
joy."

Delta's left eyebrow rose into a characteristic arch.
"Happy-go-lucky?"

Connie harrumphed. "Fine. I'll settle for carefree."

Smiling, Delta downed the rest of her coffee before
handing the mug to Connie. "Carefree?"

Connie nodded.

"It sure beats the hell out of being called a rhino."

Grinning like a Cheshire cat, Connie started for the
kitchen. "You've been called far worse, my friend. Far,
far worse.

3

When Delta entered the station, she welcomed the familiar sound of organized chaos. She loved this building with its mad scientists laboring in forensics on one wing while beat cops, detectives, and undercover cops hauled in suspects down another wing. At any moment, this place might erupt in a cacophony of noises more varied than the chords in an orchestra. Accompanying this auditory discord was an energy which blasted through her like an explosion. This building, this department, this space in time was the heartbeat that gave law enforcement individuals a reason to wake up. This was the vibrant excitement that captivated them, body and soul. Nothing compared to a squadroom in a police department. Nothing could touch her like the adrenaline rush she got every time she came through those doors. And in the fourteen hours she'd been away from her beat, so much had changed in that world; a world which relied on her to keep it safe; a world which needed her strength and integrity. It was her world and that's precisely why she loved it.

"Hey, there," Connie greeted her, not looking up from the computer monitor. "Did our morning dose of coffee get you through the day?"

Delta grinned. The question meant: Did we help assuage your fears? Pulling up a chair and sitting backwards on it, Delta rested her chin on its back. "Very much. Thanks."

"Don't thank us, thank my uncle, Juan Valdez."

Delta didn't need to look into Connie's face to know when another one of her far-fetched family sagas was being tossed into the pool. As usual, as one of their bizarre friendship rituals, Delta took the bait. "Juan

Valdez? You mean that Colombian coffee grower on television?"

Connie nodded. No grin, no twitch, no facial movement at all. It was clear that Connie was not going to give this one up easily.

"The very one. Did you know that his donkey is now twenty years old? He got Pedro as a gift from one of the growers when he first started his business."

"Pedro?" Delta studied Connie's face, expecting her to crack. When she didn't, Delta moved closer.

"Sure," Connie replied, her fingers still flying across the keyboard. "Pedro's been in the family longer than any other pet. Juan goes everywhere with him."

Delta leaned closer. "Okay, Tonto, you can smile now. This is the farthest you've gone into one of your stupid family folk tales. I have to admit—I'm impressed."

Connie's fingers stopped in midair as she turned to Delta. "What are you talking about?"

"Oh, come off it, Con. I've swallowed your Gypsy aura-reading schtick, your Hungarian hatmaker ploy, and your 'my great grandfather was an Indian scout for Custer' routine. But I am not, do you hear me, I am *not* about to buy that the Mexican coffee grower on TV is in any way related to you and your extremely diverse family. No way." Crossing her arms over her chest, Delta shook her head.

Connie shrugged and continued typing. "Fine. I don't care if you believe me or not. His picture is on the wall in my mother's house. And besides, he isn't Mexican, he's—"

"Colombian. I know."

"Well, if you know that, then you'll understand why I love coffee so much. Uncle Juan used to make all sorts of delicious coffee treats; coffee cake, coffee bread, coffee ice cream, coffee toffee—"

"Enough!" Delta cried. "I give! You win! I believe your silly-ass story. Just please stop prattling on about your cousin."

Connie looked hurt. "It's uncle. He's my uncle."

"Then how come this is the first I've heard of him?"

"You never asked. Besides, you never believe me."

Before Delta could usher her next comeback, a large, deeply Italian-looking young man strutted over to them.

"Evening, ladies," he opened, flashing his best Prince Charming smile. Tearing open a bag of chocolate chip cookies, he held it out to them.

Delta looked in the bag and shook her head. She had never had a partner quite like Tony Carducci, who ate and ate and never seemed to gain an ounce. Tony had a physique most men envied, and an insatiable appetite for anything sweet.

"No thanks," Delta replied, watching Connie pluck a cookie from the bag. "You'd better watch your waistline, Chief, or you're gonna wind up with secretarial spread."

"I'm eating for two."

Delta's left eyebrow rose in its characteristic question mark. "Oh? Since when? Until you know for sure, knock that shit off."

Tony stopped chewing his cookie and stared at Connie. "Are you preg—"

Delta waved him off. "Don't listen to anything she has to say tonight, Carducci. There's a full moon and Con gets more far out than usual."

Connie crammed the rest of her cookie in her mouth and spoke with her mouth full. "Hey, speaking of full moons, did you know—"

Delta covered her ears. "Run Tony! Run for your life. She's over the edge, whacko, 5150, nuts, loco. She has a reservation for a rubber room, a straight jacket, and all the valium she can handle. Run, before she lures you into her storytelling web."

Tony started backing away. "Man, I never know when you guys are kidding. If you ask me, you're both crazy." With that, Tony and his cookie bag headed for the muster room.

"Well, of all the nerve," Connie said, grinning.

"Hmph," Delta offered, her grin matching Connie's. "They just don't teach manners in the academy anymore, do they?" Delta turned her chair around and put one foot on it. Tony wasn't the only one who couldn't keep up with their verbal sparring. After seven years on the force together, and countless hours of off time, Connie and Delta worked together like a well-oiled machine. What one lacked, the other made up for, and it had been that way from the very start. Still grinning at Connie, Delta remembered back to Connie's first day on the job.

No one really knew what a research and data specialist was, but most understood it was a bogus term the captain or the chief had used to obtain Connie's immense talents. Consuela Dolores Maria Rivera spoke five languages, held a degree from MIT, earned a black belt in karate, and belonged to MENSA, a club for geniuses. By anyone's standards, she was an exceptional catch. And on that first day, she had earned her wings within the hour.

Delta remembered Connie standing at the computer watching someone try to extract information about a prominent city official who was suspected of being involved in a money-laundering scheme. The money he laundered was supposed to have come from a methamphetimine house that Vice had been watching for weeks. After ten minutes of watching the person at the computer come up empty-handed, Connie politely brushed him aside, sat down, and let her fingers start flying over the keyboard. Suddenly, she was tapped into the mainframe in City Hall.

"You can't do that," the computer operator said.

Connie didn't flinch. "Can and have."

"But—"

"Don't worry about it. I'll take the heat. If the captain has questions, I'll give him answers. It's simple math."

Delta had liked her instantly. She was full of the same fire and passion as Delta, and didn't mind bending rules to get what she needed. Connie enjoyed a challenge and rose to the occasion every time one was presented to her. Delta liked this about the short Latina woman whose IQ was well over the line to genius. But unlike some other brainiacs, Connie had a heart and soul as well, and Delta soon learned to love both.

Several weeks after they met, Delta finally asked Connie what everyone in the precinct was wondering. Why would someone with multiple degrees from a prestigious university like MIT go into the poor-paying field of law enforcement?

"In the barrios, my people are dying every day by violent crimes. When I graduated and returned home, my best friend spit in my face because I had found a way out. I had done what they all dream of doing. My friends, most of my family, and the other people I really cared about accused me of selling out. Like so many other ethnic minorities, my people were jealous, and instead of cheering me on, they wanted to hold me back and accused me of trying to be white."

"What happened?"

"I thought about what they said. Sure, I have a degree and an ethnicity that will open a lot of doors, but what about an obligation to my people? What about the ones who aren't as fortunate as I was? So, I looked around and decided I'd give law enforcement a chance to utilize my talents."

"And are they?"

Connie grinned. "Not fully, but they'll get there."

Her honesty and integrity were only two of the reasons Delta admired Connie Rivera. And soon, admiration at first sight became a friendship that no man or woman could sever. If there was anyone Delta would give her life for, it was Connie.

Connie turned from her work and caught Delta's expression. "Now, don't go getting all soft on me before you brave the criminal element out there."

Delta shook the memories away like someone shaking water from an umbrella. "Soft? I was still thinking about Juan Perez."

"That's Valdez."

"Wasn't that a boat?"

"No, that was the Exxon Valdez. Pronounced 'deez.' Geez, don't you ever read the papers?"

Pushing the chair under the desk, Delta turned and lightly touched Connie's shoulder. "Why should I? I have you."

Connie grinned, but didn't look up. "You're kissing my butt, and that always makes me nervous."

Delta laughed. "Well, save your nerves for the baby."

Connie looked up at Delta, a warm smile replacing her mischievous grin. "You mean BIP?"

"BIP?"

"Yeah. Baby-in-progress."

Nodding, Delta glanced over Connie's shoulder at the monitor. Some time ago, Connie had ceased playing computer adventure games during the lull in her work day; they were too painful a reminder of a case they both would rather forget.

"I'm calling Megan as soon as I get home. I'll send her your love."

"Good. You have a safe night out there, Storm, and don't take any wooden nickels."

Delta started to walk away and then suddenly stopped. "You know, my dad used to say that to me. What does that really mean?"

Connie turned back to the computer and chuckled. "Wooden nickels are useless, silly. It means don't get fooled."

"Me, fooled? Never." With that, Delta sauntered into the muster room and found her partner doing what he did best: flirting. Standing in the doorway, Delta shook her head. When she'd been bucked back to Training Patrol for some of her off duty maneuvers, Tony had been her first and only trainee. He had come to her cocky, arrogant, sexist, and impossibly male. But, like a cardboard character being blown to life, Tony Carducci revealed a complex soul beneath all the mousse and cologne he slapped on daily. He possessed integrity, loyalty, and more importantly, he had the desire to grow beyond the caricatured rookie Delta had first met. He'd come through when Delta needed him most. When the time came to put it all on the line, Tony Carducci didn't hesitate, and that had made all the difference in the world.

Before she could say anything to him about his reputation as a flirt, the desk sergeant ambled up to the podium and called everyone's attention. Muster went slowly, as it usually did at the end of fall, when rashes of burglaries, robberies, and auto thefts occurred. Like animals preparing to hibernate, many criminals began stockpiling their goods and drugs to prepare for winter. The usual California Indian summers meant they could stretch out their criminal activities that much longer.

As Delta took notes, she marveled at how the weather affected the crime rate. There would be one more major marijuana harvest before year's end, so all the dope dealers would be buying larger quantities. Colder weather meant less home invasions; even thieves tried to stay out of the cold. Car jackings went down as well during the cold months, but rapes were as high as ever. Like a broken scale, crime teetered and tottered to the different winter winds and summer breezes. Yet, whether teetering or tottering, one thing remained constant: the criminals were winning.

For every crack house they busted, seven more opened. For every burglar caught, a dozen more went unpunished. In the never-ending battle against crime, it was no contest. Beat cops, detectives, and special units alike worked their asses off to barely make a dent. To many, it felt like pedaling backwards; but to Delta, there were signs of hope.

Her hope came in the form of arrests she'd made when shutting down a child pornography ring. Her teeter stayed up when the FBI, who bungled the initial bust, redeemed themselves with their incredible interrogative finesse, their networking abilities, and the arrests of almost forty others connected with the ring.

The message the FBI sent to that particular brand of criminal was simple: don't fuck with our children. And the media loved it. But then, the media had always favored anything Delta was involved with.

And involved she had been. She found herself mindful of the promise she had made to Miles, her first partner, at his gravesite. She swore she would take care of the corner of the world his children lived in, and she did just that. It had taken her two near death experiences and the shooting of two suspects, but again, Delta Stevens had come out on top.

Now, several weeks later, Delta and her buddies were on to new cases. Now, they were returning their attention to the locals and trying to find ways to make their beats safer; a task which was becoming more difficult all the time.

"What's going on in there?" Tony asked, pointing to Delta's head.

"Nothing. Just thinking about muster, that's all."

Tony drove for a while longer without a response. When too much silence passed between them, he became too uncomfortable to let it go on.

"You don't have to share anything with me if you don't want to. Just know that I'm here if you wanna talk. I'll be here for the next nine and a half hours, so any time you want to dump a load of mind trash, go for it."

Delta did not return Tony's gaze. Instead, she nodded and drew deeper into herself, deeper into her thoughts; this was something Tony Carducci was finally beginning to understand. But that understanding didn't appear overnight. It had taken him a while to get used to the idea that his partner wasn't only a woman, but a woman who belonged to the ten percent club. Eventually, he accepted their differences, and with that, he made an attempt to understand a lifestyle and orientation that couldn't be further away from his. His attempts earned him a lot of points. Tony was neither patronizing nor intrusive. When he realized that Delta and Megan's relationship went through the same kinds of peaks and valleys as his own, he stopped viewing them as some social anomaly. Now, Megan and Delta were just another couple trying to keep everything together.

"Carducci," Delta said as they cruised through the dark streets. "Don't you ever get tired of being single?"

Tony thought for a moment before answering. This pause was a new revelation from a man who used to blurt whatever stupid thought popped in his head. Tony Carducci had come a long way, and this made Delta glad she had saved his career.

"Sometimes, sure. It's not the greatest. Is being alone starting to get to you?"

Delta shrugged. "Good days, bad days."

Tony nodded his understanding. "Today one of those bad days?"

"Is it that obvious? Don't answer that."

"Hey, man, I know what it's like when the lovin's there one minute, and in the next minute, it's gone. All of a sudden, a hug is a big deal."

Delta remembered a break up she'd had four years ago. She did nothing but eat Chinese food and read magazines for weeks. One day, Connie sat down with her and explained what Delta was doing. Connie said the body gets used to being touched, to being stroked and caressed. And when the touching stops suddenly, there's a sort of withdrawal the body experiences, something called "skin hunger." That skin hungers, even aches for human warmth is why so many inmates have same sex lovers while incarcerated, then return to their straight world upon release. Four years ago, Delta wondered if this was another one of Connie's tall tales. Now, she wasn't so sure.

"I'd give you a hug, Delta, but I don't think it would help."

This made Delta grin. "No, it wouldn't, but thanks for the thought."

They drove in silence for some time, until Tony slowed down in a dark alley. Delta turned and studied him for a moment. "Do you want to find that one special someone to settle down with someday? You know, that one certain love who steals your heart?"

Tony nodded slowly, but did not look at her. "Had one once."

"Really? What happened?"

"I guess you could say she was the one who got away."

Delta aimed her spotlight at the doorstep where one of her favorite homeless men usually sequestered himself from the cold night air. She was surprised he wasn't there. Checking her watch, she made a mental note to swing by and check again in a couple of hours.

"She got away?"

"Yep. Gwen was the love of my life. She meant more to me than all the others put together. And," he paused again, grinning, "I don't think I need to remind you just how many that is."

Feeling no need to comment or boost his ego, Delta waved him on to tell the rest of the story.

"I don't even know what happened," Tony continued. "We'd been going out for about six months, and I was having a blast. We did almost everything together. She loved football and could beat any of my friends in pool. She was really a great friend."

"Sounds like it. So, what changed?"

"I don't know. Things were moving along, and then one night, right after making love, she said we were through. Finished. Over."

"Just like that? No explanation?"

Tony shook his head. "She said she'd fallen in love with someone else. How and when she could have done that, I don't have a clue. We were together all the time. When I asked if I knew him, she wouldn't answer. Just said it was best to go our separate ways."

Delta reached out and lightly touched his arm. She had watched Tony stare death in the face with less emotion than he was sharing now, and she hurt for him. Affair pain was all too familiar to Delta, and it didn't matter whether you were straight, gay, or in between, being cheated on was the shittiest feeling in the world.

"So, you just said goodbye?"

Tony nodded and sighed loudly. "There wasn't anything left to do. She didn't want me anymore. I asked her what I had done wrong, but she just kept saying to let it go. To this day, I don't know what I did. All I know is I lost the only woman I've ever thought about marrying."

The *M* word brought Delta out of her seat. "Marry? You were going to marry her?"

"I hadn't asked her yet, but I was planning on it." Tony chuckled bitterly. "At least I didn't look like too much of a chump, huh? The only stupid thing I did was buy a pool table so that we could stay home and play pool instead of always going to some bar." Tony flicked off the spotlight and kept talking. "She always kicked my butt in pool. And you know what? I never got pissed. She was so beautiful when she studied the balls and the angles. God, I miss those times."

"You were really in love with her, weren't you?"

"Yep. I still carry her picture." Digging into his back pocket, Tony pulled his wallet out and removed a picture. "Want to see?"

Delta smiled warmly as she turned the small dashboard lamp on and aimed it toward Tony's picture. Taking the picture by the edges, Delta peered closely at this object of Carducci's greatest passion. Gwen appeared to be in her early twenties, petite in stature, a bottle blonde who wore her long hair straight down. She was standing next to a pool table, holding a pool cue in one hand and a bottle of beer in the other.

"She's cute," Delta said, allowing her eyes to linger as if she was studying a mug shot. There was something haunting about this picture, but she couldn't put her finger on it. "And you haven't seen her since?"

"Nope. Right after we broke up, I went to all of our old hangouts hoping to see her, but I never did. I finally gave up and moved on. My buddies were happy about that. Said I'd been acting like a fool."

Delta handed the picture back and flicked the lamp off. "You weren't a fool, Carducci. You were in love. Love makes us all crazy sometimes."

Tony grinned. "Sometimes?"

"Most of the time. What would you have done if you saw her?"

Heaving another heavy sigh, Tony replaced the picture and put his wallet back. "I guess I'd just want some answers. Del, I did all the things women say they want from a guy. I sent roses, took her to bed-and-breakfasts, made her dinner, cleaned house, took her to see those mushy women movies, and all that other shit, and it still wasn't enough. I just want to know what more I could have done."

Delta hid her incredible surprise. She could hardly imagine Tony Carducci even knowing what a bed-and-breakfast was, let alone spending the night at one. It was evident that her narrow opinion of the man needed a minor adjustment. "And she never told you why it was over?"

"Nope. She packed her things and headed for greener pastures, I guess."

Delta stared out the window and felt her own sliver of pain still imbedded in her heart. Some years earlier, she'd walked in on her lover and best friend in *her* bed one afternoon. Apparently, the tryst had been going on for some time, but Delta was either too busy or too stupid to notice.

"Affairs suck."

Tony smiled at her, a deeper understanding flowing between them. "Yeah, and so do cheaters."

Suddenly, the radio came to life and Delta took the call.

"S1012, you have a 1-0-0 going off at 139 Wolfe Avenue. Possible 4-5-9 in progress. R1112 will back up. Copy?"

Flipping the lights on, Delta felt her heart rate accelerate as a burst of adrenaline surged through her. A burglary-in-progress was a dangerous call. Since few burglars were ever caught in the act, their reactions to being caught were as unpredictable as the weather. Some immediately gave up, some jumped out of second-story windows, and some...well, those who had already been to the Big House often fought back with frightening tenacity. It all depended on what kind of burg it was; there were druggy burgs, juvenile burgs, and professional burgs, any one of which could pull a gun out and start shooting. A 4-5-9 in progress meant cops might scare a perp into doing something neither of them wanted to happen. It was a call Delta never took lightly.

"This is S1012 with a 10-4 on that 4-5-9. We're about two away and will make our approach from the east side, over."

"Affirmative, S1012. R1112, do you copy?"

After everyone was assured of where everyone else was going to be, Delta hung up her mike and glanced over at Tony. "You *do* know which side of Wolfe is the east side, don't you?"

Nodding, Tony grinned slightly. "I do now, boss."

4

Delta knew her beat better than her own neighborhood. She knew the back streets and alleys that dead-ended, as well as which side roads offered the greatest protection from snipers or ambushes. Her knowledge came from years of practice and experience, and it was now up to her to teach Tony as much of that knowledge as possible.

"All right, Carducci, a 4-5-9 in progress isn't something to mess around with. A burglar is a completely different kind of criminal than one you've faced so far. Unlike a robber, who rips people off, a burglar burgles because he doesn't want a confrontation with anyone. Burglars most often choose unoccupied homes in order to avoid contact with the victim."

Tony nodded as he accelerated through a red light. "Okay."

"So be careful. If he's there, he could surrender right away or come out shooting."

Tony nodded as he reached down and turned the lights off. "Anything else?"

Delta grinned. Oh, how he had changed. But then, killing a man had a sobering affect on both of them. Taking another life, no matter how right or just the situation had been, had changed them. No longer was Tony so eager to jump into a brawl without thinking it through. No longer did he push his badge in people's faces or abuse the authority given to him. The new-and-improved Tony Carducci was a boy who had come to her as a reckless youth and blossomed into a more mature, much wiser man.

Tony parked the car several houses away and carefully got out. As they moved closer to the sloping driveway, Delta stopped at the tall, iron gates blocking their path.

"Damn."

"What's the matter? Let's just climb over."

Delta shook her head. "It isn't that. Our burglar is really going to feel trapped if we happen upon him. Trapped perps fight the hardest."

"Let's not give him that chance."

Delta grinned like a teacher whose worst student finally got the answer right.

After climbing the gate, Delta landed gingerly while Tony thudded to the ground, his size eleven shoes slapping the pavement loudly.

"Geez, Carducci, would you rather just yell to him that we're on our way?"

"What?"

"Forget it." Okay, so he still needed some work.

Squatting down, Delta radioed that they were about to move in and directed backup to the opposite side of the house.

"Let's go," Tony whispered, taking a step forward before Delta rose and stopped him.

"Relax, will you? Check to see if there are any flickering lights."

"Flickering lights?"

Delta shook her head in disgust. "I swear to God, you must have slept through the Academy. Flickering lights, Carducci; the kind flashlights make. No good thief ever leaves home without one."

A minute crept by. Then two. Delta nudged Tony and pointed to a window. "Watch." Turning her face so she could talk into the mike attached to her collar, Delta instructed backup to hit their sirens. "If there's a thief in that house, they're gonna blast outta there like a cannonball."

Tony smiled widely. "Cool."

After two more minutes, Delta rose. "Well, it doesn't look like there's anyone home. Now, let's have a looksee, shall we?" Unholstering her .357 magnum, Delta started to the side of the house.

"All that and *now* you take your gun out?"

Delta grinned. "What is it with men and their guns? Is it some kind of a phallic thing or what? If it were up to you, and thank God it isn't, you'd all walk around town holding it in your hand."

"It? Are you talking about our guns or our di—"

"You know exactly what I'm talking about."

Tony nodded and smiled, but said nothing more.

"If there's a burglar in there, and he is too scared to come out, I want him to see that I mean business. Always assume there's someone in there just waiting to shoot us."

Tony hesitated a second before drawing his weapon. Tony Carducci had one of the keenest eyes and softest strokes of anyone coming out of the Academy in more than a decade. It had been his incredible marksmanship that carried him through the rigors of Academy life. It was said that he could shoot the head off a gnat at thirty yards, and after what they had been through together, Delta believed it. He was a natural. All the SWAT team was waiting for was a little smoothing of the rough edges and then off he'd go. It fell upon Delta's shoulders to do the majority of the buffing.

"Looks like the front window's busted," Tony said.

Delta squinted through the darkness of night and saw a hole in the window. "Yeah, but not big enough for anyone to get through. That's odd." Pulling out her flashlight, Delta shined it at the hole. "See the wires running the length of the window?"

"Yeah."

"Someone must have been testing to see if this place was as secure as the label on the window."

"Then you don't think there's anyone in there?"

Delta grinned. "I didn't say that. But there will be shortly." Pointing to the iron gate, Delta watched as it slowly creaked open to allow a huge Cadillac to roll in.

"The Clampetts have returned."

Tony looked at her. "The who?"

"Forget it, Tony. Way before your time."

After the Clampetts parked and let them in the house, they turned off the alarm and called the alarm company. While they attended to business, Delta's eyes roamed from a Ming vase to the marble entryway, and up to what she was sure was a Picasso. The house had the look and feel of a professional decorator, yet it didn't have that "lived in" look. If she were a burglar, she'd come to this house a couple of times a month just for rent money.

"Everything appears to be in order." Jed Clampett said as he reentered the room. "All my coins, my guns, my belt buckles—"

"Belt buckles?" Tony asked.

"Hell, yeah, son. Been collecting them since I was knee high to a grasshopper. Got my first one from my granddaddy. I don't know what I'd a done if someone woulda taken those."

Suddenly, Mrs. Clampett came rushing down the stairs clutching her chest with one hand and waving the other frantically in the air. "My ring! My diamond wedding ring is gone!"

Jed turned around and shook his head. "She loses that blasted thing every other day. I swear, you'd think it was one of those cubit zuchronums the way she leaves it laying around."

Mrs. Clampett landed on the marble floor with a heavy thud. "Oh, hush up, Jerome. I know exactly where I left it and it isn't there. I checked all over the bathroom and it's gone. Vanished. Stolen."

Delta flipped her pad open and clicked her pen. "You left a ring in the bathroom?"

"Not just any ring, Officer—" she leaned forward so she could read Delta's nametag. "Stevens. A 1.5 carat diamond ring from Van Clees' Arpels. Jerome gave it to me for an anniversary present."

Delta jotted this down. She found it slightly amusing that the "aw shucks, we ain't that rich," attitude was now replaced by the much more apt "my 1.5 carat diamond was stolen." Delta wasn't sure which posture bothered her the most.

"What else is missing?"

Mrs. Clampett shook her head. "Nothing."

"Excuse me?" Delta said, lowering the pad.

"My emeralds and rubies are still in my jewelry box. My pearl necklace is still draped over my vanity. I don't think he took anything else."

"Now, honey," Jerome said, patting his wife patronizingly on the back. "No thief is gonna come in here and steal just one diamond ring. There's at least six figures' worth of jewelry in your box, and you're telling us he only took one ring? I think you must have just misplaced it."

"I did not. I know where I left it and it's gone."

"How about we take a look upstairs?" Delta said, clicking her pen. "Maybe we can sort through this from up there."

Coming to the top of the stairs, Delta's eyes roamed across the top floor. This was a beautiful home filled with antiques, expensive-looking chandeliers, and colorful oriental rugs. Even an amateur thief wouldn't walk away with just one ring. Besides, how hard was it to carry a jewelry box?

"You'll have to excuse my wife, Officer. She has an overactive imagination. Some kid threw a rock through the window and that tripped the alarm. Period. Amen."

Delta did not acknowledge this as she walked into the first two bedrooms and studied each window. All four windows were locked.

"Whatcha looking up here for? You don't think a burglar would climb all the way up here, do you?"

Delta grinned. "You'd be surprised." Leaving the second bedroom, Delta continued checking windows until she came to one which was slightly open. "Was this window open when you left?"

Mrs. Clampett nodded. "We always leave it open so we can hear the doves coo. They make the prettiest sound."

Taking her flashlight back out, Delta shined it on the window frame. "These windows aren't tied into the alarm, are they?"

Jerome shook his head. "Didn't see the need for it, being as it's two stories up and all."

Delta followed the beam of her flashlight with her eyes. The dust on the windowsill was displaced. Tony bent over and looked from the same angle Delta was looking. Although the lights were on in the house, nothing could touch the strength of a six-celled flashlight pinpointing in a direction.

"What is it?" Tony asked.

Delta pointed to the windowsill. "Someone, or something, was up here. Could have been the doves, might have been a cat, but it's unlikely. See how dusty the edges are? But then look at this patch right here? Someone entered through this window. Get on the horn and tell dispatch that the Burg Unit might want to take a look at this."

"Then, my ring *was* stolen?"

Straightening up, Delta clicked the flashlight off. "It's possible. The Burglary Unit will be out to have a look, and they can compare what they find and see if it matches any other home invasions in the area."

Jerome shook his head. "It would take a might desperate person to climb up two stories, don't you think?"

Delta grinned at him again. "And that's exactly what most burglars are. Look, folks, the Burglary Unit will be here shortly. Don't touch any of the windows or anything that you think is out of place. You might want to go through your jewelry box again to make sure nothing else was stolen."

"Thank you so much, Officer Stevens. I really appreciate your concern."

Delta nodded to her before gliding down the stairs and out the door with Tony right behind her.

"Odd couple," Tony said, shaking his head.

"Odd case. What would possess a thief to climb all the way up here and then leave without taking the jewelry box?"

Tony frowned. "Not enough time?"

"Oh, they had plenty of time. Assuming they got in from the top window, the alarm wouldn't have gone off. They could have been in there for hours. What else?"

"Revenge?"

Delta shrugged. "Maybe. The broken window sort of suggests that, doesn't it?"

"It's too obvious though, huh?"

"Not necessarily. Don't be afraid to examine the obvious, Carducci. Anything else?"

"Drugs? Maybe he was too wired to think clearly."

"But he was calm enough to climb all the way up there? Hardly. Keep going."

Tony rubbed his chin. "I give."

Delta grinned. "How much is a 1.5 carat worth?"

"I don't know. Five, ten grand."

"Uh-huh. And I'm sure it's insured."

Tony's eyes lit up. "Oh, now I get it."

Sliding her flashlight back through the ring, Delta shrugged. "It's just one of the possibilities."

Tony grinned at her. "Always the open mind, huh Delta?"

Delta returned the smile. "Always."

5

When Delta returned home, two cats began rubbing up against her before she could even get the door closed. Used to be, she frowned upon sudden attention when her shift was over. She needed some down time. But with Megan in Costa Rica, any kind of attention worked for her now. Delta never minded living alone. After she kicked Sandy out, Delta rather enjoyed having the time and space to herself. When she fell in love with Megan, Delta was finally ready to have someone share that space. Much to her surprise, Megan had preferred to keep her own apartment, and they occasionally spent the night in their own homes. This had somewhat irked Delta in the beginning, but as usual, there was logic behind Megan's thoughts.

"Lesbians often get so immersed in their relationships, they forget who they are," Megan had explained one night after a wonderful evening of lovemaking. "Our identity gets so wrapped up in the "we" that we start losing the individual's identity that we originally fell in love with. I don't want to make that mistake, Delta. I've only recently discovered who the real me is."

Delta didn't want to understand, but she did. It was the last time she'd ask Megan to move in with her. If Megan came back from Costa Rica and still wanted separate homes, then so be it.

"Well, hello everybody," Delta said, offering her standard greeting to the cats. "Hungry?" Delta opened the refrigerator and smelled the milk before pouring it in two saucers. Aside from the milk, the only other contents in the refrigerator were Diet Pepsi and tortillas. "And how was my night, you ask?" Snatching Megan's picture out from under a refrigerator magnet, Delta sat on a barstool and stared at it. She never imagined she could love someone as much as she loved

Megan. After too many broken hearts to keep track of, Delta had given up on finding that one special person who could love her for who she was and not for who she could be. Delta Stevens was a cop. It was what she had always wanted to do, and it was what she did best. She loved it.

Yet, she loved Megan, too, and this separation was killing her.

While staring at the picture, Delta instinctively reached for the phone. She'd waited as long as she could for Megan to return her last two calls. Surely, the lawyer she was interning for didn't have her working at, what time was it over there? Four-thirty in the morning? If Megan wasn't in now, she'd surely have something else to worry about.

Finally, on the fourth ring, a sleepy voice answered. It was not Megan's. *"Bueno?"*

"Terry?" Delta asked, feeling slightly guilty for waking her up so early.

"No, it's Liz. Who's this?"

"It's Delta. Delta Stevens. Is Megan there?"

"Sure. Hang on a sec."

Delta sighed and resisted the urge to kiss Megan's picture. She grinned to herself as she wondered if other women acted as goofy.

"Delta?"

The silvery sound of Megan's voice melted the cold anxiety in Delta's heart. God, how she missed her. "I'm sorry I woke you."

"Don't be. I'm so glad you called. Is everything all right?"

Delta's stomach pitched at the tenderness in Megan's voice. She sounded so happy. "I just wanted...no, I needed to hear your voice."

"Honey, is something wrong? Are you okay?"

Delta closed her eyes and pictured Megan playing with a long strand of her blonde hair. "Nothing's wrong, baby, I just miss you so much, I ache. I needed to hear your voice."

"You're such a sweety. I miss you, too. You sure you're okay?"

Okay was such a relative term. "Yeah. I'm just feeling a little lonely tonight. Coming home to an empty house is getting old; especially after work."

"How is work?"

"Slow. The only thing that happened tonight was a burglary, and the perp took one diamond ring. It reminded me of the time we went ring shopping. Remember the saleslady's face when she realized the rings were for the two of us?"

"She sure soured fast, didn't she? I thought I'd die when you told her that her closed mind just cost her a healthy commission."

Delta grinned. "I particularly enjoyed when she mumbled 'sinners' under her breath. God, we had fun that day."

"Actually, you had more fun shopping for the perfect salesperson."

"Never did find her."

"Nope."

"Never found the rings, either."

A tenuous silence filled the gap between them. "Is that what's bothering you, Del? That I left before you could get a ring on my finger?"

"Sort of."

"Honey, what is it with lesbians and rings? A ring won't make me any more committed to you than a marriage certificate. We've been through this."

"I know," Delta said, feeling stupid for even bringing it up. What was the matter with her tonight, anyway?

"Sweetheart, don't you worry about me falling for anyone down here. My actions let these macho gauchos know that this is one little señorita who is unavailable. I've made it perfectly clear to everybody that I'm here for business only. You don't have to worry about me riding off into the sunset with one of the natives."

"That happens when you don't return my calls. It starts making me crazy."

"Stop being crazy, silly. Days run into night here before I even know how much time has gone by. I'm working really hard, sweetheart, that's all. And when I do slow down to where I can call, you're usually at work."

"I just miss you."

"I know. But you have to remind yourself that I'm not down here on vacation. I'm learning more in a day than I would in a classroom for a month. Juan Carlos has been generous with time off for side trips, and...well...I've been on one of those trips for three days. That's why I couldn't get back to you. There were no phones where I went."

"Where'd you go?"

"Do you remember when we went to Wild Animal Kingdom and I got to hold that scarlet macaw?"

How could Delta forget? That bird clicked and preened and did everything but mate with Megan. It had been love at first sight. "I remember. Why?"

"They fly in pairs down here and are as common as our sparrows and robins. It's the most incredible thing I've ever seen. They're so beautiful in the wild."

"Are there blue and gold ones, too?"

"No, they're in Hawaii. The scarlets are the ones here, and they've just made it to the soon-to-be-endangered list. With the destruction of rain forests and the number of people still smuggling them into countries like the US, their numbers are dwindling. It's getting pretty serious."

"Smuggling? People smuggle birds?" Delta picked up a pen and started doodling.

"Uh-huh. These guys used large nets to knock them down and capture them. Then they drug them, roll them in newspaper, and cram them all in a box."

"That's horrible."

"Yes, it is. And only one in seven make it out of that box alive."

"How sad."

"Delta, to see them fly...to watch them talk to each other, preen each other, and raise families is something I'll never forget. They mate for life, you know."

"I didn't know that." Delta was smiling wider than she had in weeks. "So, Dr. Greenpeace, where does this all lead?"

"I've been out there in the heart of the rain forest, Del. Juan Carlos's cousin and I spotted some poachers."

Delta stopped her doodling and sat up. "Poachers?"

"Yep. We're trying to ascertain who their connection is here in Orotina."

Ascertain? Already, Megan was beginning to sound like a lawyer. "To what end?"

"Hopefully, to jail. That's what we'd—"

"Whoa, Megan, wait a minute here. You're hanging out in the jungle spying on poachers?"

"It's not a jungle, it's a rain forest. And we're not spying, we're tracking."

"Megan, sweetheart, listen to me. Hunting poachers sounds a bit dangerous."

"We don't confront them, Del. We just track them and report them to the authorities."

"Delta, last year, in one of the reserves, out of ninety pair of scarlets, only eight babies achieved adulthood. Eight. At that rate, they'll never survive."

Delta was up now, pacing in the living room. In their two years together, Delta had never heard Megan sound so determined, so involved. "And you think that tracking this poacher will lead to the buyer?"

"Yes. We want the poachers out of Orotina. And if you could hear them chattering to each other, if you could see how beautiful they are in flight, you'd want to save them, too. I can't leave here, Delta, without giving something back to these people, to this place. It's incredible."

Delta stopped pacing and found herself grinning. Two years ago, Megan Osbourne seldom saw the light of day, let alone the need to help something living in it. Now, she was growing and changing so much, Delta was beginning to understand what had driven Megan to Costa Rica in the first place: the need for an adventure of her own. She wasn't just finding herself; she was looking for that one thing that makes her heart beat faster. She wanted to give something back to life, and she had finally found her true calling. Delta understood callings.

For a cop, adventure, danger, risk, were all part of the nightly routine. Seldom did a night go by that didn't have Delta's heart pounding or her neck sweating. Seldom did an evening pass without some risk, some challenge before her. Around every corner, with every call, danger was near, hovering, lurking, threatening harm to those wearing a badge.

Now, it was all finally making sense to Delta. Megan's college life and her life working at the bookstore lacked adventure and excitement. Her days came and went without that jolt of adrenaline. Being in college was the safest place in the world, and it had bored her. No wonder she jumped at the chance to accept a student internship in another country. Megan wanted to experience something utterly new to her. And here it was, wrapped up like a macaw in newspaper. A ready-made adventure that promised the kind of thrill and excitement Delta had every night.

"So, tell me what you're going to do to help?"

"Well, right now, we're investigating who is setting up the poachers. We have a few leads, but nothing substantial, yet."

"Who's *we*?"

"Augustine, Juan Carlos's cousin. He came over as our tour guide, so we could experience the rain forest from a native's point of view. But when he started telling us about the number of macaws being killed by poachers, I expressed an interest to learn more. Augustine is a very sweet kid, Del. I don't believe he's even eighteen yet, so don't start worrying about him, okay?"

"A kid, huh?"

"With a heart of gold. He's been really wonderful. I've learned so much. Del, I just want to make a difference. I want my life to have an impact on something besides the tiny corner I've spent it in. You—you make a difference every night of your life. For two years, I've watched you affect the people around you. I've spent a lot of time admiring it, even envying it. So, I started looking at my own life—you know, tearing it apart to find what I've been missing. Well, what I found wasn't what I expected to find. I never realized how shallow my life was until I got here. I thought college was the great mind-expanding experience that was going to broaden my worldliness. Now, I laugh at how naive I've been."

"I wouldn't call it naive, honey."

"I would. Before you came along, I thought love was the missing link in my life. Then, thank God, you came and changed that. But the missing piece wasn't love. So I tried school, thinking that was it. No again."

"What was it?" Delta asked, feeling like she already knew the answer.

"Something to be invested in. Delta, I needed something that moves me like being a cop moves you."

Leaning her head back on the couch, Delta nodded.

"Del, do you understand?"

"Sweetheart, for the first time since we've become lovers, I understand it all too well."

"I love my law classes, my relationship with you, my transformation from caterpillar to butterfly, but I need to make a difference."

"And now, you are."

"I am, and you know what else?"

Delta couldn't help smiling at the excitement in Megan's voice. "It's taken me thousands of miles and a lot of money to finally recognize how you could love your job so much. Delta, forgive me for being such a fool. All this time, I thought I was jealous of the time and energy you put behind your badge. But that wasn't it. I was jealous because being a cop gives meaning to your life. It's why you live so fully. It's the heart behind who you are. I was jealous because I didn't have that. I didn't have something that drives my spirit."

"And now you do." It wasn't a question.

"Yes, honey, now I do. There's a thrill in knowing that I'm a part of saving a species. There's a challenge, even a risk involved that excites me. I finally get why you do what you do; why you take the risks you take."

Delta sighed heavily. Her head felt light. "Megan, all I've ever wanted was for you to understand why I work so hard."

"And I do. Ironic, don't you think? I needed to go far enough away to see the big picture."

"Hey, as long as that picture still includes the two of us together. But does this mean I have to move to Costa Rica?"

"Of course not. But I'm not through here. I think it's just the tip of the iceberg for me. I've simply discovered the symptom of my doldrums, now I need to find a cause I can work at every day."

"No one understands the importance of causes better than I."

"God, Del, I'm so relieved you understand. I didn't even know where to begin to tell you what was happening to me."

"It's the new and improved Delta Stevens. I've grown some since you've been gone, too."

"But I liked the old you."

"Believe me, she's there, too."

"I love you, Delta Stevens. I love you even more for putting up with me."

"It comes with the territory."

"I'm lucky, then."

"So am I."

For a moment, silence traveled across the lines until Megan yawned into the receiver.

"You sound tired. I better let you go."

"Yeah, I've got a long day ahead of me."

Delta nodded, wondering how many times in her career she said that to a lover. "Well, don't take any chances out there in the jungle, you hear me?"

Megan laughed. "It's rain forest, and I won't."

"Good. Well, I'll be waiting with bells on. Nothing else. Just bells."

"Mmm. What a scintillating thought. I hope I dream about that when I go back to sleep."

"I love you, Megan. Come home soon, okay?"

"I love you, too, Delta Stevens. And thank you. Thank you for being so understanding. You take good care of yourself."

"You got it." When Delta hung the phone up, she sat for a very long time in the near darkness of her house. For the first time in a long time, she knew they were going to make it.

6

Taylor landed lightly on her feet and pulled the rope up quickly behind her. She knew the alarm would not engage for one minute, so she had to work fast. The dog hadn't been a problem; she merely climbed right up the front of the house in a matter of seconds. It never ceased to amaze her how safe people with dogs believed themselves to be; so safe, they'd leave windows, even doors unlocked because good ol' Fido was out in back, and who would be so foolish as to try to get past Fido? But she had learned long ago that a dog was only a deterrent if it was stationed *inside* the house. A guard dog in the backyard only meant one thing to a thief as proficient as Taylor; she'd have to go in some other way.

Pulling her gloves tighter, she gently opened the jewelry box sitting on the chest of drawers. How many women, she wondered, made no real attempt to secure their jewels? Was it laziness? Lack of money for a good safe? Or was it just a secular belief in security systems? Whatever the case, Taylor was a wealthy woman because of it.

And this house was the perfect example of why. Right there in the open sat a monstrously ugly jewelry box practically screaming at her to peek inside. The owners of this house obviously felt very secure in the knowledge that they had Fido *and* a security system; neither of which deterred Taylor.

Peering inside the jewelry box, Taylor pulled out a tiny penlight from her utility pouch and cupped her hand around it. When the small beam of light hit the sparkling gems, Taylor immediately cringed. Most of the jewels inside were hideous pieces of costume jewelry. A few were real, but for the most part, these were cheap imitations. Who would wear shit like this?

"Where is it?" Taylor asked, pawing through the box. She stood with her hands on her hips and surveyed the room. Moving over to the night stand, she bent down and shined her tiny flashlight across the top.

"Bingo!"

Laying next to the alarm clock, in a tiny plastic bag, was a large, square emerald ring with two triangular diamonds on either side. "What a beauty." Carefully picking up the bag, Taylor dropped it into her pouch before turning back and closing the jewelry box.

"Two down, three to go." Zipping up the pouch, Taylor stepped back to the window, tossed the rope down, and quickly lowered herself to the ground below. As her feet hit the pavement, the alarm went off. Snatching the rope, Taylor yanked it and it fell at her feet. Looking around, she wiped her gloves off and smiled to herself.

"This just gets easier by the minute."

7

"You're in a mood tonight," Tony offered as they pulled out of the station parking lot. "What gives?"

"Talked to Megan last night."

"Yeah? How's she doing out in the jungle?"

"Really well, and it isn't the jungle, it's a rain forest."

"Well, whatever it is, I'm happy you're in such a good mood."

Delta leaned her head back on the headrest. She could still hear Megan's voice as it danced across the phone lines. "I listened really hard to what she had to say, and I finally get it. God, Carducci, all the woman wants is to contribute something. And I've been sitting here thinking she might leave me."

"And she won't?"

"This isn't even about me. Megan's coming back to me. What more could I ask for?"

"Does this mean you're going to lighten up some?"

Delta nodded.

"Thank God. You may say you don't suffer from PMS, but it's felt like that for months."

Punching him lightly on the arm, Delta started shuffling through her reports.

"They get any prints from the Clampetts?" Tony asked.

Delta studied the reports sitting on her lap. "Possibly. There weren't any fingerprints, but they did get a foot impression from the grass below the window." Delta pulled the report closer to her face. "Now that's interesting."

"What?"

"By the size and width of the impression, they're speculating it could be a woman."

Tony's head jerked around. "A woman?"

Lowering the report back to her lap, Delta raised an eyebrow as she looked over at him. "Yeah, so what?"

"A woman supposedly climbed the side of a very tall two-story house just to steal one lousy ring?"

"Maybe it was hers to begin with. Or are you having a problem with the fact that a woman climbed up the side of the house, Mr. Man?"

"Come on, Delta. We both know that most women lack the upper body strength of men. I mean, *you* can climb anything, but you're not—"

"Not what, Carducci? You just can't admit that a woman can do anything a man can."

"Except piss on a wall."

"Depends on where she's standing."

Tony sighed. "I didn't mean—"

"Oh, I know exactly what you meant, Mr. Limbaugh. I just hope you don't buy the farm someday because it's a woman holding the gun on you."

"All right. I give! What else does the report say?"

Delta suppressed a smile. "To your credit, however, questioning a speculation is the best thing to do. It could just as well be a small man or even a teenager."

"But they don't think so?"

Delta shrugged. "Don't know what to think yet. The report says she must have scouted the place earlier to know that the alarm wasn't connected to the second floor."

"Then it was someone who knew them?"

"Possibly. But still, who would pass up all that other jewelry, whether they knew them or not? No one's going to do all that work and then pass up that kind of score."

"Do they think it's drug related?"

Delta shook her head. "Huh-uh. I think they're settling on the idea that this was the work of a pro."

"But a pro wouldn't have left all those other jewels."

"That's the part that doesn't fit for me. It's quite a little puzzler, this one."

Tony slowed the car and inhaled deeply. "Why do I get this sinking feeling right here in my stomach?"

Delta laughed. "Oh, don't worry, Carducci. We're not going after her. Something tells me she'll come to us."

▽   ▽   ▽

The next three hours were filled with the usual traffic stops, suspicious persons calls, and the never-ending patrolling of the beat. It was a quieter night than most, with only one domestic dispute and one drive-by shooting. Delta was beginning to think the criminals had taken the night off. It wasn't long before she realized what a stupid thought that was.

"S1012, we have an audible at 3331 Byron. What's your twenty?"

Delta picked up the mike. "This is S1012, we're about three away. We'll take it."

"Copy S1012."

Tony turned and snorted. "You want that call because you hope it's her, huh?"

"Her? Her who?"

When they arrived, they silently crept to a row of hedges. "You stay out here in front. I'll check the side gate." Picking her way through the darkness, Delta paused at a six-foot wooden gate with a sign on it. Squinting to read the sign, it read BEWARE OF DOG. "Great." Using the gas meter, Delta stepped up to look over the gate and into the backyard. She heard the dog before she saw it coming and immediately dropped back to the pavement.

"Shit!"

"What is it?"

"A dog. A big dog." Meeting Tony back by the hedges, Delta shrugged. "No lights or signs of movement from the house?"

Tony shook his head. "Nothing. It's probably just the wind."

"Well, with the big dog in the back, the only way in is probably through the front part of the house."

"Or...," Tony replied, looking up at the second-story windows.

Delta pulled her flashlight out and shined it on the windows. One in the front was slightly ajar.

"Damn."

"You think she got us?"

Delta shrugged, flicking her flashlight off. "It's possible. It fits her MO."

Tony shook his head. "I still have a hard time believing our perp is a woman. I mean, there are easier houses to break into. Why the second-story ones? Why ones with alarms? If she is a pro, she's not a very good one."

Delta went to the front door and knocked loudly before announcing, "Police!"

"What are you doing? There's no one in there."

"Just making sure." When no one answered the door, Delta radioed dispatch that all was clear and asked them to notify the security company to turn off the alarms before the neighbors became angry. Leaving her card on the door, Delta returned to the car.

"Why the second story, Del? Just answer me that."

Delta followed his gaze up to the second story. "It may not even be her, Carducci."

Tony shifted his eyes to Delta's face. "Maybe not, but I can tell by that look in your eyes that you think it was her."

Shrugging, Delta snatched the keys off Tony's belt and ducked into the driver's seat.

"Delta?"

"Hmm?"

"It was her, wasn't it?"

"Carducci, we don't even know if anything was stolen."

"That's not what I asked. You think she hit this house tonight, don't you?"

Delta turned and nodded. "Yes, Carducci, I do. And if she did, she's good."

"Good enough to beat us?"

Delta looked over at Tony and grinned. "Not a chance."

8

"Hey, Chief," Delta said to Connie when she came through the station doors.

"Connie glanced up from the computer and smiled. "Hi there." Connie's eyes suddenly narrowed as she scrutinized Delta's face. "What's up with you? You're looking a hell of a lot perkier tonight than of late."

Delta pulled a chair up and sat down. "I am. Megan and I talked last night, and everything's going to be okay."

"Damn you, Storm, Gina and I have been trying to convince you of that for months. You can be such a thickheaded jackass sometimes.

Delta held her arms up in surrender. "I know, I know. And I've been unbearable lately, but Megan finally put it in words I could understand."

Connie folded her arms across her chest. "So, when are you going to start listening to me?"

"Pretty soon, okay? Con, it was a great conversation. I finally realize what Megan's been searching for."

"Herself?"

Delta nodded. "In a way. She's gotten involved in the preservation of macaw parrots."

Connie's eyebrows shot up. "Preservation?"

"Yep. She's investigating poachers who are smuggling the birds out of the country."

Connie completely turned to Delta now. "Investigating? Storm, what, exactly, is Megan doing?"

Delta shrugged, slightly alarmed by the tone in Connie's voice. "I don't know. Why?"

"Smuggling exotic animals out of Central and South America is as big as drug smuggling, and sometimes it's just as dangerous."

"Dangerous?"

"Hell, yes. There are stiff sentences in some countries for poachers and people attempting to remove the animals from the preserves. It's a big business down there."

"How big?"

Connie frowned as she thought. "A scarlet macaw in this country sells for anywhere between two and five grand. A hyacinth macaw can go anywhere from ten to twenty thousand."

"Dollars? You're kidding."

"I told you—big business. Other exotics run high as well, but the scarlet is in greater demand because it's so pretty. You ever see one up close?"

Delta shook her head. "No."

"They're beautiful. They have white beaks, about a four-foot wingspan, and can live to be seventy years old. They're really popular here, but even more so in the United Kingdom and Australia, where breeding in captivity isn't proving to be very successful."

"But how much danger could Megan really be in?"

Connie shrugged. "In Africa, if you accidentally interrupt poachers killing elephants for their tusks, they'll kill you in a heartbeat. No questions asked."

"Well, I don't think she's trekking into the rain forest after anybody. At this point, I think she's checking around town for information."

"Well, relay what I've told you about the seriousness of poaching."

Delta's heart seemed to constrict inside her chest. "Will do. She's got a good head. I trust that she won't get herself into any real danger; just excitement."

"Speaking of which, what's going on in that beat of yours? Anything new and fun to play with?"

"Maybe. I think we have a real professional thief who enters the second story of alarmed homes. She gets in and out in a—"

"She?" Connie grinned deliciously.

"Uh-huh."

"Is she good?"

Delta nodded. "Very. I can't be sure yet, but I think she only snags big ticket items. Leaves the nickel and dime stuff. She's quick, light on her feet, and she is a climber."

"Interesting. Anything else?" Connie did not need to take notes; she absorbed data like the hard drive on a computer.

"Size seven shoe, weight between one ten and one thirty. She knows how to climb and rappel. That's about it for now."

"Want me to check NCIC and see what comes up?" Delta's eyes sparkled. Oh, how she loved to play with Connie. "Would you? There's something about this that keeps gnawing at me."

"I'll get right on it."

"Thanks, Con." Grabbing her gear, Delta headed for the door.

"Oh, and Del?"

"Yeah?"

"Don't waste any time telling Megan to be careful. Remind her she's not in Kansas anymore."

Grinning, Delta walked out the door.

9

When Delta heard ringing she thought it was in her dream. It took her a minute to realize it was her phone. "Hullo?" she said, hoping to hear Megan's voice on the other end.

"It's me," came Connie's voice instead. Delta reached over and turned the clock radio toward her. It was nearly 8:00 a.m. "You want to hear this now or later?"

"To wake me at eight, it better be good." Delta sat up and rubbed the sleep from her eyes. "You been working all this time?"

"Yeah. Couldn't sleep. Look, I found a thread and followed it to a big ball of yarn. You know how I get."

"Yes, I do, and I love you for it. Whatcha got?"

"Some really interesting things started showing up as I rummaged through the old computer chips. First off, the 459 you went to last night on Byron was a burglary."

Delta slapped the bed with her hand. "I knew it! What did she get?"

"Oddly enough, she only took an emerald ring."

"That's it?"

"That's it. I have the report sitting right in front of me. Nothing else was touched. You said she was a big ticket kinda girl, but there were other pieces in there of more value. Very curious, indeed."

"Maybe the alarm stopped her from taking what she really wanted."

"Maybe. The victim did say that she didn't think the emerald was in the jewelry box with the rest of her valuables, so maybe that's why it was all she got."

"It's possible. What else?"

"Well, you were right about the entry being the second story. No prints, though. This hit is very much like the last. The Burg Unit is sure it's the same thief."

"You think she's a pro?"

"Most definitely. The direction the investigation is headed in is that both pieces were bought at Van Clees' Arpels, a distinguished jeweler on Rodeo Drive, but the diamond was bought over ten years ago."

"Yeah, besides, doesn't everyone in southern California buy their jewelry at Van Clees' Arpels?"

Connie chuckled. "I have a friend checking some other files to see if there are any other suspected female perps whose MO fits our gal."

"What do the dicks think?"

"It's split. Wayne thinks it's an insurance thing, since both were insured, and Hap thinks there's some kind of sexual twist to it."

"It figures. That's all Hap ever thinks it's about. What's your take?" Delta pulled the covers up to her chest and listened to the sound of Connie's fingers as they flew across the keyboard.

"Too early to call. I'm fascinated by the near fact that it's a woman. And she's either incredibly arrogant or very stupid. She's struck twice in one week on the same beat, at houses that had far more valuables than what she left with. Is this a Robin Hood thing? I'm full of questions."

"Any questions that she'll hit again?"

"Count on it."

10

After spending the better part of the afternoon in the library thumbing through various books on rain forests and raising exotic birds, not to mention a pile of *National Geographics,* Delta appreciated the bustling sounds and living energy of the station. But the moment the doors closed behind her, she knew this energy was different. Something was wrong. The strength of the tension which hung in the air stopped her like a clothesline tackle. This wasn't the everyday energy she was used to. Something big had gone down while she was sequestered in the library reading about ecosystems and marine biology. She looked over to find the one person she knew would have immediate answers. Delta was alarmed to find that Connie wasn't at her desk.

Grabbing the first uniformed officer who was hustling by, Delta stopped him. "What went down, Randolph?"

"Didn't you hear? Some whacko took a few shots at the DA."

Delta's blood ran cold. "What? Who? Is she all right?"

Randolph shrugged. "I don't know. Happened about an hour ago."

Delta released him and headed for the captain's office. District Attorney Alexandria Pendleton wasn't just the DA. To Delta, she was a dear friend. If someone out there was attacking her...

Bursting through the door without knocking, Delta stopped abruptly upon seeing the captain, the chief of police, and one of the DA's clerks staring at her.

"Excuse me, Captain Henry, but I just heard—"

"Ever hear of knocking, Stevens?" the captain asked sharply.

"I'm sorry, sir, I just heard the news. Is the DA okay? I mean, was she hurt?"

The aide looked down at his shoes, and the chief cocked his head as if trying to read some hidden message within the apparently innocuous question. Captain Henry motioned for Delta to close the door. "Officer Stevens, here, is a devoted admirer of the DA's work," he explained to the chief and the aide. "She's put away a fair number of Steven's collars. To Delta, he answered, "Yes, Stevens, she's fine. Fortunately for her, the perp was a poor shot. Got off a few rounds that missed entirely."

Delta swallowed hard as her heart continued racing. "I'm sorry for barging in, Captain. It's just that Alex, I mean, Ms. Pendl—"

"Go way back," the captain finished for her. "I'm aware of your connection with her, Delta. Just try knocking next time."

Delta nodded. "Any arrests yet?"

"Not yet, but we're working on it."

Delta knew by his tone that she wasn't about to get the straight scoop from him; at least, not yet. "Once again, I apologize for the intrusion." Backing out of the room, Delta closed the door and exhaled slowly. The thought of a gunman pointing a weapon at Alex gave Delta goosebumps. Alexandria Pendleton wasn't just a good DA, she was a great woman; someone Delta cared deeply for. Delta didn't appreciate the fact that some asshole was bold enough to take potshots at her friend, district attorney or not. Who would have done such a thing, and how had they escaped discovery?"

There was only one place to go for the answers, but Connie wasn't at her desk. Where in the hell was she?

Rounding the corner, Delta ran headfirst into her answer.

"Where in the hell have you been?" Connie rasped, pulling Delta into the women's locker room.

"I could ask the same of you."

"I've been working my tiny ass to the proverbial bone all afternoon in the basement. In between potty breaks, I've left a hundred messages for you. Have you heard?"

Delta nodded. "I've been at the library all afternoon."

Connie's eyebrows raised. "The library?"

"Long story. Why were you in the basement?"

The basement, which wasn't really a basement, but a room full of a decade's worth of microfilm, was where many detectives and would-be sleuths went to solve old crimes. There were microfilm machines, an ancient Xerox machine, and a dinosaur computer, along with hundreds of mug shot books. It was a dark, windowless, musty smelling room which justly deserved the title, "the basement."

"I've been looking to see who's been paroled in the last month that Alex put away. I've also been assigned the unenviable job of locating every perp she put away before she made DA. Goddamn, that woman's been successful."

"Where is she now?"

Connie shrugged. "No idea. They're keeping quiet as to her whereabouts until they get a better handle on it. I think it surprised the hell out of her people and they're running scared."

"Had she received any death threats or anything like that?"

Connie nodded. "Her aide received three death threats, but felt is was his job to keep them from her."

"Of course. If Alex had received death threats, she would have told me about them."

"Instead, her people felt it more prudent to view them as harmless and just ignore them. They felt death threats might harm her re-election."

"Damn fools!" Delta raged, shaking her head. "How could they be so stupid?"

"It's an election year, Del. People lose all common sense when it comes to this kind of stuff."

"That's not all they might lose; their damn jobs should be on the line. Can you find out where they're keeping her?"

Connie shook her head.

"Any idea of how this played out?"

Connie nodded. "She was coming out of the court-house this afternoon, when some shithead took three shots at her. All three rounds missed."

Delta's muscles tightened as she listened.

"We've recovered the rounds. They're from a .44 Magnum, Model 29, eight-inch barrel."

"The Dirty Harry," Delta remarked, offhandedly.

"With a hunter's barrel. Still, he missed."

"Thank God for that. And he got away..."

"Eye witness reports are so varied. He could be a six-foot-tall Iranian, or a five-foot-two Asian."

"Great. So, where does that leave us?"

Connie walked over to the door and locked it. "I can see that you're getting ready to go to the stables to retrieve your white charger, and I know there isn't a damn thing I can do about it. Well, let me at least remind you that Alex is a public figure and this is a very public campaign. Everything must be done by the book. She cannot appear to receive preferential treat-ment just because she was a potential victim. You could do her more harm than good by galloping to the rescue."

Delta fiddled with a lock on one of the lockers. "How can I do that, when I don't even know where she is?"

A sly, incriminating grin slid slowly across Con-nie's face. "So, is that my first assignment? To find out where she is?"

Delta looked up from the lock and grinned. Connie knew her better than she knew herself. Maybe she couldn't ride up on her white charger right now, but that didn't mean she couldn't lend a helping hand. "Can you?"

Connie's grin slid into a smile. "Already have. Well...sort of. I don't know where she is right now, but I know where she'll be at 10:00 tonight."

Delta stepped closer. "Tonight?"

Connie nodded. "The aide followed me to the basement and left a message for you to meet her at Pauline's tonight at 10:00."

Delta nodded. "Pauline's at 10:00?"

"Yep, and just you. She needs the shooter found ASAP so it doesn't appear to the public that the DA can't take care of herself. How will the public view her if she doesn't come up with a suspect?"

"But I thought you said—"

"I did. She needs everything done *publicly* by the book. The media, the press, and the public must not think she's getting special treatment. But she needs a suspect, Storm, and I'll bet a month's salary she needs you to help find one."

Suddenly, the political ramifications of the shooting hit Delta head-on. "Without a suspect, Alex will look incapable of defending herself."

"Exactly. That will give Wainwright the perfect opening to attack her publicly."

"Which could kill her chances of re-election."

Connie unlocked the door. "Either way you cut it, Alex is in trouble, Del, and she needs us. Only this time, we have to keep our involvement under wraps, or we could seriously jeopardize the election."

Delta thought about this for a moment. She couldn't imagine life without Alex as the district attorney. "Then let's not do that. I'll find out how she wants to handle it. No matter what, we'll play it her way."

Connie opened the door, but stopped. "Del?"

"Yeah?"

"You can't afford to get caught with your hand in the cookie jar this time."

Delta's left eyebrow raised. "Are you speaking personally, or professionally?"

"Both. Don't get busted putting your nose where it doesn't belong, and don't let your hormones run your body."

"Connie!"

Connie closed the door and stepped right up to Delta. "Don't play that game with me. You'd have to be in a coma not to see the flames that fly between you two. With Megan out of town, I don't want to see you do anything you might regret."

"Consuela Rivera, have you any idea how much I love Megan?"

"Yes. I also know an attraction between two women when I see one." Connie held up her hand to stop Delta's response. "Deny it all you want, Delta Stevens, but there's something deep between you and our DA, and it's my job as your best friend to keep you from sinking in it. *Capishe?*"

Delta nodded and grabbed the door handle. "Think what you want, Chief, but I am not about to risk my relationship with Megan for a fling with Alex."

"Good. You call me after your meeting with her, okay?"

Delta started out the door. "You know, sometimes, you're worse than my mother."

11

Delta looked at her watch. It was four minutes to ten, and the flashing blue neon sign to Pauline's was reflecting off the hood of the patrol car. "I need to check in on a friend of mine, Carducci. Mind waiting?" Tony shook his head. "Nah. Just don't be too long. I haven't eaten since breakfast."

Delta nodded as she got out and entered the building next to the restaurant. It was one of those old plazas where the shops were linked together by tiny halls and indoor alleys. It was the perfect place to enter because anyone watching would not be able to see where she was really headed.

Walking quickly past a tennis shop, a jewelry store, and a Chinese restaurant, Delta stepped through a side entrance next to the service elevator. When the door closed behind her, Delta's eyes quickly adjusted to the candlelit restaurant. Pauline's was a very dark, very private place, where booths had high backs and the only lighting came from the fat, round candles sitting on the tabletops. There was a light behind the expansive antique bar, but other than that, the place was incredibly dark. The ambiance was half the reason people came; Pauline, herself, was the other half.

Pauline was a grandmotherly woman, stout in build, with salt and pepper curls on her head. Everyone who knew her adored her, and it seemed as if everyone within ten blocks knew her. During World War II, she had been a riveter and supervised the building of more than fifty battleships. One of her dearest friends was Gloria Steinem, and Pauline had submitted numerous articles when *Ms. Magazine* was just a fledgling monthly. Because of her varied acquaintances, the crowd at Pauline's was just as mixed.

When Pauline's husband died some twenty years ago, she took the inheritance and opened her own restaurant. She'd been prospering ever since.

"Hey there, good looking!" Delta said, embracing the older woman. "You look wonderful."

"You're such a smooth talker, Delta Stevens. Where the hell have you and your lady friend been?"

Delta pulled away and straightened her tie. "She's been out of town awhile, but the moment she gets back, we'll be in for some of your homemade dessert."

Pauline raised her eyebrows and grinned. "So, while the cat's away, eh?"

Delta followed Pauline's gaze toward the back room. "Oh. It's not what you—"

"Say no more, love," Pauline interrupted, touching her fingers to Delta's lips. "It's not my place to judge you, honey. And if I did, I'd have to give you a ten on your choice of companions. Even with that silly wig on, I can tell she's beautiful."

A hot flush spread up Delta's neck and to her cheeks. "Pauline, I—"

"Never keep a lady waiting. Now get going before you make the other customers nervous."

Smiling her thanks, Delta pushed open the black curtain leading to the back room and found Alex sitting in one of the booths with her hands around a mug of coffee. Delta barely recognized her with the dark wig on.

Sliding across the booth, Delta wrapped her large hands around Alex's, which were warm from the heat of the mug. "You okay?" The candlelight flicked and danced from the air movement.

Taking off the phony glasses, Alex smiled weakly. "I'm fine. He missed." There was a hint of fear in her gray green eyes as she locked stares with Delta.

"He? You sure it was a male?"

Alex nodded. "I saw him as clearly as I'm seeing you."

Delta pulled her small pad from her breast pocket and clicked her pen on the table. "Description?"

Reaching across the table, Alexandria laid her hands on Delta's. "You're such a sweetheart, but you're already on overdrive, and I'm not sure you're in any position to help me this time."

Delta leaned back, away from Alexandria's intense gaze.

The black wig covering her long auburn hair did not hide the real beauty behind the disguise. Her lavender blouse was accentuated by dangling purple and silver earrings which rocked gently whenever she spoke. Her jawline was long and strong, framing well her sturdy Roman nose. There was a beauty in her strength and strength in her beauty few women could carry off as well as Alexandria did; Delta admired both qualities.

When they first met, Alexandria was investigating Delta's involvement in bringing down the men who had killed Miles Brookman, her partner and best friend. Alexandria had dug, pulled, twisted, and cast all manner of light on Delta's story about that night when Delta fired a fatal bullet into a man sent to kill her. Alexandria did her job, and she did it better than anyone Delta had ever seen. What Alexandria discovered in her search for the truth was how honest Delta Stevens really was. When the trial was over, the two became instant admirers of each other's integrity.

"You know I'll do whatever I can, Alex. Just say the word."

Alex smiled warmly, displaying thousands of dollars worth of perfection. "You know, for someone who prides herself on her unpredictability, you can be awfully predictable sometimes."

"Only my hairdresser knows for sure. I'm a little partial to the current DA. I'm not ready to break in a new one."

Alexandria finished her coffee and set the mug on the table's edge. "That's good to hear because...," Alex's smile disappeared, "because I'm not ready to give it up. At least, not quite yet."

Delta shifted her body weight and folded her hands on the table. "Explain."

"This could really turn the tide in Wainwright's favor, Delta. When this hits the news tonight, I'm not going to be looking so swell."

"Because?"

"First off, it happened right outside the courthouse and the press were everywhere. Flashbulbs popped all over the place. God, how I dread tomorrow's papers."

The waitress came over and filled Alexandria's mug and offered to serve Delta, but she declined.

"Anyway, my people obviously got right on it. We've spoken to the chief, and he believes it could be someone I put away who's now out on parole."

Delta studied Alexandria's face as she spoke. She was incredibly calm for a woman who had just survived an assassination attempt, but there was something behind the words that bothered Delta.

"I get the feeling there's a 'but' in the air. You don't buy the chief's scenario?"

Alexandria shook her head. "I saw him so clearly, Del. I saw him as clearly as I'm looking at you. I spent hours with Jonesy at the computer drawing up his picture. We have a good likeness of the shooter."

"And?"

"And I have a photographic memory where people are concerned. I never forget them. That man wasn't anyone I've ever convicted."

"You're sure?"

Alex nodded. "Positive. Even if the beard is fake or he shaves it off, I've never seen that man before today."

Delta watched as Alex poured cream from a little white carafe. "I'm sure you're great with faces, Alex, but when a guy's pointing a gun at you—"

Alexandria held up her hand. "That's just it, Del. That's the reason I called you. I saw his face because he moved the gun."

Delta shook her head. "I don't follow."

Looking at the cream as it disappeared into the coffee, Alexandria struggled with the words. "I haven't told this to anyone else, Delta, but I swear, I think he intended to miss me."

"What?"

Alex nodded and lowered her voice. "I saw the barrel of the gun move just before he fired. I think he never intended to kill me, just scare me a bit."

"A bit?"

"I know it sounds strange, Delta, but think about it. He had me cold. I saw how close he was, yet he missed all three shots. And why only three shots? If he really wanted to kill me, why not squeeze off the additional rounds?"

Delta nodded. "And why not use an automatic? Why a dinosaur like the .44?"

"If he was truly serious about killing me, why not use a high-powered scope and shoot me from half a mile away? Why right there in front of the courthouse with all the press there?"

Running her hands through her hair, Delta conceded. "Damn, I feel like I just walked into the middle of a movie. You're suggesting that it was a staged attack."

Alex nodded before sipping her coffee. "That's precisely what I'm suggesting. I've gone over it and over it all day long, and too many things simply don't add up."

"The attack has political underpinnings."

Alex shrugged. "I've been getting death threats—"

"So I've heard."

"I'm sorry, Del, but we couldn't take the chance on it leaking to the press. I don't need those vultures picking at me during this election. Wainwright is an arduous opponent as it is with all his moneyed backers. We couldn't take any chances, I'm sorry."

"What's done is done. What do you need from me? You want me to see if it's someone connected to Wainwright?"

Alex shook her head. "No. I want you to make sure it isn't someone from within."

"You're kidding."

"No, I'm not. I need to be sure I don't have someone close to me who is actually with Wainwright. I can't ask any of my people to check it out because how would that look if the press got ahold of it? Worse, what if one of my people is on board with Wainwright? I need someone I can trust."

Delta grinned. "You know you can always trust me."

"Yes, I do. I need answers and I need them quickly. I can kiss this election goodbye if I can't prove to the voters that I can take care of myself. How is it going to look if I appear incapable of protecting myself? The shooting, if it was staged, is the perfect election weapon. If I don't get a suspect, and soon, I'm a goner."

Delta didn't want to admit it, but Alex was right. A DA who appeared helpless in her own defense didn't stand a chance of winning the confidence of the public. And with the amount of backing Wainwright possessed, the battle would be tough enough without this thrown into the stew.

"What if it is someone on your staff?"

"We'll let the public relations department cross that bridge. What I need is a suspect charged with attempted murder. And I need an investigation with discretion; the kind of discretion only you can provide."

"Then, you're not really interested in the trigger man; you want who's behind him."

Alex nodded. "If we find out who that is, give me some time for damage control, and see if we can't turn this around to my advantage."

Delta looked deeply into Alex's eyes. "I'll do whatever I can, Alex. You know that."

"We have to move quickly, Del, or—"

"Or else we'll have a new DA who's more interested in his financial connections than with convicting criminals. I read you, Alex. Wainwright's a slimeball who talks out of both sides of his mouth. He should be a politician."

"That's just it. Wainwright will use his office to further his own political ambitions. He doesn't give a rat's ass about crime in River Valley."

Delta reached across and took Alex's hands in hers. "You can rest assured that I'll turn over a bunch of rocks and see who crawls out from under them. In the meantime, beef up your own security with people you know you can trust."

"Like you?" Alex smiled a very different smile that did not go unnoticed by Delta.

"Yeah. Like me." Rising, Delta lightly touched Alex's wig. "I prefer your real color." Delta hugged Alex tightly, then stepped back and smiled at her. "I'm just glad the asshole missed."

Alexandria grinned. "Me, too. I was wearing a new suit."

Delta picked up Alexandria's hand and kissed the back of it. "You be more careful out there, you hear me?"

"You, too. The last time I asked for your help—"

"Ancient history. This is what good friends are for. I'll get back to you as soon as we have something."

Delta parted the black curtain and walked back through the restaurant. Pauline was mixing drinks for a gentleman, and she waved as Delta walked out the door.

"Come back soon, Delta."

Delta saluted her acknowledgment before stepping out into the crisp night air. Once outside, she strolled down the alley until she came to the front of the buildings, where she pretended to check all the front doors. When she came to the patrol car, she found Tony clipping his fingernails."

"Sorry, it took longer than I thought."

"How is she?"

Delta cocked her head in question. "Who?"

"Come on, Del. I'm not stupid. I've been with you long enough to know that God, himself, couldn't keep you from Pendleton's investigation."

"It's *her*self, and so what?"

Tony turned. "So what? So what about lesson two hundred and twelve? The one about trusting your partner? Or was that just a bullshit line from the FTO training guide?"

Taken aback by his anger, Delta held up her hands. "You don't understand—"

"Because you won't even let me try. Damn it, Delta, I've killed a man protecting you. You trusted me with your life out there, and I came through for you."

"Yes, you did."

"Then why can't you trust me to help you help her?"

Delta turned the interior light on as she turned to face him. Yes, she had trusted him with her life, and he had, indeed, pulled through for her. He had executed his role to perfection; no questions, no hesitations, no missed marks. He had risen to the challenge and succeeded.

"It's not that."

"No? Then what?"

Delta studied his face for a moment. He had grown so much in the two months they'd been together. He had toned down his macho man demeanor, and had done everything she asked of him. Why then, shouldn't she trust him?

"I'm sorry, Tony. I haven't been very fair, have I? I demand complete loyalty and trust and have only given you a fraction of mine. Trust isn't something that comes naturally to me. I've been burned too many times by people I thought I could trust."

"I won't burn you, Delta." The words were said so softly, so quietly, Delta wasn't sure they'd come from Tony's mouth. "Del, you taught me right off the bat that whatever is said in this car stays in this car. Give me a chance to prove to you that I'm not the same jerk I was when we first started working together."

Delta peered deeply into Tony's eyes. Yes, he had changed. The reality of snuffing out a beating heart hit Tony hard, and he did a great deal of self-examination for weeks after.

And now, here he was, with his hat in his hand,
asking his feminist, lesbian partner to once again put
her trust in him. Tentatively, she laid her hand on
Tony's forearm. "You're right, Tony. You're not the
same guy I saw at Harry's that night."
"Then give me an opportunity, Delta. That's all I
ask. I'd at least like the chance at bat. Don't I deserve
that much?"
At that very moment, Tony Carducci changed forever in Delta's eyes. Suddenly, the boy transformed
into the man before her; not because he killed a man
to save her life, not because he finally learned how to
determine east from west, but because he cared. Tony
Carducci cared, and that made all the difference in the
world. Inhaling deeply, she told Tony everything that
was going on with Alexandria.
"We're on a very short leash, you know," she said
when she had finished outlining what Alex needed
from them.
Tony nodded. "I know."
"If we get busted nosing around this investigation,
you can kiss your SWAT team dreams goodbye. Hell,
for that matter, you can kiss the dog pound goodbye."
"Then let's not get caught."
Delta looked over at him and grinned. "Ah, Grasshopper, you catch on quickly."

12

The vibrations from the powerful bike felt good beneath Taylor, as she cut the Harley engine so she could coast up to the dark house. Long ago, she stopped being surprised by how few people actually turned on their porch lights when they left their houses at night. What else was it for if not to scare the burglars away? And how many times had Taylor faced motion detector beams and high-powered floodlights which were not turned on? What was the use?

Rolling silently up to the targeted house, Taylor grinned beneath her black helmet. Of the neighboring houses, neither had their porch light on, creating a sort of black hole appearance on this side of the street.

Checking her watch, Taylor realized she had to work quickly; not that time mattered here as much as it did in Chicago or New York. It was so much easier working nights in California. It was a burglar's dreamland; warm nights, long driveways, plenty of night life for the natives, and neighbors who were not about to get involved. Yes, she could plant roots here, if she wanted. However, even warmer climates beckoned her once she had completed this final challenge of her illustrious career.

Turning the Harley around so it faced the street, Taylor readjusted her gloves before trying the front door. It was locked. Moving to the side yard, she easily scaled the fence, threw her rope up and over the fireplace, pulled it taut, and swung to the side of the house to start her ascent. When she came to the window, she checked it and found it locked as well.

Holding onto the rope with one hand, Taylor unzipped her pouch and retrieved a small box. From the box she pulled out a tiny suction cup, which she licked before placing it on the window. Then, she extracted a silver device resembling a math compass. With a flick of her wrist, the compass whirled, cutting a flawless circle in the glass. When the compass came back to where it had started, Taylor tugged gently on the suction cup and out popped the perfectly round piece of cut glass. Next, she reached her arm through the newly made hole, unlocked the window, and let herself in. She did this all in less than a minute.

"Ah, Taylor," she said to herself, "you haven't lost your touch." Putting her tools away and withdrawing her penlight, Taylor quickly made her way to the bedroom, where she searched through two jewelry boxes until she came to a long, slender gray box.

"Ding, ding, ding," Taylor said, plucking the box from the bottom of the wooden jewelry box. "And the winner is...me!" Opening the box, Taylor put the penlight in her mouth and shined the light on the gold necklace with ten deep blue gemstones set magnificently in gold settings. Of the hundreds of pieces of jewelry Taylor had stolen, this was one of the most incredible pieces she'd ever seen.

Looking at her watch, Taylor placed the necklace in her pouch. Creeping downstairs, she set the empty gray box on the kitchen table and exited through the front door. It was a crisp, clean night that might be considered a summer night in London or New England. Oh, how she had grown fond of California's weather.

Stepping out the front door, she double-checked all her zippered pouches before straddling the Harley. Then, with great flair, she slammed her visor shut, gunned the powerful bike, and squealed down the street, smiling grandly as she pulled behind a patrol car at a stop light.

"Ah. Sweet, sweet irony."

13

Tony was humming an indistinguishable tune when dispatch came over the air. "S1012, we have a 459 at 19 Virgil Way. See the man."

Tony picked up the mike. "This is S1012, we copy." Hanging up the mike, Tony turned to Delta. "Think it's her?"

Delta smiled. "It's possible. Virgil isn't exactly her type of neighborhood, though."

"Virgil Way?" Tony asked, interrupting her train of thought. "I don't remember ever seeing that street sign before."

Delta shook her head. "You wouldn't because there isn't one. Virgil is one of those streets that looks like an alley but is really a narrow road. There are a few houses down Virgil, but you can't see them from the cross street." Pulling down a dark side street, Delta slowed when she came to the corner. "See? That little road is Virgil. Blink, and you'll miss it."

"Is it a cul-de-sac?" Tony asked, squinting through the blackness of a poorly lit street.

Delta nodded.

"She's taking a chance hitting a court, don't you think?"

"Not really. Take a good look at this street. No lampposts, no porchlights, no stores, nothing. It's dark, dark, dark. Getting in and out undetected, especially by foot, would be a piece of cake." Delta pulled into the driveway and then backed up so the car was parallel to the house. Two men stood in the doorway with their arms around each other's waists.

"Officer! Over here!" the thinner one yelled, waving to them as if they wouldn't know which house to go to. The thin man suddenly released himself from the other man's grasp and ran up to Delta. "My necklace! They stole my beautiful lapis necklace!"

Delta exited the car and stared at Tony, who shrugged.

"Lapis, sir?"

"I'm so glad you're here. Please, come in. Come in and see what those...those horrible hoodlums did to my home!"

Walking up to the other man, who resembled a young Harrison Ford, Delta made the appropriate introductions and handed him her card. "Your house was burglarized tonight?"

Harrison nodded. "I think we made it home just in time because they hardly took a thing, and I have some extremely expensive computer equipment."

Delta glanced over at Tony, who had positioned himself so that she was in between him and the two men. Pulling her notebook from her pocket, Delta glared at him. If he understood the meaning behind the look, he chose to ignore it, because he maintained a good two arms length away from the men.

"Did you just return home?" Delta asked Harrison.

Both men nodded. The thin man kept staring at Tony, as if he sensed Tony's discomfort.

Turning to Tony, Delta motioned for him to go upstairs. "Tony, why don't you take your homophobia upstairs and determine where the point of entry is."

"My wh—oh...yeah, sure." Scooting around the back of Harrison, Tony disappeared into the house and up the stairs.

After watching him go, Delta turned her attention back to the two men. "I make it a habit not to apologize for my partners, but just know that he is in the process of his humanity training and sometimes has setbacks."

Harrison laughed and put his arm around the thin man. "Randy and I have skin of leather by now, Officer. But thank you for sending him off. There's nothing worse than feeling uncomfortable in your own home."

"I couldn't agree with you more. Now, if you don't mind telling me what you discovered when you returned home."

Stepping into the house, Harrison started to speak first. "We just came home from the theater and—"

"Was the alarm ringing?"

"Not when we arrived. When we got to the door, it was open."

"Do you remember closing it?" Delta asked, quickly jotting down his words.

"Oh, yes," Randy offered, "I always lock the door. Stephen always drives, so it's my job to lock the door. It was definitely closed and locked when we left."

"Okay. When you came home, did you see or hear anything?"

"No, I went directly upstairs to make sure that my grandmother's brooch was still there." Randy flustered, "Oh, I would have died if anything had happened to that."

Delta tried not to smile. Men whose voices were more feminine than hers always made her smile. "And, I take it, it was left untouched."

Randy drew his hand dramatically up to his chest. "Thank goodness, yes. I simply don't know what I would have done."

Stephen tightened his grip on his partner. "We've checked the entire house, and the only thing missing is Randy's necklace."

"And it's such a beautiful necklace. I kept it in the box Stephen gave to me for our anniversary. That's the box there on the table. We didn't touch it because we're hoping they left their fingerprints on it."

Delta grinned as she squatted down to examine the box. "Well, we'll have to wait for the Burglary Unit to dust for prints, but not touching it was wise." Standing up, Delta jotted more information down before looking around the room. This hit already had the feel of her female cat burglar.

Suddenly, Tony appeared at the top of the stairs nodding and beckoning Delta with his hand. Delta excused herself and joined him at the top of the stair-case. "What is it?"

"She came in through the window all right. In this bedroom."

Delta followed Tony into the bedroom and saw the perfectly round six-inch hole in the window. "She sure is a pro, isn't she?"

Tony nodded. "I'm getting tired of her already."

"You have to hand it to her, she's well equipped." Delta examined the window frame and floor beneath the window.

"What are you looking for?" Tony asked.

Delta shrugged, but didn't take her eyes from the carpet. "She may even be better than good, but there's something we're missing."

"What do you mean?"

Slowly rising, Delta turned to him. "Don't you find it odd that she puts so much energy into getting inside, only to steal just one piece of jewelry? What's up with that?"

Tony scratched his head. "That *is* pretty weird."

"Right. What's her point? Why those specific pieces. I mean, lapis? What in the hell is lapis?" Starting back down the stairs, Delta rejoined the two men who were now sitting on the couch. "We'll file a report on this, but I suspect the Burglary Unit will want to take a closer look."

Delta shrugged. "Was the necklace insured?"

Randy nodded. "Stephen makes sure that every-thing valuable is insured."

"Well, you may not get the necklace back, but at least they didn't steal your brooch."

Rising in unison, the men shook hands with Delta, but ignored Tony. "Thank you so much, Officer. You've been extremely kind."

Delta nodded once. "That's what you pay me for. You can do me a favor, though, and make my job a little easier by installing a floodlight on the porch. This is one of the darkest streets on my beat."

"Will do," Stephen said, escorting Delta and Tony to the door. "I'll be sure one goes up tomorrow."

Heading toward the car, Tony sighed heavily. "I'm sorry, Del, but those two gave me the creeps."

Delta stopped in her tracks. "You were about as subtle as a bull in a china closet. Damn it, Carducci. Just when I think your puny mind has opened some, you pull this shit."

"I can't help it."

"That's the sad part."

"Oh, come off it, Delta. How many straight men do you know who openly accept fags?"

Delta bristled. "Gay men, Carducci. The respectable term is gay men. And there are plenty who are open-minded enough not to care about anyone's sexual orientation."

"I'm open-minded enough."

"Oh, really?" Reaching the car, Delta noticed a lavender note stuck under the windshield. "What the—?" Carefully taking it by the right corner, Delta pulled it out and flicked it open. "Lapis lazuli—an opaque, azure blue to deep blue gemstone of lazurite. From the Latin: stone."

"That little bitch is—" before Delta could finish, a loud, thundering roar ripped through the air. Looking up from the note, Delta saw a single headlight at the top of the street glaring down at them. The sound, loud and reverberating, could only be one machine: a Harley-Davidson.

For a moment, Delta waited to see if the bike was moving; it wasn't. It was just idling loudly. In the dim light of the street, Delta could see little, save the single headlight beam and the silhouetted outline of a small figure straddled atop the large bike. Delta estimated the biker to be about fifty yards away.

"Hit your spot, Carducci," Delta ordered, knowing full well who was perched on the motorcycle. In the flash of a second, the bike and its rider were brilliantly illuminated; the harsh glare of the spotlight danced off the black leather jumpsuit, shiny black helmet, and polished chrome pipes. Before Delta could utter a single word, Taylor waved, grabbed the handlebars, and roared away.

"Let's get her!" Tony yelled, jumping into the car.

Delta looked at the note in her hand before climbing into the driver's seat.

"What are you waiting for, Del? Come on!"

Delta reached over and clipped the lavender note to her clipboard before starting the car. "Relax. We're not going to be goaded into a chase."

"Why the hell not? What's wrong with you? She's probably laughing her head off under that helmet."

Putting the car in drive, Delta sighed. "Yes, she probably is."

"Then why aren't we going after her?" Tony's voice was caught between whining and pleading.

Delta ran her hand through her hair. "She's long gone, Carducci. That bike would kick our butts without even trying hard. Forget about it."

"Forget about it? You're kidding, right?"

Delta gripped the steering wheel tightly. No, she wasn't kidding. She had already been burned once tonight. She wasn't about to make a fool of herself chasing after a vehicle that could go places the patrol car couldn't. Glancing over at the note, Delta grimaced.

That thief. That woman. She'd had her hands on Delta's patrol car. She'd been here, watching Delta's investigation, gauging her reactions, trying to goad her into a needless chase. What was going on with this woman? Who was she, and why in the hell was she messing with Delta?

"Delta? Hello? Is anybody home?"

Delta tapped her finger on the clipboard. "She's a bold woman, Carducci. She's challenging us. She sat out there, watched us work, and for some reason, tried to get us to chase her."

"Then, why didn't we?"

"Ever ride a motorcycle, Carducci?"

"Sure."

"Ever been on a 1340cc Harley?"

"Well...no."

"I have, and believe me, we would have eaten her dust and really given her something to laugh at. No, we're not going to get into a high speed chase over a bunch of colored rocks. It's not worth it."

Tony cracked the knuckles on his right hand. "Well, she sure is making us look stupid."

Delta nodded. Yes, she was. For a second, Delta wondered what was beneath that helmet and black leather jumpsuit. She'd seen that outfit somewhere before, but couldn't quite put her finger on where. "She's good, Carducci. Sometimes, you just have to acknowledge the truth."

Tony slowly turned to Delta. "You know, if I knew you better, I'd think you kind of admire our burglar."

Delta laughed. "I hardly think so. Admire is a tad strong for me. I've just always appreciated women with chutzpah."

"Chutzpah?"

"Guts. That woman has iron guts."

"So, how do we bag ourselves Old Iron Guts?"

Stepping on the gas, Delta answered, "Patiently, that's how. She's going to slip up, and when she does, we'll be there."

14

Pulling into a parking stall labeled *compact,* Delta watched as the pink neon sign of the Leather and Lace bar flickered on and off. The L and L had risen quickly as the prominent lesbian bar in River Valley. It was a place for today's lesbian, women who were no longer trapped by gross stereotypes or molded out of societal archetypes of what dykes should look like. The L and L drew women who were career oriented, who were single mothers, college students, artists and writers, established business women and an assortment of other females who refused to be jammed in a box. Various meetings were held on any given night, and there wasn't a weeknight that went by when there wasn't a softball, rugby, basketball, or volleyball player sitting around reliving her game. The L and L had a mixed bag of women and, for this reason, it had become the fulcrum of the lesbian, feminist, and bisexual women's community.

Hopping out of her truck, Delta pulled her leather jacket out and pushed her arms through the sleeves. The leather creaked, as all new leather jackets tend to. She loved her new jacket, which had come to her as a gift from the parents of the little girl she had saved from a near fatal fire.

One last check in the window, Delta ran her hands through her hair before zipping up her jacket all the way. She had lost a little weight since Megan had left, and it showed in her face.

"If anyone asked me, I'd say you were looking pretty fine," came a purring voice from behind her.

Whipping around, feeling foolishly vain, Delta looked over the roof of a BMW that had pulled up beside her. A striking face surrounded by blond hair was smiling back at her.

"If I'd known that women like yourself come to this bar, I'd have visited it much sooner."

A stupid smile appeared on Delta's face long before any intelligent words could find their way out of her mouth. "Actually," she began, watching as the blond slammed the door and sauntered seductively around the back of the BMW. The short, five-foot-three, one-hundred-ten-pound woman wearing black stretch pants, black pumps, and a white waiter's jacket made her way in front of Delta. "I, uh, don't usually come here, myself, but my lover is out of town, and—"

"And the mice will play, won't they?" the woman said, brushing up against Delta before leaning against the truck. This was the second time she'd heard that stupid phrase in less than twenty-four hours.

"Well, not this mouse."

The woman's right eyebrow lifted as if independent of her other facial features. "No? What a shame. Then what is a gorgeous creature like you teasing the rest of us for? If you were my lover, I'd never let you out of my sight, let alone into a lesbian bar by yourself." Toying with her hair, the woman took a step toward Delta, close enough for Delta to smell the spicy aroma of her perfume. "If you get my meaning."

Delta grinned and tried to move back, but her butt was already against the other car's door. "You're quite a flatterer." The eyes Delta gazed into were not unlike her own: deep, almost emerald green.

"A flatterer flatters. I simply tell the truth. There's a difference," Green Eyes smiled. "But then, I'll bet you're just as brilliant as you are good-looking."

"Are you alone?" Delta asked, immediately realizing how that sounded. God, it had been so long since anyone had come on to her, she wasn't sure what to do or say anymore.

"Do you want me to be?" Now, Green Eyes was practically rubbing up against Delta, and the chill of the night air was quickly replaced by a sudden warmth. "Look," Green Eyes said, as if reading Delta's discomfort. "If you get inside, have a few drinks, and change your mind...about playing, I mean...then look my way. I'll know."

Delta nodded stiffly. "Sure, but—"

"Shh. No buts. Life is so much more fun without buts, if onlys, or should haves, don't you agree?"

Nodding mutely, Delta stepped around her. "Well, I seldom live by the rules or the buts or the should haves, but this time, I'm going to have to make an exception. My friends are waiting for me."

"I'll bet they are."

"Have fun tonight," Delta said as she made her way to the door.

"Oh, I already have. As a matter of fact, you're the most fun I've had in a long time." With that, Green Eyes laughed and followed Delta into the bar.

The L and L was busier than usual, and Delta surveyed the room to discover why. There was a pool tournament on one end of the room, a dart match on the other, and an AIDS walkathon sign up at the bar. The bar had finally come into its own.

After pushing her way through the crowd, Delta peered over everyone's heads searching for Connie and Gina. When she didn't find them, she spotted two lovers staring into each other's eyes while sitting at the table Delta used to call home when the bar was aptly named the Dirtbag. It never ceased to amaze Delta how ritualistic bar goers tended to be. Some danced all night, with or without partners, while others, like herself, preferred to sit at the tables chatting and watching the younger women strut around like peacocks. Still, there was always the set that hung around the pool table, seeing who could rule the table for the night, while others roamed like sharks in search of food.

Reaching into her pocket, Delta pulled out a ten and flipped it on the table, breaking the lovers' prolonged gaze. "Drinks are on me if you'll let me have this table."

Both women looked up at her questioningly.

"Sentimental reasons," Delta said, shrugging. What she couldn't tell them was that she, too, had established some pretty bizarre rituals since becoming a cop; one was that she always had to face the door whenever she was in a restaurant or out for the evening. It had been etched in her mind in the academy that she should always be aware of who was coming and going. This particular table gave her a perfect view of the front and back doors, the bar, and the pool table. Call it paranoia, call it cautious, Delta never sat with her back to the door.

The two women looked at each other before the slighter one nodded. "Sure." Snatching the bill in her right hand, she reached for her girlfriend's hand with her left. "Time for dancing anyway."

Watching them walk arm in arm, Delta felt the familiar sting of loneliness. God, how she missed Megan.

Still studying the crowd, Delta spied a petite blond bending over the pool table eyeing her next shot. It seemed everyone around the table was interested in the blond who stood erect, chalked up her cue, and slowly bent over to take aim once more. When she blasted the purple four ball into the corner pocket, Delta's expression changed from bemused to impressed. Her admiration of the blond escalated when she went on to clear the table without ever giving her opponent another shot.

"Not bad," Delta mumbled to herself, watching the next challenger cross her name off the board. She was a large, extremely masculine looking woman who handed the blond a beer before kissing her on the lips. "Her mate," Delta uttered, completely taken in by the scene. It seemed as if everyone in the bar was watching them. When the blond smiled at the challenger, Delta leaned in for a closer view.

"No way," Delta said, leaning forward for a better look. "I'll be damned. I think it is." Rising from the chair, Delta stood for a moment before moving closer. She wanted to be sure—absolutely sure—before saying anything. After all, she hadn't really looked at the picture that closely. Still, Delta had a memory for faces, and the pretty blond wasn't likely to be one she'd soon forget. And, even if her eyes had deceived her, there was no fooling her gut.

It was Gwen; Carducci's ex-girlfriend. Alive and well, and playing pool in a lesbian bar. How interesting.

Before she knew it, Delta was standing in front of Gwen, ignoring the acid stares from her girlfriend.

"Excuse me," Delta opened, for lack of anything clever to say, "is your name Gwen?" The bar seemed to come to a standstill as everyone watched the girlfriend's reaction.

"Beat it, sister, she's taken," came the gravelly smoker's voice of the girlfriend.

Delta ignored the voice and the woman it belonged to. "This isn't a come on or anything like that. I saw a picture of someone who looks like you, and I was just wondering if maybe you were her."

The blonde's reddish eyebrow rose in question. "Well, on whose picture might that have been?"

"He's a colleague of mine." Delta sensed the overpowering jealousy emanating from the girlfriend, but continued to ignore it. The blonde, however, did not. Stepping up to Delta, she smiled coyly.

"You got a name, sweetheart?" Her voice betrayed both her attraction to Delta and her affinity for igniting fireworks in public places—neither of which made Delta comfortable. Perhaps she should have left well enough alone.

"I'm not looking for trouble. I saw a picture of a woman who resembles you." Delta felt the air close in around her as the girlfriend moved in.

"If you're not looking for trouble, Cowgirl, you ought to just keep on moving right along."

Cowgirl? Hell, she supposed it was a better cut than fluffball. Either way, Delta hesitated for a moment, deciding whether or not it was worth finding out if Carducci's long lost lover was, in fact, a lesbian.

"You deaf or something?" The girlfriend stood right at Delta's shoulder.

Deciding against further aggravating anyone, Delta thought maybe showing her badge might earn a little cooperation.

As Delta reached for her wallet, a small hand slipped into hers while an arm slid around her waist. "There you are, sweetheart," Green Eyes purred into her chest. "I thought I'd lost you."

Speechless, Delta couldn't even muster up a smile.

"After five years, you'd think I'd know she was making friends at the pool table," Green Eyes said kissing Delta's neck; this settled the big girlfriend down in a heartbeat.

"Hey," the girlfriend said, smiling a smile that looked somewhat awkward on her face. "Sorry if I jumped the gun. Bars kinda make me nervous, know what I mean?"

Delta glanced down at the thick, outstretched hand thrust at her before taking it firmly in hers. "Unfortunately, I do. No respect for relationships."

"Exactly," she said. "Now, what was it you thought Gwen might know?" The girlfriend stepped next to Gwen and wrapped her meaty arm over Gwen's shoulder.

Delta grinned slightly and tried ignoring the fingers caressing her back. What would Connie and Gina say if they saw this? She hated even thinking about it.

"His name is Tony Carducci." Delta knew by the rush of blood to Gwen's face and the way her eyes dilated that she was the one in the picture.

"Yes, I knew Tony," Gwen said, casting defeated eyes at the girlfriend. "We dated once."

"Dated?" Delta asked. Oh, how two stories could be so very different.

"I suppose he thought there was more to it than that, but that was it. Don't tell me he still carries my picture around."

Delta pried one arm from off her waist and tried not to look down at the face smiling up at her. "I suppose he has a good reason to."

Gwen turned to her girlfriend and asked if she would buy her a beer. The girlfriend looked at Green Eyes hanging on Delta and nodded before trudging away.

"Look—"

"Delta."

"Look, Delta, poor Tony caught me at a time when I was just discovering who I was and what I was about. I couldn't very well tell him I was exploring my sexuality. I cared about him, but...he just wasn't what I needed at the time."

"But you never told him the truth, did you?" Delta pried the other arm off her as she spoke. Green Eyes seemed to relish her role.

"I couldn't. It would have devastated him."

"Maybe, but at least he'd know the truth. As it is now, he just has a lot of unanswered questions. Don't you think he deserves to have them answered?"

Gwen looked into Delta's face. "How is it you know him so well?"

"Yes, dear," Green Eyes added. "How long have you known Mr. Man?"

Gwen laughed. "Obviously you know him very well. How do you tell a macho man like Tony Carducci that you'd rather make love with a woman? As much fun as we had, he was still the most narrow-minded, pig-headed man I'd ever met. When I met Brandy, I really struggled with whether or not to tell him the truth. And if you know Tony as well as I did, you'd know that the truth would have hurt him more."

Delta nodded slightly, remembering her own ex-lover's very same words. They were pathetic then, and they were pathetic now. People who withheld the truth to "keep from hurting someone" were the lowest form of life in Delta's book. It had happened to her, and it hurt like hell. But cheaters often rationalized their dishonesty by stating, rather gallantly, that they lied to protect their lovers. Just the idea made Delta wince.

"You hurt him, Gwen. And it may be hard to believe, but Tony is still wounded."

"Wounded?" Gwen took the beer her girlfriend handed her. "We must not be talking about the same guy. Tony's ego was incapable of being wounded."

"Maybe he's changed."

"So? What do you want from me?"

Delta stared down at Green Eyes, who again had both her hands around Delta's waist. Just what in blazes was going on here? And where in the hell was Connie?

"What she wants," Green Eyes began, "is for you to understand that he can't let go because he's blaming himself. All she's asking is for you to free him from the doubt that you, my dear, inflicted upon him."

Delta looked up from Green Eyes and nodded. "That's all it will take, Gwen. Tony isn't the same man you went out with. He...his views about gays and lesbians have changed."

Gwen studied Delta with skepticism. "And who changed him? You?"

Delta shrugged. "Circumstance changed him."

"What are you to him, anyway?" Gwen asked.

"We're partners. We're cops." Without even looking at the girlfriend, Delta could sense her surprise.

Gwen, on the other hand, smiled. "So, he finally made it? It was all he ever talked about."

Delta nodded.

"Then, I take it that having a lesbian for a partner has broadened his horizons?"

Grinning, Delta stuffed her hands in her pockets when Green Eyes reached for her hands. "Sort of. Tony's an okay guy, but there's a pain in his voice when he talks about you."

Gwen's facial features suddenly softened, her posture opened, and she seemed to hear what Delta had been saying. "I don't know if he can accept that I left him for a woman, but I'll give it some thought."

Delta shrugged. "Won't cost you anything to be honest with the guy. He deserves that much."

Someone from the pool table area handed her a stick. "Look, I'm up. I'm not promising anything, but I'll really think about it."

Delta nodded and, again, pried Green Eyes' hands off her waist. "Thanks for your help. For a minute there—"

"You could have taken the big one out without even breathing hard...although watching you breathe hard could be a lot of fun."

Feeling the heat rise in her cheeks, Delta sighed loudly. "Well, thanks for the help."

"No, thank *you*. It's definitely been a...far more interesting evening than I imagined."

Delta looked down into Green Eyes' face and smiled. "What did you say your name was?"

Standing on her tiptoes, Green Eyes kissed Delta's cheek. "I didn't." And with that, she slipped off into the crowd, leaving Delta staring at her back.

"What's your pleasure, good-looking?" came Connie's voice from behind her.

Delta wheeled around and hugged Connie tightly. "Man, am I glad to see you!"

"Whoa, Kimo. You been drinking too much Pepsi, or what?"

Delta pulled away and smiled broadly. "I just needed a hug, that's all."

"Then give me one," Gina added, stepping up to Delta, who gave her a squeeze.

"Missing Megan?" Gina asked, lightly brushing some stray hairs from Delta's forehead.

"Uh-huh. This one woman sort of came on to me and I suddenly wished that Megan was here to fend her off."

"Sort of came on to you?"

Delta laughed. "Long story. Can I buy you two drinks?"

Connie and Gina exchanged secretive glances.

"What?" Delta had known the two of them long enough to know this "Boy-do-we-have-some-special-news-to-tell-you" look they shared between them.

"Tonight's a champagne night," Connie answered, grabbing the nearest waitress and ordering a bottle of champagne.

"Champagne? Don't tell me..."

Connie grinned from ear to ear. "Yep. We is. The insemination from the Native American took."

Delta wrapped her arms around both of them and hugged them tightly. "The doctor or home pregnancy test?"

Gina blushed. "Home preggers for now. I have an appointment with Doctor Weeks tomorrow morning to confirm."

"I can't believe it! I mean, I believe it, but...a baby? We're having a baby!" Delta pushed through to her table, but found it occupied. "Excuse me, but this woman is pregnant and really needs to get off her feet." Immediately, both women jumped out of their chairs. "Thanks."

After taking their seats, Gina reached out and took Delta's right hand and Connie's left. "Let's get one thing perfectly clear right here and now. I will not be coddled and pampered like some china doll for the next nine months, do you hear me? I am pregnant, not helpless."

"No, dearest, you're not," Connie said, bringing Gina's hand to her mouth and kissing one knuckle. "But our fun will come from taking especially good care of you."

Delta nodded. "That's right. Besides, it's in the pregnancy manual. Rule ten, Section C, states all of the rights and privileges of the family of the pregnant party. It's our right to spoil you and you're obligated to let us."

Gina looked at Delta with mock irritation, but still couldn't keep her own smile from appearing. "Pregnancy manual? Oh, sweet, sweet, Delta, you've been hanging around Connie far too long."

Connie laughed. "She's right, Del. Pregnancy manual is right up my alley."

The waitress appeared with a bottle of champagne and three glasses. "Can I have some seltzer water?" Gina asked. Then she turned to Connie and Delta. "Absolutely no alcohol during the pregnancy."

Connie nodded before filling the two glasses with champagne. "Page one, Rule two."

As Connie bent over to kiss Gina, Delta warmed all over. So many things were changing so fast for the three of them. Megan was away in the rain forest somewhere "finding herself." Connie and Gina were preparing to embark on a major life-changing adventure of their own, and Delta was...just what was Delta doing? Waiting. Waiting for Megan to come home. Waiting for Carducci to be able to stand on his own. Waiting to see if she really did have room for anyone else in her life. The changes and the unknown were both exhilarating and frightening.

Raising her glass, Delta toasted. "To great friends, greater love, and the greatest miracle of all." Clinking the glasses together, the three women tossed back their drinks.

"Tonight," Connie said, reaching for the bottle, "Gina is the designated driver."

Delta refilled her glass and gingerly sipped it. She wasn't overly fond of champagne except when celebration filled the air, and then, it seemed to whisk down her throat before slamming into her head. "Then we'll get a definite date of arrival tomorrow?"

Connie nodded. "We're hoping so. Just think, Del. We're going to have a little papoose running around. Won't that be a kick?"

"Sounds great—until four in the morning, braces, principals, and homework. I'm glad it will be the two of you doing all the work while I stand on the sidelines and cheer."

"Well, don't put your sweats on yet, Punkin' because if we decide to have a home delivery, we want you there with the camera rolling."

Delta felt the blood drain from her face. "I hardly think so. No way. Uh-uh. Not me."

"Not so fast, Storm," Connie released Gina's hand and laid her hand on Delta's forearm. "You can face lunatics with guns and knives, but you run away from a woman having a baby? You've been shot at, stabbed, punched, kicked, and spit on, yet you shy away from the most beautiful act in the world?"

"Not shy away, Chief, but run as fast as I can. The very thought of seeing all that blood and...and stuff. " Delta shuddered. "I'm sorry, Con, but this is one caper you're going to have to do without me."

Connie crossed her arms defiantly. "I think not. Whatever your hang-up, you have nine months to get over it."

"I can't."

"Why not?"

Delta was beginning to feel very warm. "In high school, I was the only one in the class who fainted during a film showing childbirth."

"You fainted?"

Delta flushed. "Dead away. Woke up with the teacher waving smelling salts across my face. It was horrible."

"The fainting or the film?"

"Both. Man, when I realized that was the head popping out, I thought I was going to die."

"But you fainted instead." Connie could barely contain herself.

"Honey, if Delta doesn't want to be there—"

"Oh, it's not that I don't want to, Gene. I'd just die if I fainted on you two."

Connie took Delta's free hand. "At least consider being in there with us? I don't want to experience the most important moment in my life without you."

Delta gazed back into Connie's penetrating brown eyes and knew that no matter what came, no matter how scared or grossed out she might be, she would never let Connie down; whether it was on the streets or in the delivery room.

"I'll think about it."

Just then, the waitress approached and handed Delta a fresh glass of champagne. "I didn't order th—"

"No, you didn't," the waitress interrupted, motioning toward the door. "That blond woman with the gorgeous green eyes sent it over. She told me to tell you...let's see...for you not to worry, that your paths will cross again, and it was a pleasure to finally meet you."

"Finally meet me?" Delta muttered more to herself than to the waitress.

"That's what she said."

Accepting the drink, Delta raised the glass in the air toward Green Eyes and nodded at her. Green Eyes smiled and blew Delta a kiss before disappearing out the door.

"Uh, Ms. Stevens," Connie said, waving her hand in front of Delta's face. "Is there something you should tell us?"

Delta grinned before bringing the glass to her mouth. "I'll never tell." As Delta took a sip, something sparkled up at her from the bottom of the glass. At first, she thought it was just a reflection of the bubbles, but when she held the glass up to the light, she knew exactly what it was.

"Goddamn it!" Delta cursed, jamming the glass in Connie's hand. "Don't lose that!" Pushing her chair over so hard that it tipped over and hit the ground, Delta shoved and excused her way through the growing crowd until she was standing outside. After looking in four directions, Delta stopped, closed her eyes, and listened to the sounds of the city. Surely, it was too cold for her to be on her motorcycle. When Delta did not hear the rumbling of a Harley, she ran into the parking lot and discovered the BMW was gone.

"Damn her to hell!" Delta shouted, kicking a half-full Coke can across the lot, splashing her shoes and pant leg. "Hello, Storm, you jerk. Is anyone home?" Staring out at the city lights, Delta felt the familiar pang of being truly had. "How could I be so stupid?"

Shaking her head, Delta made her way back to the bar and found Gina and Connie waiting for her at the door.

"All right, pal, what gives? Who was that woman, and why in the hell were you running after her?"

Taking the glass from Connie, Delta tipped it, dipped two fingers into the bubbles, and fished out a very wet, very beautiful 1.5 carat diamond ring.

"I don't believe it," Connie said, covering her mouth.

"She gave you that ring?" Gina asked.

Delta shook her head. "No, Gene, she gave this ring *back*. The woman who sent that drink over is the jewel thief who is haunting my beat."

Connie looked at the ring, looked at the door, and then focused intently on Delta. "Well, Kimo, it would appear that our little thief has thrown down the gauntlet."

Delta stared out the window, feeling the unfamiliar sensation of defeat. "So it appears."

15

When Delta arrived at the station the next night, she pulled the ring from her pocket and set it in front of Connie.

"Well?" Connie asked, not taking her eyes from the computer.

Delta shrugged. "It's the same ring, all right. There's a bill of sale from Van Clees' Arpels's and I had the salesman examine it under the loop. It's our ring."

Connie paused the computer and rubbed her eyes with her fists. "I need glasses. So, what you're saying is that she climbed the house, stole this ring, followed you to the bar, and then gave it to you?"

Delta could only nod.

"She certainly put a great deal of energy into making sure the ring got to you. Odd."

"Very."

"Maybe she just has a crush and this is her way of meeting you. Afterall, you *are* somewhat of a celebrity."

"Oh, shut up. It's not like that at all."

Connie cocked her head. "Oh? A woman steals a ring and then gives it to the cop from whose beat it was yanked, and you don't think she might have a crush? Well, I can tell you what it isn't. It isn't greed, need, or revenge. That leaves...hmmm...passion."

"Don't make me kill you, Chief."

Connie grinned. She hadn't heard Delta say that in years. "All right, then, how about the thrill of the hunt?"

Delta nodded. "That's possible. The hunt and the chase."

"She's enjoying this."

Delta shook her head slowly. "Damn, Con, she literally slipped through my fingers. She was right there." Delta reached out for an imaginary Green Eyes.

"Right there, and I missed her. She was all over me, and I watched her walk. Am I losing my touch, or what?"

Laying her hand on Delta's shoulder, Connie shook her head. "Of course not. But give credit where credit is due. She's good. Very good. And she wants you to know just how good."

Delta stared at the sparkling ring still sitting on the desk. It was huge. "Well, she was good enough to get in and out of my grasp before I knew what hit me. I'm so mad at myself, I could scream."

"How were you to know? How many lesbians have you busted in your career?"

"One."

"Exactly. You were in familiar and comfortable surroundings around women you know and trust. How were you to suspect that a woman flirting with you was the jewel thief you've been looking for? Give yourself a break here."

Delta shrugged. She wasn't feeling any better. "Still..."

"Still, shmill. Delta, you may have lost her momentarily, but you got the most important clue she left."

Delta's eyebrows knitted together. "The ring?"

"No, goofball. The motive, *her* motive. Don't you get it? She's enjoying playing with you."

Delta thought back to something Green Eyes had said to her. "You know, she did say something about me being the most fun she'd had in a long time."

Connie grinned. "Exactly. Now, let's take a look at the big picture." Connie pulled out a clipboard and pen and flipped the page over. "Okay, in the first break-in, she went through the second story without setting off the alarm, only to chuck a rock through the window before leaving."

"You don't know she was the one who threw the rock."

"Yes, I do. And so do you. She threw that rock in order to bring you to that house."

Delta shook her head. "Chief, you have absolutely nothing to go on there."

"Maybe not as it stands by itself, but let's look at break-ins number two and three. She breaks in and exits through the front door, leaving it ajar so the people, who don't have an alarm system, will know they've been robbed. Furthermore, she leaves the empty jewelry box in plain view so they know *exactly* what she stole."

Delta paced across the room. "It's way too much supposition, Con."

Connie slammed her fist on the table. "What's with you, anyway? You've busted a lot of people on a hell of a lot less."

"I just think you're jumping the gun, that's all. She isn't Elson Zuckerman, the computer madman we dealt with before, you know."

Connie bristled. "What's that supposed to mean?"

"It means that she isn't out to get me or anything. She's just a thief. Period. Everything you have here is just conjecture."

Connie's eyebrows rose. "Oh? Then you take a look." Handing the clipboard to Delta, Connie folded her arms across her chest and waited.

"Okay," Delta started as she looked at the notes. "Let's say, for argument's sake, that she started the alarm *after* she took the ring."

"And?"

"And she purposely left the front door open."

"Keep going."

"And she left a note on the window of my patrol car."

"And she waved to you, Del. Don't you see? Each time, she came closer and closer until finally, at the bar, she actually made physical contact with you. Come on, Del, she's playing you like a violin. Why is it so hard for you to see that?"

"Maybe I don't want to."

"Don't want to what? See it, or admit it?"

Delta shrugged. "Both. Neither. I don't know."

Connie gently took the clipboard from Delta and set it on her monitor. "What's eating at you?"

Delta sat back down and sighed. "I don't know. The last thing I need right now is some perp trying to get the better of me."

"Some perp?"

"All right, this particular perp. I feel burned. Set up. I hate that."

Connie smiled softly. "Does this thief's particular gender have anything to do with the temperature level of your blood?"

"I hardly think that's an issue."

"Delta—"

"All right, all right. Maybe. A little. Damn it, Con, this...this..."

"Woman?"

Delta closed her mouth and frowned. "Yes. This woman is making a fool out of me."

Unfolding her arms, Connie placed her hands on Delta's shoulders. "That's it, then, isn't it? She's a woman who is as good at what she does as you are at what you do." Connie stepped closer. "And you're caught between wanting to bust her and wanting to admire her tenacity."

Delta couldn't look at Connie. "You make it sound so—"

"True? I know you, Delta Stevens, and I'll bet that the burr up your butt is about your true feelings about this woman. Who could help but admire her moxie? The woman's got guts."

"Guts? Geez, Con, she pawed all over me, gave me a good look at her face, engaged me in conversation, and even came on to me. I'd say she possesses more than just moxie."

Connie grinned. "Yes, and no matter what you say right now, I know that you admire that in a woman, even if she is breaking the law."

Delta looked up at Connie's grin and shook her head. "She's still a criminal."

"Pshaw. Your criminal is willing to take chances and enjoys unnecessary risks. And because of this little fact..." Connie opened her desk drawer and pulled out a folder. "I've had a psychological profile done on her." Delta quickly rose. "You had a psych done on a thief?"

Nodding, Connie opened the folder. "Someone owed me a favor, and I had nothing better to do, so I asked if she wouldn't take a look at our little gem collector. Want to hear?"

Delta sat back down. "Do I have a choice?"

"No." Sitting down, Connie inched closer. "She was just a jewel thief until last night, but crossing the boundary into your life has changed things dramatically. She may be bright, sexy, and articulate, but that doesn't mean she isn't dangerous. After all, she did follow you. She did have you alone in the parking lot. And if you're not going to recognize her as a possible threat, then I will."

Delta bowed her head in defeat. "What did you find?"

"Well, I am happy to say that she isn't psychotic. According to the report, she's between twenty-five and thirty-five, lives alone, was probably raised by an older sibling or a relative other than her parents. She exhibits compulsive behavior as well as impulsive tendencies. She's meticulous and well-educated, but probably wasn't focused enough to complete college with a degree. She's single, has been burglarizing for quite some time, probably since her youth, and has kleptomaniacal characteristics."

"Does that mean she has to steal?"

Connie shook her head. "It means she wants to. My buddy thinks she enjoys the thrill, and given the fact that she gave the ring back, her actions pretty much support that line of thinking."

Delta nodded. So far, there was little she could disagree with. "Anything else?"

"She's a loner. Crossing the physical boundaries in the bar doesn't necessarily mean she's a lesbian. It actually shows more of an obsessive behavior than anything sexual."

The light went on in Delta's attic. "It's that obsessive part that worries you."

"Yep. Del, she either tailed you from home, bugged your phone, or has been following you for some time."

"Either way—"

"That makes her dangerous."

"Anything in the report about other pathologies?"

Connie set the file down and shook her head. "None. She isn't likely to respond violently if cornered, but that still doesn't mean she isn't dangerous." Connie reached out and touched Delta's arm. "If she wanted to, she could have taken you out right there in the parking lot."

"But that wasn't what she was after."

"No, it wasn't. She's into head games. Your head in particular."

"You think I'm going to let some woman—"

"A beautiful woman."

"Okay, a beautiful woman. You really think I'd let some beautiful woman mess with my head? That right is reserved for Megan."

Connie tried not to smile, but failed. "I just want you to be aware of all the possibilities. Take her as seriously as you would a male thief, okay?"

"Okay."

"Promise?"

"Promise." Gently pulling away from Connie's grasp, Delta tapped the folder. "Gee, Chief, a little worried about me, or what?"

"I've seen that look, Storm. I had just cause. There's more to this case than simply jewel thieving, and you know it. It's my job to make sure you're armed with all the facts before you go out into the cold, cruel world."

"I read you loud and clear."

Connie's smile broadened. "Good. I want my child to have plenty of memories with her special *Tia*."

"Aunt?" The idea of being an aunt hadn't ever really sunk in until now.

Patting Delta's shoulder, Connie winked at her. "Get used to it. In nine months, you'll be Auntie Storm for the rest of your days."

"Auntie Storm, eh?" Delta rubbed her chin in a theatrical pose. "I like it."

"Me, too. And I want you to live long enough to watch her grandchildren graduate from college."

"I have to live that long?"

Connie smiled and nodded. "I insist. And until then, you keep your head on straight."

"Will do."

"Oh, and one more thing."

"Yes?"

"Try to remember that you already have a beautiful woman in your life, okay?"

Delta nodded. Just because Megan was away didn't mean she couldn't look, did it?

Did it?

▽   ▽   ▽

"Stevens, the captain wants to see you when you're through."

Delta turned from Connie and cast a disparaging glance at the captain's office. God, how she tired of being summoned to the "principal's office" every time she turned around. Ever since the Zuckerman case, every little thing she did outside the standard rules and regs was scrutinized under a microscope, brought to her attention, pounded into stone, and then handed to her like Moses' Ten Commandments. And it was beginning to bother her.

"I'm through," she said through grit teeth.

"Kimo—"

Delta held her hand up to stop Connie. "Save it, Chief. I've learned the magic of selective hearing. They obviously still feel the need to drum a few things into my pea-brain."

"Yeah, well, don't take it personally."

Poking her head into the captain's office, Delta forced a grin. "You wanted to see me, sir?"

Captain John Henry was an Old Spice caricature of a man, with a big, barreled chest, Popeye arms, and a handlebar mustache. He looked more the role of a sailor than a cop, but fortunately for her, he had the temperament of neither. Delta's run-ins with him were not nearly as explosive as his predecessor, mostly because Captain Henry was a very fair, very honest man. Even when he had sentenced her to Training Patrol, he hadn't done so without doing some research into Delta's background. When Delta and Tony shot and killed two child pornographers, he quickly rescinded his initial orders and immediately put her back on the street.

Still, he had called her to his office, and that always made her uneasy.

"Come in, Delta. Have a seat."

Delta grinned. "I prefer to remain standing, sir."

Captain Henry looked at her and shook his head. "Based on your identification, Jonesy made a composite of the jewel thief. Did you finish with your full report to the Burg Unit?"

Delta nodded. "Yes, sir. They have everything I know."

"Good." Captain Henry leaned forward on the desk. "That was quite a little confrontation you had with her, wasn't it?"

Shrugging, Delta held her hands behind her back. "I wouldn't exactly call it a confrontation, sir. It was more like two ships passing."

Raising his large bulk from behind the desk, the captain strode over to the window and looked out. "You know, that's what's bothering me. She didn't pass you; she made a direct hit. She hitched up with you, made personal contact, and I don't like it. Not one bit."

"I couldn't help it, sir."

Captain Henry turned from the window, his features softer than she'd ever seen. "Oh, I'm not blaming you, Delta. I'm not questioning what happened, where."

"Then what *are* you questioning, sir?"

Taking the seat next to Delta, Henry pulled on his mustache. "Delta, you are one of the finest officers to come through those doors. Your scrapbook of new articles must be two-feet thick. Your picture has been in the paper more times than all your colleagues put together. A lot of the younger guys really look up to you. To put it bluntly, you're sort of the star of our team."

Delta had absolutely no idea where he was going with this. "I just do my job, Captain."

This made him laugh. "Delta Stevens never *just* does anything. You have quite a reputation among law enforcement and the media alike."

"Captain, I appreciate all of this, honest I do, but it's late. Could you make your point?"

"My point is, I don't like the direction this case is heading. I don't like the fact that she has established contact with one of my officers."

"I don't believe she's dangerous, sir."

"You don't know that. She's followed you and probably knows where you live. She's stalking you, Delta."

Delta felt the hair on the back of her neck tingle, and she looked impatiently at the captain.

"Once she established contact with you, the rules changed, and we're not going to play by her rules. If this woman is counting on you to show up at her burglaries, then we need to take the wind out of her sails."

She was about to hear the words she feared most. "I don't believe it. You're taking me off the streets, aren't you?" He might as well be stabbing Delta with an ice pick. "But I didn't do anything!"

"I am aware of that, and you'll return as soon as we've assessed the situation. You may not be alarmed by her actions, but the department is. Until we're sure you're out of danger, we're going to pull you."

Delta paced over to the window and peered through the mini-blinds. The ice pick felt more like a pickax. "What about Carducci?"

"He stays. It isn't him she's after."

Delta didn't turn from the window. "If I were a man, would you still yank me?"

"Delta, don't insult either of us with that sexist bullshit. This isn't personal. It's procedural. I'd do it for any of my officers."

Delta nodded. "So, you yank me. Then what?" Delta slowly turned and leveled her gaze at the captain.

"We make catching her a priority. Along with, and you're not going to like this, a guard posted at your house."

Delta turned. "No way. I don't need a baby sitter. Captain, I'm a cop—"

"And I'm your captain, and I say we post a guard. You know, Delta, if anyone is being sexist here, it's you."

"How's that?"

"You don't feel threatened because she's a woman. If she were a man who had invaded your space, do you think you might handle this differently?"

Delta opened her mouth to respond, but stopped. Hadn't Connie just said the same thing? Was it possible that they both were right? Delta hated the thought. "I don't know."

"Right. So, in cases like these, we follow procedures. Now, I know you're not very good at that, but this time, you'd best make an exception. I don't want to see you ditching the guard, sending him on errands, or otherwise getting in his way."

Delta bowed her head and nodded. "Yes, sir."

"Oh, don't look so glum. Just to show you what a fair kind of guy I am, I've given you an assignment I think you'll enjoy."

"What's that, sir? Meter maid? How about animal control? Oh, I know, I can run errands and make coffee."

Captain Henry smiled patiently. "I've had the opportunity to watch you work for more than two months. And, well, to be honest with you, you're every bit the renegade cop I was warned about." Captain Henry waited for Delta's retort. When none came, he continued. "I would be a fool to underestimate you on any level, including your incredible sense of loyalty. So, given your penchant for rule-bending, I'm putting you on an assignment I'm sure you're probably already on."

Delta tilted her head. "Already on?"

"Yes. I want you to find out what asshole tried to kill our DA."

"Excuse me?"

Captain Henry moved back behind his desk and opened a folder. "I've been studying your file for some time, Delta, and three things became glaringly obvious: one, you never quit; two, you're loyal beyond reason; and three, you pay back your debts. Put all of these together with your relationship to Alexandria Pendleton, and you know what I came up with?"

Delta shrugged.

"That it would be easier to find a snowball in hell than to find you following my directive to stay clear of this investigation. How'm I doing?"

Delta looked at him, but said nothing.

"That's what I thought. I know that you're not about to sit idly by while some shithead takes a shot at Pendleton. And, for once, I can't say I blame you." Reaching into the folder, the captain pulled out a dogeared, yellowing newspaper article and handed it to Delta. Taking the article, Delta skimmed it and realized it was of a well-known 1985 drug bust. The arresting officer was a young officer by the name of John Henry. It was his second year on the force. The lawyer who prosecuted the case was an even younger Alexandria Pendleton.

Delta looked up from the article, not quite knowing what to say.

"You're not the only one who owes her, Delta. Pendleton put my name on the map with that case, and it's probably the reason I'm sitting on this side of the desk."

Delta looked down at the article before handing it back. The pieces were all falling into place. When Delta was bucked back to Training Patrol, the captain was initially going to take her off the streets altogether. It was at Alexandria's request that Henry put her on the streets as a Field Training Officer. At the time, Delta had wondered what it was that gave Alex so much clout. Now, she knew.

"Delta, Alexandria is a cop's DA. She's a tough, hard-hitting, low-ball player who does her damnedest to help make sense of our jobs. She gave me a reputation that leapfrogged my career. I owe her."

"I know how that feels."

"I'm sure you do. But you see, I have two problems here. One, I have an officer being stalked by some nutcase thief. The other, some asswipe is trying to whack a good DA during an election year. There's a way for me to cover all my bases without having to juggle the duty roster."

Delta nodded. "I see."

"Besides, I know you'll leave no stone unturned in your investigation, and that's what this needs; some-one who will be devoted to finding the perp. We can't have this sniper go unchecked. He's already done dam-age to her campaign, and the thought of that windbag Wainwright heading up the office makes me sick to my stomach."

"Me, too."

"Good. Then as far as anyone knows, you're on special assignment until we can roust up your little admirer. And for God's sake, watch for tails. I don't like the thought of you in the morgue, either."

Nodding, Delta reached for the doorknob. "I'll do my best, sir."

"You do that. In the meantime, report directly to me by nineteen hundred hours and don't discuss this with anyone. Not even Rivera."

Delta opened the door. "Oh, there's one more thing. Does it have to be a male you post at my house?"

Captain Henry grinned. "What's the matter, Delta? You shy?"

Half-turning, she grinned right back. "No, sir. It's just been a while since there was a man in my house." With that, Delta left an open-mouthed, speechless captain sitting behind his desk.

16

Sitting down at Eddie II in her den, Connie punched buttons and numbers until the computer came to life. "Okay, Del, I've run through all the parolees Alex put away, and only two have stayed in the area."

Delta nodded and looked up from a file she'd been reading. "What about recent incarcerations?"

Connie typed data in and waited. "Numerous. Two minor felons beat a rap, but we have a fix on them, and they weren't anywhere around at the time." Connie printed up a list and then handed it to Delta. "These are all the cases she's won."

Delta whistled as she took the list from Connie. "She's been busy."

"And successful. Look how many received maximums."

Delta handed the list back. "What's your take on this angle?"

Studying the list, Connie slipped it into a growing file. "I think it's a possibility that one of her perps came after her, but it's a slim one."

"Why slim?"

"It doesn't add up. A perp who wanted Alex dead would find any number of ways to get her, don't you think? A dark alley, her car, her house, even her office. How many low-level scumbags would do something as sensational as try to shoot her in front of the media with their cameras rolling and a huge crowd watching?"

"Point taken. You don't think it was revenge."

Connie shook her head. "Nope. This wasn't some whacko shooting the place up. If it was, he would have gotten off more than three shots."

Delta nodded. "Another good point. How are we coming on the list of Wainwright's employees?"

Clicking the mouse, Connie changed the monitor. "It's a long list, Del, and as varied as the pasta choices at Prima Vera's. He's got some big money behind him."

"Sure he does. The office of DA is just a stepping stone for him on the way to Congress. Wainwright couldn't care less about law. It's politics that float his boat."

"As evidenced by some of his more republican backers. It's the greenbacks who are anchoring him to shore. Look at these guys."

Delta leaned over and followed Connie's finger as it pointed to CEO's, bank presidents, Hollywood executives, and various stock market honchos. "Yep, his intentions are pretty clear. They get him into office, and he pays them back when he gets to the big house."

"He wouldn't be the first man to buy his way into office."

"Nor would he be the first to kill his way in, either."

Clicking the mouse twice, Connie changed the screen to various groupings of the names on the previous screen. "We can do backgrounds on all these guys, Del, but the bottom line is that there's plenty of money in this crowd to afford a hit man."

"Then we dig until we find out who has connections to that kind of source."

Turning toward Delta, Connie grinned. "I feel sorry for the guy who meets up with you."

Delta grinned. "What kills me is that Wainwright is such a shitty lawyer. Look at his track record."

Suddenly, Gina came in from the kitchen carrying two cups of coffee. "You know, loves, once the baby arrives, that sort of language must disappear from both your vocabularies."

Taking her favorite Phantom of the Opera mug from Gina, Connie looked appropriately chastised. Delta snickered.

"And that goes double for you, *Auntie*."

Her mug poised in midair, Delta grinned. "Or what? You'll send us to our rooms without dinner?"

Delta and Connie looked at each other like two little girls who enjoyed taunting their mother.

"No. You two would enjoy that too much. But mark my words: you have eight months to practice changing your he-man vocabulary."

Connie set her mug down and pulled Gina to her lap. "Okay, sweety, we're sorry. What Delta really meant was that Wainwright is a poopy lawyer."

Delta laughed. "Somehow, that loses something in the translation."

Pulling herself out of Connie's grasp, Gina feigned hurt. "Fine. I see trying to talk to you two when you're like this will get me nowhere. Happy hunting."

Watching Gina return to the kitchen, Connie sighed. "God, I love that woman."

Delta nodded. "Yeah, she's a good thing."

"Can I tell you something really bizarre?"

Delta's eyebrow shot up. "As long as it isn't some wild tale about your heritage."

Connie laughed lightly. "Do you think it's odd that I find pregnant women sexy?"

Delta stared at her. "You mean, women with their big, round bellies out to here turn you on?"

Connie nodded. "Isn't that bizarre?"

"Yeah, but so are you. Does this mean that I should start knocking before I come in?"

"Oh, shut up. Where were we, anyway?" Turning back to the computer, Connie grabbed the mouse to release the screen saver floating across the monitor. "Wainwright and his band of moneyed men. What's our next step?"

"See what the dicks have come up with. Glean their files, see where their investigation is headed, and then go from there. They have the manpower for the kind of extensive checks we need to run. Let them do all the work."

"And you?"

"I'm going to run a check on everyone in Alex's campaign. We can't rule out the possibility that Wainwright planted someone in Alex's organization."

"Or that someone with a vendetta is out to get her."
Connie rose and stretched. "You think this is an inside job?"

"Hard to say. Either way, Alex's career is in trouble if we don't come up with the shooter. The press is already having a field day with the notion that she can't defend herself, so how can she defend us. Like she goes out there with a gun and badge to keep peace. God, how I hate the press."

"Sounds like a planted story to me. Too pat, know what I mean?" Connie returned her attention to the monitor. "So, the way we're looking at it, we have either a revenge theory or a conspiracy angle."

"Right."

"I don't have to tell you that both are going to be a bitch to prove."

"Remember your vocabulary."

Connie grinned. "And you remember to stay out of trouble."

Delta stood and finished her coffee. "Who, me?" Smiling, Delta handed her mug to Connie before opening the front door. "You don't call me Storm for nothing."

17

The doors to the Property Crimes Division looked
like they hadn't been cleaned in years. The last *I* in
Division was missing and there was a slight crack on
the bottom of the frosted glass. Delta wondered if all
the budget cuts meant the janitorial staff had been the
first to go.

Carefully pushing the door open, Delta stepped
into a large room. Unlike the rooms in the rest of the
station, PCD was a brightly lit area as quiet as a
library. Evidence was being examined, people spoke in
hushed whispers, and investigators hovered over crow-
bars, screwdrivers, hammers, and other telltale pieces
of jigsawed investigations. There was a waiting room
air about the room as technicians waited for matching
prints, entry mark matches, and other assorted identification. This was one of the labs where crimes were
solved. The other lab, a place Delta hated more than
the dentist, was the forensics lab, where most homi-
cides and violent crimes were solved.

"Officer Stevens!" a young investigator whispered.
"Over here!"

Delta looked up to see a thin, short, blonde kid
coming toward her. He was wearing a white lab coat
and black-rimmed glasses. Delta took a quick look to
see if he was wearing a pocket protector. He wasn't.

"Christian, right?" Delta had worked with Christian on a case when she first came to the force. Miles
had introduced him as the Whiz Kid because at thirty-
two, he looked half his age, with six times the IQ.

"Same old me, Delta. How are you these days? I
keep reading about you in the paper." Christian wiped
his hand on his lab coat before shaking her hand.
"Miles would be proud."

As always, whenever she heard his name, Delta
warmed inside. "I hope so. And you?"

Christian shrugged. "Crime's up. So is my work-
load." Releasing Delta's hand, Christian pushed his
glasses back up the bridge of his nose. "So, what's this
about?"

"There's some speculation that our jewel thief has
an agenda that includes me. I need to know if she's
stealing prior to setting off the alarms."

Christian's eyebrows knitted together. "Before?"

"Yeah."

"I don't have any data that would indicate that, no.
Of course, that's not saying it isn't possible. But that
would mean—"

Before Christian could finish, three uniformed officers stepped from an adjoining room marked "Biologi-
cal."

"If it isn't the infamous Delta Stevens," one officer
quipped. "Got any more fatal obsessions knocking on
your door?"

Har har.

Snicker.

The three officers laughed and poked each other in
the ribs. "You gotta admit, Stevens, you really win the
prize on this one."

"Uh, come on, fellas," Christian said meekly.

"Stevens, have you thought about maybe changing
that men's cologne you wear? We hear it drives women
wild."

"Or is that your goal?"

"Fuck off, York," Delta said, stepping up to the
shorter man. "Before I do something you might regret."

One of the officers came to York's side. "Maybe it's
a dyke thing, eh? An ex-lover or a lesbo scorned."

"Don't push it, Baker."

York backed up a step as Delta leveled her gaze at
Baker. "Don't push her, Bake. You ever hear what she
did to those other cops that pissed her off?"

The third cop, a rookie, nodded, but said nothing.

"Where's your Dago bodyguard now, Stevens? Heard he roughed Miller up defending your 'honor.' Is there honor among dykes?"

Delta stepped right up to Baker. "God gave men dicks, Baker, so they wouldn't be complete assholes. Unfortunately, you're both."

The other cops started to laugh, but then stopped.

"You're a homophobic asshole who's not worth two seconds of my time, so if you don't mind—"

"But I do mind, Stevens. I mind very much. It's bad enough we gotta let you people into the military, into our schools, and even into our churches, but—"

"Shut your mouth, Baker," Delta warned.

"Or what?"

"Come on, Bake," York pleaded, touching his arm. "You made your point."

Baker pulled away and stood eye to eye with Delta. "No. Come on, hotshot. You think that just because you're a dyke, you can take out a man? I'm so fucking tired of hearing about all this gay rights shit I could—"

Before she could stop herself, Delta brought her left knee into his groin, doubling him over. Then, she grabbed him by the neck and slammed his head against a wall.

"Listen up, you sorry sack of shit. The next time your tiny mind closes and your big mouth opens, I'm going to be there to slam it shut. So, if you don't want this dyke to humiliate your manly pride in front of your buddies like I'm doing right now, you'll keep your prehistoric ramblings to yourself. You understand me?"

Baker could do nothing except grunt and hold his crotch.

Releasing his throat, Delta pushed him away from her and into the arms of York and the rookie, who didn't know quite what to do.

"I don't recommend messing with me today, guys. As you can see, I'm not in the mood."

Both men held their hands up as if being arrested. "Don't worry. No problem."

"Then get him out of my sight." Delta watched the two men half-carry, half-drag Baker out of the building. She hated losing her cool like that, but she wasn't about to stand there and let some redneck walk all over her. Returning her attention to Christian, Delta grinned at his slack-jawed appearance. "Don't worry, Christian, he'll live."

Christian gulped. "Yeah, once they remove his gonads from his throat. You're just like everyone says you are."

"Oh? Who are 'they,' and what are 'they' saying?"

"Uh...nothing bad, really. Just that you live up to your reputation. I sure hope I never get on your bad side."

"Not to worry, Christian. You're one of the truly good guys in my book."

Christian blushed. "Thanks."

"So, anyway—"

"Sorry, Delta, but there's simply no way of knowing if the alarms are set off after the burglaries have occurred."

"Okay, what about point of entry?"

Christian led Delta over to a six-foot-long lab table. Various items were tagged and laying face up. "The POE is consistent with each burglary. We have the piece of glass she cut out, pictures of all window frames, and assorted treadmarks, but other than that, the evidence is pretty slim. She's a clean one."

"Clean?"

Christian nodded. "No prints, not one strand of hair, not one eyewitness other than yourself. There were no other identifying marks other than the shoe imprint, and all that did was give us her size and weight. If you're looking for hard evidence, I'm afraid we're lacking where this one is concerned. She's good."

Delta nodded thoughtfully. "Can you give me some soft evidence?"

Christian cringed and Delta knew why. It was his job to find and evaluate concrete clues. Anything beyond the tangible facts were out of his realm and nonproductive. Techies stayed away from the abstract, the obscure, and speculative. Unless they could smell it, touch it, or see it, it didn't exist for them.

"Such as?"

"Why is she only taking one item?"

"One that we know of." Christian grinned the grin of an evidence techie.

"Fine then. So let's *assume* she's getting away with only one item. What does that tell you?"

Rubbing his chin, Christian pulled a pencil from his pocket and drew a circle. "My best guess?"

Delta nodded.

"She knew what she was after prior to going in. She isn't merely selective, she's precise. She's passed up way too many valuable items, some of which were more valuable than what she took."

"Interesting."

"All three items stolen were bought at Van Clees' Arpels."

"Excellent. We can check employees." Delta pulled her notebook out and wrote this down.

"Not really. Van Clees' Arpels does extensive background checks on all of its employees, so that angle could yield us zip."

"Any other similarities?"

"None. Not even in her taste of jewelry. She's stolen different color jewels, different styles, different cuts, and different gems. If there's a pattern, I can't tell you what it is. She leaves virtually no concrete clues, yet enough abstract ones to spin my brains into muck."

"What about NCIC? Anything there?" The National Crime Information Center was like a magic wand to those who knew how to thoroughly utilize the system. Christian was one who did, although he wasn't nearly as proficient with the ins and outs as Connie was.

Christian removed his glasses and cleaned them. "We don't believe she's ever been caught or done time. No one in the system matches her speculative height, weight, or MO. There was one—"

"Who?"

Christian put his glasses back on. "She died two years ago."

"What about the Harley? Any leads?"

"Interestingly enough, not one dealer in California has reported one stolen."

"You're assuming it was."

"Clearly, we were wrong. It appears she may have either borrowed it, owns it, or stole it outside of California."

"Harley doesn't make that many bikes in a year—"

"Delta, you didn't get the make, the year, the color, anything. The bike could have been bought in the seventies for all we know. Still, we'll run a check on Harleys bought in the last ten years by women. Again, that's assuming it was bought by a woman."

"In other words, it's a big, fat zero."

Christian shrugged. "So far, yes."

"Is there anything to go on at this point?"

"You might want to visit Van Clees' Arpels yourself and just eyeball the employees."

"I take it you're leaning toward the thief having some kind of connection to Van Clees' Arpels?"

Christian shrugged again. "It's the best lead we have so far."

"Maybe I'll do that."

"If you do, be forewarned; the manager at Van Clees' Arpels is quite a package. He made it clear that he would not tolerate anyone 'pointing the wicked finger of guilt' at his staff."

Delta smiled. The intimation was that the manager was a flamer. "Did he really say that?"

"It's what I heard."

"Thanks." Reaching for the door, Delta turned and smiled. "Thanks for your time, Christian. As always, you've been invaluable."

Blushing, Christian held the door open for her. "And as always, you've given the department something new to talk about."

Winking at Christian, Delta stepped outside. Maybe the redneck jerks were right...maybe she should change her cologne. Grinning, Delta headed back to Connie's.

18

"So Chief, how's your end?" Walking into the family room, Delta dumped an armload of books and newspapers on the floor.

Connie answered in a singular grunt. "I'm stumped. Wainwright's people are almost too clean. They're too true to be good."

Delta started to correct Connie's misuse of a quote, then realized she probably had intended it to come out that way. "Give me a sampling."

"Try this: a coordinator for the AIDS project, the VP of the March of Dimes, the president of the local Elk's lodge, and a contingency of people who might show up someday on the *Lifestyles of the Rich and Famous*. No parolees, no ex-cons, nothing dirty. *Nada*."

Delta blew out a breath. "Almost too neat and tidy for my taste."

"I procured a list of everyone in Alex's organization as well."

Delta went to the kitchen, retrieved a Diet Pepsi, and popped the top. "You think it was an inside job, don't you?"

"I think," Connie said slowly, "that Wainwright doesn't command such an awesome following by being stupid. He has his hands in many pots. All of whom would hightail it out of there if a scandal this big were ever in the open." Opening a manila folder, Connie pulled out a thick stack of computer paper. "I had every name on the list run through NCIC. Oh, while I was at it, I also had your thief run through."

Delta sipped her soda. "Been done. She's clean. Whoever she is, she's never been busted."

"I've taken a different angle, but I'll let you know more when I get the results. Since you continue defending her—"

"I don't defend her."

"One report from NCIC and you're ready to assume she's never been busted? That's hardly the Delta I know and love."

Delta shrugged and stared at the bubbles in the can. "You've got it all wrong, Con. I just don't care for assumptions. If we're going to go after her, I want facts."

"Then facts you shall have, Kimo." Connie changed the subject, "I have a schedule of Alex's proposed events and speeches. Because of public access to her agenda, I think it would be wise for her to make some unannounced stops along the way. You know, throw a few curves, shake up a few things. Since we don't know if the suspect intends to make another attack, she needs to be semi-unpredictable. Think you can convince her to do that for a while?"

Delta nodded. "If she wants to live."

"Good. The key now is for her not to trust anyone within her organization. Everyone is suspect until we get a lead. So far, all we have is a high-powered weapon that would have blown an eight-inch hole out the back of her."

"I wonder why he only shot three times."

"My guess is the sound attracted attention. The bullets were scattered all over as if someone had jostled his arm."

"That's interesting. You'd expect they'd be close together."

"Well, she was moving; she was coming from the courthouse heading south downstairs. He fired before she came to the end of the stairs, where she met with the media."

"So, if he would have waited, what, two, three more seconds—"

"He would have had a shot at a nonmoving target."

"But he didn't wait."

"Nope."

Delta looked down at a black and white photo of the courthouse steps. "I wonder why not."

Before Connie could answer, the doorbell rang. When Connie opened the door, a boy about nine years old stood with a rolled up newspaper in his hand.

"Good morning, Eric. Since when did you start door-to-door delivery?"

Eric smiled and his freckles seemed to jump around his face. "Your friend said it was your birthday, and she gave me this to give to you."

Suddenly, Delta was at Connie's side. "What did she look like?"

Eric looked up at the sky, as if the answer was written in the clouds. "She was short. Almost my size. Had long blonde hair down to about here. She was...pretty." Eric held the paper out to Connie in one hand and a small, gray velvet box in the other. "Happy birthday, Miss Rivera."

Taking the box, Connie forced a smile. "Thank you, Eric."

"Have a nice day. I love it when it's my birthday." Leaning over, Eric picked up his bike and rode away.

Closing the door, Connie held the box out to Delta and said sarcastically, "Gee...I wonder who this is from."

Taking the box, Delta walked back into the den. "She must have followed me here."

"But she's not dangerous, is she?" Connie folded her arms across her chest. "I've already had some asshole abduct my lover, Del. I am not ever going to go through that again."

"I hear you."

Connie stepped up to her and looked hard into Delta's face. "Do you? Because so help me, if this little twerp harasses me in any way, I'll take her down with or without your help. *Capishe?*"

Delta nodded. In all the years they'd known each other, Connie had only gotten angry with Delta once. This posture now made it once and a half. "Maybe I've underestimated her."

"Maybe. And that, my friend, is how good people get hurt." Connie unfolded her arms and moved next to Delta. "You gonna open it? I can already tell you what's in it."

Opening the box, Delta revealed a gold necklace with the initials *DS* in gold. In between the two letters sat a large emerald. "Oh, shit," uttered Delta, staring down into the box. "I think we've got trouble."

Taking the box from her, Connie snapped it shut. "You think? Jesus, it's about time. I was getting tired of thinking for two of us."

Delta looked up and blushed. "I'm sorry, Chief. I guess...I don't know."

Reopening the box, Connie took the necklace out. The emerald threw green light like a prism throws rainbows. "It's actually quite stunning. I'm surprised she went this far out on a limb."

"You mean by coming here?"

Connie shook her head. "No. By having this made, she's left us a huge clue. If we find out where it was made, we may be able to track her down."

"You think she's careless enough to leave her real address at a jewelry store?"

Connie grinned slightly. "Careless isn't the adjective I would use. Fearless is more like it."

"She can be a thorn in my side professionally, but personally—"

"That's just it, Delta. This *is* personal. Don't you get it? She's enamored with you. She went to a lot of trouble to have that ring converted into a necklace for you. She's in love."

Delta jumped up and paced over to the window. "Give me a break, here. In love? With me? Right."

Connie continued. "The thefts are incidental. It's *you* she's really after."

"Well, I don't give a shit if she steals the Hope diamond for me, I'm not going to stand around while some thief trails me and interferes with my personal life. Enamored or not, she's crossed the line."

Connie put her arm on Delta's shoulder and pulled her back to the computer. "Just hear me out for a minute, okay? First, she follows you to the bar, makes physical contact, and then leaves the diamond. What does that tell you?"

"That she wanted me to know she was the thief."

"What else?"

"That she Snuffy-Smithed me."

Connie's eyebrows raised. "Snuffy-Smithed?"

Delta chuckled. "My grandfather used to say that whenever he was dealing with dishonest people."

"And you make remarks about *my* heritage?"

Delta shrugged. "We're Okies, what can I say?"

Connie held her hands up to surrender. "Say no more, please. So, she wanted you to know that she—"

"Snuffy-Smithed me.

"Whatever. What else?"

Delta thought for a moment. "Her line about me being the most fun she'd had in a long time."

Connie's face broke into a grin. "Right. Consider yourself her entertainment. Can you imagine the adrenaline rush she must have gotten out of standing next to you, indeed, hanging on you? She's an adrenaline junkie."

Delta cocked her head. "A what?"

"An adrenaline junkie. Her motive is excitement, the thrill, the danger of being caught. Like skydivers and bungy-jumpers, she's into this because it pumps her up. Part of the game for her is riding the edge. It was riding an edge to have Eric deliver the box. She was right outside this door, and yet, we still didn't see her. At this moment, she's probably riding the crest of adrenaline. It's like a drug to her."

Delta shook her head. "An adrenaline junkie, eh?"

Connie nodded. "I was reading a report about them a couple of weeks ago."

Delta's left eyebrow rose. "Oh? Any reason in particular?"

Connie rose and poured herself a cup of coffee. "Yeah, because a person I love happens to be one."

Delta opened her mouth, but the words could not travel out of her brain. So, someone else was worried about the chances Delta had been taking recently.

Bringing her coffee back, Connie rubbed Delta's thigh. "Don't look so hurt. Gina and I were watching a movie a while back about these guys who were surfers, skydivers, and rock climbers, you name it. If there was danger and risk involved, they did it." Connie took a sip of her coffee before reaching for Delta's hand. "Gina made a comment that you were a lot like them. That you loved the risk, the thrill of possible death. I was appalled when she said it, but then she pulled out one of her psychology abstracts, and, sure enough, it described you to a tee. There's a name for people who like the razor's edge."

"Adrenaline junkie? I don't think so."

Connie smiled warmly and when she spoke, her voice was soft. "You're fearless, Delta. Even your fear of fire didn't keep you from going into a house you had no business entering. You're the kind of person who goes to Six Flags Magic Mountain and rides the shit-your-pants rides. You soak up thrill like a sponge. That's one of the things that separates you from other cops; you're not only incredibly adventurous, but I think you enjoy the challenge of death."

"That's absurd."

"I wish it were, but you fit every category. That's why I think this woman chose you. You're cut from the same cloth."

Delta rose and walked over to the window. "Don't you think you're reaching just a little?"

Rising, Connie joined her. For a minute, only the clock could be heard. Then, more quietly than Delta had ever heard, Connie whispered, "Honey, you gave up your gun."

Delta turned and faced Connie. Giving her gun up was a subject they had never discussed. She had done it, breaking all the rules, and was one of the few cops to live to tell about it. "So?"

"So, Gina and I became a little scared for you. For your safety. I needed to know how you could do that, what gave you the courage to toss your life on the ground like that. Reading that abstract gave me the answers I was looking for."

Delta looked down into Connie's deep brown eyes; those eyes which had never judged her, criticized her, or condemned her. Delta realized she had frightened Connie, and that hurt. "I'm sorry, Con."

Connie smiled that warm smile that said she loved Delta regardless of anything she would ever do. "Don't be. You did what only Storm would do. I just needed to make sure you didn't have some kind of a death wish, that's all."

"Isn't that what you're saying?"

Connie shook her head. "On the contrary. An adrenaline junkie doesn't want to die. The rush comes from succeeding. That's what I needed to know. And it fits you perfectly. Beating the odds turns you on. It's also what gets our thief going. She's chosen you, Del, because you're both adrenaline addicts, and this will be her greatest challenge." Connie sipped her coffee and grinned. "This is just my speculation, of course."

"Of course. And what else, oh abstract guru, are you speculating?"

Connie's grin turned wicked as she returned to the desk and pulled a yellow slip out from the file. "Glad you asked. I do happen to have a plan."

Delta sat down and shook her head. If Delta was truly an adrenaline addict, then what was Connie? Her pusher? "You have a plan already?"

Connie nodded. "Megan's last words to me were for me to take care of you, and I always do what I'm told."

"Since when?"

"Since she threatened to shave me bald in the middle of the night and tattoo Daffy Duck on my head, that's when."

Delta smiled. That was so Megan. "Okay, Kojak, whatcha got?"

"First off, Van Clees' Arpels is too obvious. She's too professional to get tripped up by a common thread."

Delta nodded. "Agreed."

"But that doesn't mean you don't go ahead with your line up."

"What next?"

"We'll get on it about this necklace. I'll give it to the guys in the Burg Unit, and fill them in. I still think that will lead nowhere as well."

"And we'll continue with the Harley search, right?"

Connie nodded. "And the NCIC report should be back later today. What are your plans for this beautiful day?"

"First, I'm going to see Alex about free-forming her itinerary. Then, I'm going to visit Felicia at the paper and see if she can bury any more stories about Alex until we have a clearer picture."

"I didn't know you and Flea were still friends."

Delta nodded. "After that exclusive I gave her, she warmed right up. If she had axes to grind, she's ground them all up."

"Good for you. Never hurts to have a city editor on your side."

"What about you?"

"I'm running some things through Eddie and waiting around for the NCIC report."

"Christian said his search didn't yield much."

"Christian is a nice guy, Del, but he doesn't politic enough. I've broadened the search to include everything from the USMS to Interpol."

"Interpol?"

Connie nodded. "Just a hunch. What's all that crap you dumped on the floor?"

"Oh, I almost forgot." Reaching over, Delta slid one of the newspapers out from under the pile. "I've been thinking—"

"Haven't I warned you about that?"

"Very funny. Do you want to hear this or not?"

"Of course. Please, think on."

"A while ago, Megan was telling me that I get so wrapped up in my work that I don't pay enough attention to her life."

"I remember."

"Well, I'm paying attention now, and I want to buy her something that shows her I wish to be a part of her life and her dreams as well."

"A gift?"

"Sort of. I'm thinking about buying Megan one of those parrots she was telling me about."

Connie's eyebrows raised. "A macaw? You're going to buy Megan a macaw?"

"Yep. I've been reading the classifieds to see if there are any for sale."

Rising, Connie bunched all the papers together and tossed them in the fireplace. "You don't buy a bird that expensive from some yahoo in the papers."

"Why not?"

"There's no guarantee it will be healthy, that it doesn't bite, that it isn't hot. Come on. You want to buy a bird for her, let's visit a few pet stores and breeders and see what we can find out."

"You'll help?"

"Of course I'll help, Pilgrim. If I don't go, who knows what cleaners you'll be taken to. I mean, I wouldn't want someone to Smiffy-Snuff you."

Delta threw her head back and laughed. "That's Snuffy-Smith, and that would be impossible with you along. Geez, Con, is there anything you *don't* know?"

Connie flashed her most brilliant smile as she locked her files away in her desk. "Sure."

"Oh yeah? Like what?"

"Like, who shot at Alex, and what our little thief is really after."

19

The phone woke Delta out of a dream of colorful flocks of birds flying high over skyscrapers while she and Megan laid in lounge chairs by a huge swimming pool.

"Hello?" She answered, hoping to hear Megan's voice on the other end.

"Stevens, it's Captain Henry."

Rolling over and turning the light on, Delta squinted from the bright light. "What's up, Captain?" Delta looked over at her digital clock to see what time it was. "Something wrong?"

"Damn right something's wrong. Your little burglar struck again tonight. *Five* times."

Delta was wide awake now. "You sure it was her?"

"Oh, yes. All of the houses hit were on your beat. Dickens, Emerson, Lawrence, Tolstoy, and Alcott. Same POE, same MO, but there's one major exception."

Delta shifted the phone to her left ear.

"She raked in. Everything. I mean, she made a killing."

"What are you saying?"

"She cleaned house. Every piece of jewelry, gone. You were right about her; we pissed her off by yanking you, and now, she's ramming it down our—my throat. Five houses. Shit."

"So, why are you calling me?" Delta could hear the captain's heavy sigh.

"Five tonight, Delta. Add the four previously, and she's burying us. Un-fucking-believable. She did exactly what you said she would."

"I really am sorry, sir."

"No, Delta, I'm the sorry one. Maybe it was hasty of me to pull you. In light of the circumstances, I'd like to rescind my original order."

"But what about the Pendleton investigation? We—I was making great headway."

"I'm sure you are. And I fully expect that you'll continue...with discretion, of course. Bring to me anything you find first. The paper is tearing her to shreds. We're going to need something yesterday."

Delta nodded as she got out of bed and padded into the kitchen to make coffee. "We're doing the best we can."

"We?"

"Uh...yeah. Me and my computer, of course."

"Of course. I'll expect one hundred percent of your attention to be on your beat, and I'm not going to lift the guard from your house until you bag that little bitch. I'll expect your full cooperation in that matter, Delta. No screwing around."

"Yes, sir. Anything else?"

"Well...there is one small thing that I was going to let slide, but because it supposedly happened off duty, I'm required to inform you."

Delta smiled to herself. She knew exactly where the complaint originated. "Go ahead."

"A woman named Gwen Anderson called and said you were 'harassing' her and her lover at one of the uh...gay bars the other night. Now, you know, what you do on your time is your business, but she alluded to abuse of authority, and that's why I have to inform you of the complaint so I can shitcan—I mean properly file it."

Delta nodded. She was starting to like Captain Henry more and more. "I understand."

"Don't get me wrong, Delta. It's pretty clear by the way she boldly pronounced the word *lesbian* that she was trying to ruin your career by outing you. When I didn't give her the stunned reaction she was hoping for, she pressed and tossed the word out several more

times. I saw through her stupid game and thanked her
for calling."

"Do you want my version of what happened?"

"Not really. Like I said, what you do on your own
time is none of my business. Just make sure it doesn't
become my business. "

"Thank you, sir."

"No need to thank me, Delta. Just be back on your
beat tomorrow night and tame that partner of yours.
He's been acting like a wild man without you. He's
made his opinion of your shift change clear to anyone
stupid enough to listen."

This made Delta smile. "Will do."

"Good. See you tomorrow night. Oh...and Delta..."

"Yes, sir?"

"Catch that woman."

"I'm gonna give it my best, Captain. Bye." Hanging
the phone up, Delta looked at the clock again. It was a
little after five. She decided that if she had to be up,
she would not suffer the dawn alone. Pressing the
auto-dial on her phone, Delta waited. After just one
ring, Connie picked up.

"Rise and shine."

"What do you mean by 'rise?' I haven't even been to
bed yet."

"No kidding?"

"My data came in from NCIC early this morning,
and I wanted to have a look-see before we connected.
Come on over morning-girl for some of my world famous coffee. What's got you awake so early, anyway?
Loneliness?"

Delta told Connie about her conversation with Captain Henry.

"Well, you got to feel for the man. He's damned with
you and he's damned without you."

"I would have liked a few more days on the street,
bu—"

"How do you feel about what she's done?"

"You mean gone on a rampage of sorts?"

Connie chuckled. "Of sorts? Come on, Del. The guys said she's rolling in it by now. She could retire on the hits she made the last two days."

"Don't we wish."

"Do we? I'd have thought you'd want to catch her."

Delta rolled her eyes. "Don't start that again. Look, let me hop in the shower, and I'll be over in a flash."

"Great. I'll toast us some garlic bagels."

"Garlic bagels? Ugh."

"It's my Italian ancestry. My grea—"

"See you soon." With that, Delta hung up the phone, shook her head, and laughed. Only Connie Rivera could make five in the morning a fun place to be.

$$\nabla \qquad \nabla \qquad \nabla$$

In less than an hour, Delta was pouring herself a cup of coffee while Connie arranged all of her note-cards, printouts, and data she'd spent all night gathering.

"After wading through tons of information from NCIC on unidentified persons, stolen jewelry, wants and warrants, etcetera, I think we may have something."

Delta nodded and sipped her coffee; next to Diet Pepsi, caffeinated coffee was her greatest vice. "You mean, besides a headache."

Connie looked up and grinned. She lived for this stuff. "I checked the records on stolen property, focusing primarily on jewels and jewelry. I think the problem our Burg Unit is having is that they're not narrowing their search enough. She isn't just a thief. She's a jewel thief, and her little two day spree pretty much proved that."

"Okay, so she's a jewel thief with a very specific MO."

"Exactly. High story entrances aren't just a *modus operandi*; they're her trademark—her calling card. It's the only real clue she's left. I think we can use it to our advantage."

"I'm following. Go on."

"I've spent all night matching her MO to locations and cities throughout the country. It appears she began her little career on the East Coast, possibly in New York or New Jersey. High-rises were her specialty there."

"Those are some really high-rises."

Connie grinned. "She's fearless. Scaling, swinging, rappelling. You name it, she's done it."

"And she's never been caught?"

Connie shook her head. "Nope."

"Impressive."

"Save your admiration for later. I haven't even gotten to the juicy parts yet. Apparently, she traveled around the New England states for quite some time, hitting high-rises and posh apartments."

"Just jewels?"

"You got it. Rubies, emeralds, diamonds—"

"Lapis?"

Connie smiled. "Actually, none on file. Until now, she stuck with only the biggies. Also, after a great deal of cross-referencing, I discovered that she usually cleans people out. This little one item shtick must be entirely for your benefit."

"Odd that she'd deviate so much from the norm. I mean, why lapis now? Surely, she could have stolen a few diamonds instead."

"Brace yourself. I highlighted all of the burg cases in the printout matching her MO, location, and dates. If she is the same thief in the highlighted sections of that printout, she's amassed earnings of well over five million dollars."

Delta's mouth dropped open as if her hinges just busted. "Five million?"

"Astounding, huh?"

"And no one has ever caught her?"

Connie shook her head. "Nope. And, brace yourself one more time. Interpol has a file on her as well."

This information brought Delta to her feet so fast, she nearly spilled her coffee. "Interpol. When you said...I mean...I never imagined..."

"Well, I did. Our little thief isn't so little. The trail first started in London, and by the time Interpol got involved, she'd stripped six European countries for an estimated net worth of nearly fifteen million dollars in jewelry."

"What happened to five million?"

"That was five just here in the states. Her total is a cool twenty million dollars."

Delta paced across the floor. "My God."

"It gets better. Interpol was reluctant to get involved until she lifted a ten-carat diamond and sapphire ring from a royal bigwig in Scotland. By then, she was already a pro. She beat a living security system in France, and to this day, they still don't know how she did it."

"Can I be impressed now?"

Connie nodded. "Feel free. She's beaten Dobermans, Rotts, camera systems, live security guards, and even light-sensitive systems that crisscrossed entire rooms."

Delta finished her coffee and stared down into an empty cup. "Then you were right. It isn't for greed. It's the challenge."

"She's a pro, and she loves what she's doing."

"Did Interpol agree that our woman is the same one?"

Connie frowned and shook her head. "The inspector I spoke with admitted there were similarities, but he seriously doubted she would have made contact with you the way she did. They say it doesn't fit her profile. Inspector Parnell from Scotland Yard doesn't want to jump to conclusions simply because both thieves are female."

"That's big of him."

"Her. She also explained that Interpol really has its hands full with all of the terrorist activity going on, so our thief isn't a high priority."

"Bullshit. She's not a high priority because she's here in the US. If she were anywhere else, they'd bust their balls to assist us."

"Now don't go getting all nationalistic on me, Kimo. They're like any other overworked, underpaid law enforcement body."

Sighing, Delta walked into the kitchen and set her mug into the sink before pouring water into it. "Whatever. What else did Inspector Clouseau have to say?"

"She said that delivering the jewels to you wasn't at all like the woman they were after. She said if we got anything else, to give her a call. Then, she politely 'rang off,' and that was that."

"In other words, do all the legwork and then call me when it's time to make the bust. I think not, Inspector Shmector."

Connie couldn't hide her grin. "Care to hear my theory?"

Delta returned to the den and sat back down. "I'm all ears."

"I think she's bored. Maybe after beating so many different types of security systems, she's trying something new. I think she's...goading you."

Delta stood up again and stared out the window. There was a gentle mist falling lightly through the trees, and for a split second, Delta wondered if that was what a rain forest was like. "An international jewel thief, huh? Imagine the chief's face when we turn her over to Interpol. He'll just die."

Connie sipped her coffee and stared at Delta's reflection in the window. "Yeah, it sure would look good for everybody."

"Where do we start?"

"The most obvious place to start is with you."

Delta turned with surprise. "Me?"

Connie nodded. "Sure. Del, she could be anywhere in the world doing whatever the hell she pleases, but she isn't. She's here in River Valley because something has drawn her here. That something is you."

Delta turned and sighed. She could no longer deny that.

"She's done this for years without anyone ever seeing her face. Suddenly, blam, there she is, hanging all over you. You're the perfect jumping off place." Connie grabbed one of the reports off her desk and began reading. "Your ID of her puts her at five-three, one-ten, and green, green eyes." Turning, Connie cocked her head. "Contacts?"

"Maybe. It was dark."

"Hair, blonde. Wig?"

Delta shrugged. "Possibly."

"Accent?"

Delta cocked her head. "Accent?"

"If she started in London, we might presume she's British."

Delta shook her head. "Not a trace. She definitely sounded American."

Connie moved back to the table and typed all of this information into Eddie II. "She's a pro. If she is British, you can bet she cut her accent loose a long time ago. What else do we know?"

"She knows where we both live. She drives a Harley and a BMW, and she's strong enough to pull herself up the sides of buildings, so she must work out."

"Excellent! We can have someone check out some of the local gyms. What else?"

"She steals only one item at a time—at least she did until she got pissed that I wasn't responding to her calls." Delta rubbed her temples. "That's all I can think of at the moment."

"Good. Are you working tonight?"

Delta nodded. "Uh-huh."

"Expect her to hit. She'll hit tonight just to let you know she's glad you're back."

"This is too weird."

"We've had weirder. What are your plans for the day?"

"I've got some snooping to do around Alex's campaign headquarters. And you?"

"Sleep. I'm exhausted."

Reaching for her jacket, Delta noticed the slight smirk on Connie's face. "What are you smirking at?"

"Oh, nothing?"

"Consuela?"

Looking up, Connie's leering grin grew. "It's sorta cute."

"What is?"

"Her crush."

"Oh, shut up."

Connie let her grin open into a wide-mouthed laugh. "Used to be, you'd have at least been flattered. What happened, old lady?"

Pulling the door open, Delta grinned back. "Megan happened."

20

The only sound Taylor heard was the rope grating and straining as she lowered herself down the side of the high-rise. She loved high-rises. She loved looking out over the skyline and watching the lights shine over the darkened streets. There was something magical about a city at night, and she adored every moment. The air felt cleaner, the perspective fresher, and the overall ambiance was one of romance, excitement, and intrigue. At night, everything transformed; alleys became dangerous black holes, capable of swallowing the unsuspecting; shadows lurked around every corner, sometimes merging with their owners to become some poor innocent person's nightmare; nothing was as it appeared under the sun. It was a world few truly knew, and none mastered. Everyone was a potential victim of the night, and only the smart or the strong survived. It was for this reason that she so loved being a creature of the night.

Inhaling the crisp night air deeply, Taylor smiled. This little city reminded her a great deal of London; with its clocktower perched among large parliamentary-type buildings. Americans may have left a great deal of England behind when they seceded, but they would forever have a love affair with British architecture.

Lowering herself a few more feet, Taylor stopped and looked out at the lights. The night's chill reminded her of Hayward's Heath, where she was raised, and she felt the slight tug of homesickness.

She did not miss the seemingly endless rain and continual gloomy weather. That eerie fog which clung to her clothes like some nebulous sap was now a distant memory, much like everything else she'd thankfully left behind.

Landing softly on the balcony of the ninth-floor apartment, Taylor surveyed the glass doors and surrounding balcony area. Just as she suspected, the balcony doors were unlocked and left slightly ajar. And why wouldn't it be? Time and time again, she'd seen sliding glass doors left unlocked simply because the owners never imagined a burglar would land on their balconies. And what kind of thief would do that anyway? Nine stories up was also nine stories down, and only the truly crazy or desperately brave would scale the side of a high-rise at night. Fortunately for Taylor, she was the latter, although there were those around the world who might disagree. For a moment, she wondered what Delta thought of her.

The thought made her smile.

Actually, she had found herself smiling a lot since she'd come to River Valley. Delta Stevens had, thus far, proven to be a very intriguing diversion, and Taylor was sure Delta would rise to the challenge. So sure, she knew that she had little time before Delta successfully tracked her down. From what she had read in her research about Delta, she was a take-charge kind of woman, who seldom obeyed rules, who acted on impulse, and who never lost control. The press seemed to love this heroine, this cop who successfully challenged her own system and won. The woman who caught a vengeful serial killer before nearly frying herself while saving children from a burning house. She was the Great Dyke Hope, and whenever a law enforcement controversy sprang up, the press ran to her for her opinion. She was gutsy, smart, and not hard to look at—which surprised Taylor. The television and press photos hadn't done Delta justice. This was a woman with the most intense eyes Taylor had ever seen. When Delta Stevens looked at you, she looked into you—to the core of your being. In a split second, she could size up someone and tell you whether this was the kind of a person who cheated on her income tax, or her lover. Which was too bad. Taylor would love spending just one night with a woman of Delta's caliber, but if she had learned anything about Delta Stevens, it was that she was loyal to a fault.

Taylor's research uncovered Delta's relationship with a prostitute who helped her break open the drug ring responsible for the death of Delta's best friend and partner, Miles Brookman. But, where was this woman now? Surely, she hadn't chosen to leave this hunk of a woman alone for very long. Delta Stevens may not have noticed how many heads turned when she strolled into the bar, but Taylor had. If her five-nine stature didn't jump start their hearts, then those bedroom eyes most assuredly did. Taylor found herself nearly swallowed up by them until she remembered that Delta could see things that weren't there. Taylor had watched the action in the bar closely enough to know that whatever those eyes took in, the mind behind them never forgot.

But then, she already knew that. That was why she'd worn that silly blonde wig and green contacts; well, that, and the fact that she knew Delta had a thing for blondes.

Looking back out over the night, Taylor sighed. Somewhere out there, Officer Stevens was driving around in her patrol car, waiting for Taylor to make her move. Waiting. Thinking about her and wanting to catch her. Too bad Delta didn't simply want her. The game would be so much more fun if Delta weren't so damned trustworthy.

"It's like great sex," Taylor whispered to the city lights. "The experience is heightened by good foreplay." Watching her breath as it left her mouth and dissipated into the cold air, Taylor turned quietly, slid the sliding glass door opened, and disappeared inside.

21

Delta glanced over at Tony and struggled with whether to tell him the truth or not. On one hand, he deserved to know, Gwen deserved to have to deal with his anger.On the other, what good would it do to hurt him like that?

Police harassment! What a crock. The cow didn't have the guts to take her on right there, so she came after Delta from behind, dealing her a sucker punch. Well, cheap shot or no, Delta was more concerned about the effects such news might have on her partner. He deserved the truth. After all, if any of her friends would have told her that Sandy was sleeping with their best friend, then Delta could have made decisions based on facts. As it was, she continued on her merry way, thinking everything was hunky-dory, and then— WHAM!—reality jumped up and knocked the wind out of her.

"You're awfully quiet tonight," Tony remarked, looking over at Delta. "I thought you'd be stoked to be back on the street so soon. What's up?"

Delta turned and opened her window a crack. "I just don't like being jerked around."

"Yeah, well, Captain Henry jerked mighty fast. The jewel thief had us for lunch, Del. We were looking like big, dumb dogs chasing our own tails. How in the hell she hit five houses in one night is beyond me. I guess she got what she came for, huh?"

Delta forced a grin. "I'm here, aren't I?"

Tony slowed down. "I'm really glad. You know, I never thought I'd say this, but boy did I hate working with another guy."

Delta's face registered surprise. "Oh?"

"Yeah. Ronhaar's butt took up half the car. He reeked of cigarette smoke. And twice, oh, God, twice, he farted and tried to pass it off as broken sewage lines. He was gross. What a pig."

Laughing, Delta patted Tony's arm. "Aw, are you saying you missed me?"

"Let's just say you never know how good you have something until it's gone. The guy ate all of his dinner and most of mine, and that was *before* we stopped at the Hot Dog Palace."

Grabbing the opportunity, Delta smoothly segued into, "Yeah, well, sometimes, it seems better after it's gone than it really was."

Tony cocked his head in question. "What's that supposed to mean?"

"Pull over for a minute."

Tony did, and when he killed the engine, he turned his upper torso so he completely faced Delta. "Did I do something wrong?"

Delta smiled tenderly. He had come such a long way. "I've been struggling with something tonight, and I don't quite know how to say it."

Tony grinned. "Do what you normally do: talk in riddles."

Delta's grin matched his. "Okay, let's say you knew that Megan was cheating on me—"

"What? She isn't, is she?"

Delta sighed in frustration. "It's an analogy, Carducci. Pay attention."

Tony nodded and clamped his lips tightly together.

"If she left me, but didn't tell me why, and you knew it was because she had been having an affair, would you tell me?"

Tony thought about this for a minute before nodding.

"Why?"

"Because you deserve to know the truth. You're the most honorable person I know. You don't deserve to be left wondering what you did wrong. Believe me, I know how that feels."

Delta inhaled deeply. "Suppose I told you that I know why Gwen left you?"

"I'd say you were crazy." Tony smiled at Delta, but when he saw that she was serious, the smile slowly faded. "How would you know?"

"I saw her."

"Where? I looked all over and never found her."

"You never saw her because she doesn't hang out in the kinds of places you two went to."

"Where does she go?"

"I saw her playing pool at the L and L the other night."

Tony didn't blink. "Oh, that. Gwen will play pool anywhere there's a free table."

Delta sighed and reached for one of his hands. "Tony, she wasn't alone. She was...with her girlfriend."

Tony pulled his hand away as if he'd been stung. "Her...what?"

"Gwen is a lesbian, Tony. She couldn't find a way to tell you, so she just up and left. I'm really sorry. I didn't know if—"

"She has a girlfriend?" Tony shook his head as if confused. "As in...lover?"

Delta nodded. "As in, I wanted her to be the one to tell you, but she pretty much blew me off and reported me to Captain Henry."

"She reported you? For what?"

"Harassment."

"What a bitch."

"My sentiments, exactly."

"So, what happened?"

Delta gave him a play-by-play description of that evening, and by the time she finished describing Gwen's girlfriend, Tony's anger seemed to evaporate. When she finished her story, he stared out the window for a moment before turning back to her and forcing a grin. "I'm glad you told me, Delta. Really I am."

"I'd want to know if Megan was cheating on me."

"What I don't get is why she didn't tell me the truth."

Delta smiled and put her hand on his. "You weren't real tolerant or understanding of people who were

different from you when we first started working together. I shudder to think of just how closed your mind
was back then."

Tony blushed. "Oh."

"But that still doesn't excuse her, Tony. She should
have been honest with you so you didn't have to carry
all that guilt around."

"Yeah, well, that's one less piece of baggage for me,
huh?"

The pain in his eyes hurt Delta. "How do you feel
about this, now that you know?"

Shrugging, Tony started the engine. "I'm a guy,
Delta. I'd be lying if I said my pride wasn't a little hurt."

"Your manly-man pride?"

Tony laughed. "Something like that. I mean, do you
know what the guys would say if they ever found out?"

"Well, they aren't going to hear it from me."

Tony pulled the car into the traffic. "A lesbian,
huh?"

Delta nodded. "Hey, she fell for a woman. Could you
have saved the relationship if she fell for another
man?"

Tony shook his head.

"Cheaters are cheaters. Either you do or you don't."

"Do you?"

Delta laughed. "Cheat? Nope. And not because I'm
some saint, either. I just think it's too much of a hassle
trying to remember all the lies and alibis. No thanks.
I'd rather spend my energy doing something construc-
tive."

"I figured you'd say something like that."

"Honesty is underrated, Carducci. Look at the dam-
age Gwen did by not being up front with you."

Tony nodded. "No kidding. And all this time I
thought it was something I did."

Suddenly, the radio spit out their call number and
crackled that there was a burglary-in-progress.

Delta grinned as her heart rate sped up. "Here's
one woman in our lives who doesn't let us down."
Picking the mike up, Delta responded that they were

on their way. In less than two minutes, they arrived at Franklin Gardens, a high-rise apartment building on the east side of their beat.

"Carducci, you call backup and have them cover the west side of the building. You take the ground floor elevators, the lobby, and the parking lot. I'm going up."

"Up?"

Delta nodded. "Up. Dispatch said the ninth floor, so that's where I'm going."

Tony reached for the mike. "Don't you think she's long gone by now?"

"Gone, maybe, but not long. I've made the mistake before in thinking she was gone, but she likes to inspect her handiwork. She's around somewhere. It's the nature of the beast." Jumping from the car, Delta started inside and took the stairs two at a time. By the fourth floor, her legs felt it. By the seventh floor, her quads and hamstrings burned. When she finally reached the ninth floor, she was standing on soggy noodles, trying to catch her breath.

"Officer! Over here!" The building superintendent in a blue jumpsuit waved his arms.

Pushing her legs down the hall, Delta's eyes scanned the building for any signs of potential danger.

"I was doing my rounds when I saw Mrs. Flanagan's door open and the apartment was dark. I called out to her, but she didn't answer. I flicked the lights on, but I didn't go in."

"You didn't see anybody?"

"Nope. But she always locks her door. Always."

Delta nodded as she peered into the dark room. "Why did you turn the light back off?"

"I watch TV. I know I should leave the crime scene the way I found it."

"What makes you think a crime has been committed here?"

"Hey, I read the papers. I know there's a ring of jewelry thieves in River Valley."

Delta cringed inside. As usual, the media only got the story half right. "Well, calling the police was a very wise move. You stay clear." Delta pulled her revolver out. "I'm going to go see if there's anyone in there."

Turning the light on with her right hand, Delta immediately saw the open sliding glass door. Carefully moving toward the balcony, Delta let her .357 lead the way as she stepped into the cold night air. The balcony was empty, save for the rope dangling against the side of the building. Looking up, Delta did not need to see where it went to know where it must have been tied. Tucking her weapon back in its holster, Delta ran back out to the hallway and radioed Carducci.

"Fourteen floors?" she asked the super.

"Not including the penthouse and the basement."

"Thanks. Watch this door and don't touch anything, okay?"

"Sure!"

Inhaling deeply, Delta brushed off the fatigue in her legs before starting back up the stairwell.

Five floors later, she emerged on the chilly rooftop in time to see a small, dark figure dash across the length of the roof and take flight before landing on the roof of the building next door.

"Damn it!" Delta yelled, wondering whether or not her rubbery legs could make the same leap. Before she had an answer, Delta hit the roof on a dead run, not stopping to think of the distance she was jumping or of how high up she was. As she neared the edge, Delta leapt into the air, covering a distance that might as well have been the Grand Canyon. In the dark, with only the light from the moon to guide her, Delta wondered for a brief second if she would make it.

When the rooftop appeared beneath her, Delta landed with far less grace than the figure before her. A shooting pain in her leg zapped up her spine as the old wound from the Zuckerman case flared up at the wrong moment. Righting her balance, Delta groaned when she realized the suspect was heading for the ledge of this building as well. Feeling another suicidal leap would be hazardous to her health, Delta ripped out her Magnum and dropped to one knee. "Freeze! Police!"

Stopping just before she reached the ledge, Taylor raised her hands in the air, turned toward Delta, and smiled. "Okay, okay, I'm frozen."

Delta guessed she was about thirty feet from the suspect. Weighing her options, she lowered the weapon slightly. "I ought to kick your ass over the side of the building. Are you insane? That jump could have killed us both!"

Taylor grinned. "But it didn't. Pumped you up, though, didn't it?"

Delta rose unsteadily and took a step forward, her .357 still poised at Taylor. "Is that what this is about? Being 'pumped up?'"

Taylor shrugged. "Isn't it?"

"I still ought to kick your butt over the edge."

"Aw, you really don't want to do that, now do you?"

"Why wouldn't I?" Delta took two more steps.

"Admit it, Delta. You're enjoying the chase. You're having more fun than anything else you've done since your girlfriend left."

"My g—"

Taylor smiled and held her hands up. "Don't worry, I'm harmless."

"Funny, Interpol doesn't think so." Delta relaxed her grip on the gun and took another step. As she did, Taylor put one foot over the guardrail.

"Interpol? You're going to listen to a bunch of stuffy Europeans? They can't find their butts with both hands. I'm disappointed in you, Delta. I thought you made up your own mind."

Delta stopped when she saw Taylor lean over the side. "Get off the rail."

"Sorry, sweets, but if you take one more step, over I go. I don't plan on spending the rest of my life in a six-by-six-foot cell. So, unless you want to put my gorgeous pieces back together, stay right where you are."

Delta reached for her radio.

Taylor leaned over the side even more. "Not that, either. Just me and you, or I'm airborne."

Nodding, Delta slowly removed her hand from her radio. "Okay, easy does it. We're at a stalemate here. What do you propose we do about it?"

"Do? There's nothing to 'do.' I'm not going to let you arrest me, and you're not going to let me go."

"But something has to give."

Taylor nodded. "And it won't be me."

"But why? Why take the risk of being caught when it would be so much easier to live the rest of your days spending the money from the jewelry you've stolen."

"Isn't it obvious?"

"Call me stupid."

"Oh, I'd like to call you, all right. Besides, it's a long story."

"Condense it for me."

Taylor nodded, still hanging onto the guardrail. "It's fun."

"Fun?"

"Sure. If you read my Interpol file, you'll know I have enough money, enough material things, enough comfort to last me five lifetimes. I have homes in four different countries on three different continents and women in every port. I have it all."

"Why not simply retire and walk away with your freedom?"

"I tried that. Got incredibly bored. Then, I saw you on the boob tube. I started following your very impressive career, and then it hit me. I'd match wits with you and see if you were as good as they say you are."

Delta frowned. "The last person who matched wits with me fell off a building much like this one."

"Yes, but Zuckerman was half a bubble off. I'm not. At least, I don't think I am." Taylor smiled before looking down. "Well, that leap was just a little scary, wasn't it?"

Delta grinned, feeling her heart race inside her chest. "A little."

"It was your interview in *Black and White* that brought me out of retirement. I saw the fire in your eyes and the determination everyone talks about, and...well...here I am."

Delta looked around to see if there was some way to get her off the ledge without killing them both. "Yes, here we are." Delta took half a step.

"You don't really want to see my lovely guts splattered all over the pavement, do you?"

"My partner gets worried when he doesn't hear from me."

Taylor checked her watch and then smiled. "A lady never overstays her welcome." Grabbing the railing, Taylor leaned way over. "You're good, Delta Stevens. Very good. And I am having the time of my life. But I cannot let you apprehend me. *Ciao, Bella.*" And with that, Taylor jumped over the side of the building.

"No!" Delta cried, seeing a flashback of Elson's miserable death. Running to the side, Delta looked over the edge. Dangling in the wind was a thick piece of nylon rope, and Taylor was nowhere in sight.

"Carducci," Delta said into the mike. "Cover the ground floor of the Hyatt."

"The hotel? Are you su—"

"Just do it! And keep looking up. She's rappelled down and disappeared around the ninth floor. Station someone at the elevators. She has to come down sooner or later."

"10-4."

Putting her revolver back, Delta pulled the rope up before heading back down the stairs. "How on earth did she get over and down before I reached the edge?" Delta muttered to herself as she took the steps three at a time with her long stride. At least going down was easier than going up.

When Delta reached the ninth floor, she knew by all the commotion that her thief had landed here. In the hallway, there were eight people standing and pointing and telling each other about the woman who had just run through their room. When the group saw

Delta, their hum turned into a roar, like a group of school children all shouting out the right answer.

"Which way did she go?" Delta shouted above the noise.

"That way." They said in unison, pointing down the hall. Sprinting down the hall, Delta radioed to Tony to block all ground floor exits.

At the end of the hall, a door into one of the suites was slightly ajar. Withdrawing her gun again, Delta gently pushed the door open. As it cracked open, Delta peered inside. "Give it up," she yelled, turning lights on as she passed by light switches. The rooms were still. Too still. Delta knew well the sensation of another heartbeat, another breath being taken in the same room. The air felt different, her nerves tingled, and her muscles tensed whenever she felt that presence. She was not experiencing those feelings now.

And then...she saw it.

For a second, she didn't know what it was. When it registered that it wasn't a part of the window, she could have kicked herself. "Carducci, move your men to the outside of the building. She's gone down the side."

"Down?"

"There's a grappling hook hanging from the window. She's gone down the side of the Hyatt. Has anyone seen anything?"

"Not a damn thing. You want us to come up and help?"

"No. Keep the ground secure. She can't go anywhere without coming down."

"Affirmative. We will maintain your perimeter."

Leaving the hook and the rope on the window, Delta went back to the group of onlookers.

"She was wearing black leather."

"He was short and fast, like a cat."

"I saw him first. He pushed right by me."

"We thought it was one of them punk rockers."

"He was a she."

As Delta waded through the overzealous crowd, one reached out and grabbed her arm.

"Excuse me, Officer—"

"I'll get all of your statements in a minute," Delta answered, pulling her arm back.

"She handed this to me as she ran by and told me to give it to Officer Stevens. That is you, isn't it?" The woman pointed to Delta's name tag.

Stopping dead, Delta took the envelope from the woman. Then, she walked to the elevator and waited for the door to close before opening it.

Dearest Delta:

I truly hope you're having as much fun as I am. Pretty soon, I'll be gone and we'll just have the memories of a really great time. Don't disappoint me, hero.

Very truly yours,

Taylor

For the remainder of the elevator ride, Delta stared at the note handwritten in bold script on lavender stationery. So, Connie had been right all along; not that that surprised Delta. When was the last time Connie was wrong? She had pegged Taylor as a bored woman finding adventure in challenging Delta's police skills. It was as simple as that. Folding the note up, Delta put it in her pocket when Tony called her over the radio.

"This is 1-82, go."

"We've got nothing here. What's your 20?"

"I'm on my way down. Cut the perimeter loose, Carducci. She's gone." Clicking her mike off, Delta stepped off the elevator and into the lobby. Yes, Taylor was gone, but not for long. She'd be back. And next time, she wouldn't get away.

22

When Delta walked into the station, Connie practically met her at the door. "She stole a topaz, didn't
she?"

Delta sighed and nodded. "Damn. I just finished the
report and—"

Connie grinned as she took Delta's hand and pulled
her over to the desk. "Remember the pattern I was
looking for?"

"You found it."

"In spades. And, I hate to admit, I'm a little embar-
rassed for not finding it sooner. Actually, it was so
simple I almost overlooked it as a coincidence."

Delta plopped down in the chair next to Connie and
waited.

"Here," Connie said, handing Delta a slip of paper.
"Read this."

Delta took the slip and looked it over. "It's the list
of jewels Taylor's stolen."

Connie's eyes widened. "Taylor? You know her
name?"

Delta nodded, returning her attention to the list.
"I'll explain later." Reviewing the jewelry on the list,
Delta read aloud. "One diamond ring, one emerald
ring, one lapis lazuli necklace, and now, add one topaz
pin. I don't see a pattern here."

"Neither did I. Not until I read the list of the five
houses she hit while you were off." Connie handed
Delta a second slip. "Now, read these."

Delta looked at the paper. It contained the ad-
dresses of the five houses Taylor burgled when Delta
was off duty. "So?"

"Read the streets off to me."

"Dickens, Emerson, Lawrence, Tolstoy, Alcott. So?"

"Look closer, Del. As a matter of fact, line them all up vertically."

Delta pulled out a pen and wrote:

Dickens
Emerson
Lawrence
Tolstoy
Alcott

"Now do you see?"

Delta stared at the paper. "The first letters spell out my name!"

Connie nodded. Now, do the same with the jewels.

Delta quickly scribbled out:

Diamond
Emerald
Lapis
Topaz

"My God, Connie, she's practically drawing a map."

Folding her arms across her chest, Connie smiled proudly. "I was really bugged by the theft of the lapis. It wasn't a jewel she had ever stolen before, and it kept nagging at me until I wrote the list of jewels stolen."

"You're brilliant."

"Not really. She helped. It wasn't until I reviewed the five hits that I realized where the lapis fit in. That's what kept bugging me all this time; why steal a lapis? When I figured it all out, I tried paging you, but you never answered."

Delta pulled her beeper out and looked at it. "My batteries need charging."

"Obviously, so do mine," Connie pointed to her temple. "I can't believe I almost got outsmarted by that little witch. It's so simplistic, it's almost insulting."

Delta grinned. "Don't take it personally, Con. It isn't you she's trying to outsmart. She may not be brilliant in the clue-making department, but she's quite adept at evading the law." With that, Delta continued with her story of the night's failed bust and showed Taylor's note to Connie. "You were right, Chief. I happen to be her new and favorite pastime."

"So I have partial redemption. Now, I want the full glory of catching her."

Delta nodded. "We will."

"Not if she keeps jumping off buildings. Geez, Del, need I remind you about Elson?"

"I don't know how she did it, but one second she was over the railing and the next second she was gone. It took me maybe three seconds to get to the edge, and all I saw was rope. She's exceptionally good."

"And exceptionally bold. I didn't think there was anyone alive who could fly in the face of authority as well as you."

"Fly. Yeah, well, that's what she seems to do. One minute she's there, the next, poof, gone."

"Well, her 'poofing' days are coming to an end. She's left a pretty big trail through the woods, and we're hot on it."

Delta quickly rose. "We are?"

"Hell, yes. I'm sure the next hit will be for an amethyst."

"Why so sure?"

A sly grin crept across Connie's face. "It's your birthstone. The lavender stationery is another one of her amateurish clues. It's an amethyst, all right."

"Have you checked with Van Clees' Arpels?"

"Uh-huh. Oh, Christian told me he got you into Van Clees' Arpels for an on-site lineup tomorrow. Not that it matters. I seriously doubt she is employed there. I think Van Clees' Arpels is a red herring."

"Judging by her sense of humor, you're probably right. But it won't hurt to check on it. Let's take a peek tomorrow and see."

"We have some other work on our agenda, so we'll have to make it a quick peek."

Delta sat back down. "What's up?"

"Alex called tonight." Connie brought her hand to her mouth like she was holding a bottle. "She's in a pretty bad way, Del."

"She's drunk?"

"Sounded that way to me. She's probably passed out by now, but it wouldn't hurt to drive by and see how she is."

"Care to join?"

Connie shook her head. "No thanks. My woman is tucked warmly in bed, and that's precisely where I'm going to be in less than an hour."

"Lucky you."

Connie grinned. "Ain't I, though? Look, I'll pick you up tomorrow morning around nine o'clock and we can check out Van Clees' Arpels together."

"Good. There are a few other places I'd like to stop at while we're out and about."

"Oh? Where?"

"McCloud's Pet Emporium. I'm going to buy Megan a macaw."

23

Alexandria had the front door of her beautiful Victorian home opened even before Delta could knock. Standing in the doorway, in plum-colored silk pajamas, Alexandria was holding a glass of white wine.

"I knew you'd come," Alexandria said, motioning for Delta to enter. As Delta brushed by her, she could smell the fruity scent of Alexandria's wine breath.

"You okay?" Delta asked, turning in time to see Alexandria's eyes linger a moment too long on Delta's rear end.

"Depends on what your definition of 'okay' is, I suppose." Walking into the sunken living room, Alexandria took Delta's jacket from her with one hand, while balancing her wine glass with the other. "The polls show that demented moron has shot huge holes in my campaign hopes. He's capitalized on the shooting at every turn. He's transformed an attempted murder into an advertisement for himself. He sickens me."

Sitting on the couch, Delta couldn't help but stare at the impeccably decorated home. Above the white marble fireplace hung two tasteful Maplethorpes, beneath which were four low, thick candles flickering against the white walls. The furniture was white leather, which balanced masterfully with the looming mahogany bookshelves lined with hardback law books. A perfect fire crackled in the fireplace, casting dancing shadows on the oriental rug laying beneath the furniture.

"What a room."

Alex laughed. "And I'd like to keep it, if you know what I'm saying."

Delta leaned her elbows on her knees. "I hear you, but I'm not sure I understand."

Sitting on the couch next to Delta, Alexandria sighed loudly. "What I mean, dear Delta, is that it doesn't matter much if you catch the shooter or even if you find out who sent him, if I lose the election anyway. The polls—"

"Don't mean squat, Alex."

"Maybe not to you, but to many, they're the gospel. My re-election is sinking, Delta, and I can't seem to stop it."

"Well, first off, you don't need any more of this." Taking the wine glass from Alexandria, Delta walked into the white-tiled kitchen and set it on the sink. An empty wine bottle stood on the butcher block sitting grandly in the middle of the gourmet kitchen. "Frankly, Alex," she said, re-entering the room. "I'm surprised at you. This isn't like you at all."

"Which part? The drinking or the quitting?"

"Both. And you're not quitting. I don't bust my ass for quitters, Alex."

"He's won, Delta. He's instilled doubt in the minds of the voters; doubts I can't assuage." The last word slurred as it rolled off her tongue. "My ad manager is trying to counter Wainwright's attacks, but it may be too late."

"It's never too late."

Alexandria leaned forward, her pajama top revealing two healthy mounds of flesh. "Got any suspects?"

"No."

"Right. Every day we come up empty gives him momentum. And the thought of losing this election is killing me." Suddenly, Alexandria's eyes filled with tears. "All I ever wanted was to be the DA, to serve people, to get crooks off the streets. I've given this office everything I have, and then some. Damn it, Delta., I'm a great lawyer."

Delta nodded. "Yes, you are. You're one of the best."

"Yes, but how soon the fickle public forgets. And Wainwright—that shithead is trying to make me look like a helpless woman. Me! Alexandria Marquee Pendleton. God, how I hate that man."

Delta sat next to Alexandria on the couch and took her hand. "People will always doubt, Alex. But if you start doubting yourself, then you're right. It's over." Alexandria looked down at her hand in Delta's. "You don't doubt me, do you?" Delta grinned. "Never." "Do you ever doubt yourself?" "Sometimes. And when I do, Connie grabs me around the collar and yanks some sense into me." Alexandria smiled. "I suppose that's why I called you over here, huh? To yank my collar?" Delta shrugged, but said nothing. "You're a good friend, Delta Stevens." Setting her hand on Delta's thigh, Alexandria's smile changed—and with it, the atmosphere in the room changed as well. "Have you any idea how much your friendship means to me?"

Swallowing back her trepidation, Delta took Alexandria's hand from her leg and held it between both her hands. Delta could tell by the pinkish tint of Alexandria's cheeks and the imprecise way her words slipped out of her mouth that this was the wine talking. "I have a pretty good notion, yes. I've always known."

"Have you?" As Alexandria scooted closer, her perfume wafted over to Delta and mingled curiously with the scent from the wine. "But have you always known how deeply or just how much?"

Alexandria's last three words sounded more like jushowmush, and Delta was certain that this strange conversation had been poured out of the bottle in the kitchen.

"Alex, I—"

"Shh," Alexandria said, placing one finger over Delta's lips. "I need to say this in case we never get to work together again." Running her finger down Delta's lips, Alexandria inched closer. "Don't you ever get tired of always doing the right thing? Don't you ever just want to throw caution to the wind and see where fate takes you?"

It was a rhetorical question; one Delta knew did not require a response. "Alex—"

"Well, I do. Defense attorneys pay witnesses off, and then reach into their dirty bag of tricks to beat me. I have to play strictly by the rules. And look where that has led me. Well, I'm sick of it. I'm no angel or saint, Delta, and tonight, I'm going to do exactly what I feel like doing, come high or hellwater."

Delta grinned at her misuse of the cliché. "And what would that be?"

Pulling Delta closer, Alexandria whispered, "That would be to seduce you, Delta Stevens."

Now Delta was convinced this was the wine talking; Alexandria was so out of character, it was the only logical explanation. Gently taking both of Alexandria's hands in hers, Delta brought them to her lips and kissed each one. Gazing deeply into Alexandria's troubled gray eyes, Delta smiled warmly as she brushed Alexandria's hair over her shoulder. There was no doubt about it; Alexandria Pendleton was one of the most strikingly beautiful women Delta had ever had the fortune of meeting. She was brilliant, sexy, and, right now, extremely sensuous as she sat here with her pajamas revealing too much cleavage. Anyone would be a fool to pass up an opportunity to spend just one night with this incredibly gorgeous creature. One night was all she was asking, and Megan was thousands of miles away. She wouldn't even know.

Slowly rising, Delta pulled Alexandria to her feet. "Which way?"

With only her eyes, Alexandria directed Delta to the hallway which led to the large, light pink bedroom. Like a picture of a Victorian bed-and-breakfast, the bedroom was decorated with white lace, a fluffy pink comforter, and tiny rose wallpaper. Not one thing appeared out of place. The four-poster, mahogany bed stood majestically in the center of the room, and Delta could only imagine the sights and sounds it had seen.

"You have incredible taste," Delta said, tossing the comforter back.

"Thanks. I've always loved the Victorian period. It's so...romantic."

"Yes, it was." Staring into Alexandria's face, Delta pulled her close and held Alexandria tightly. "Don't worry, Alex. You're not going to lose all of this; not if I have anything to say about it." Maneuvering them over to the bed, Delta laid down and patted her own shoulder. "Lay your head here for a minute."

"What about your clothes?" Alex said, slurring 'clothes.' Crawling beside Delta, Alexandria laid down and snuggled in the crook of Delta's arm.

"Later. Right now, let me just hold you, okay?" Wrapping her arms around Alexandria, Delta gently stroked Alexandria's long, auburn hair that tumbled down the back of her pajamas. Almost immediately, Delta felt Alexandria's weight go slack against her chest.

"Thank you," Alexandria mumbled before her right leg twitched.

Delta smiled and kissed the top of Alexandria's head before pulling the comforter over them with her free hand. "That's what friends are for," Delta whispered, closing her eyes. Delta's last thoughts before she drifted off to sleep were of Megan, their life together, and how deeply in love she was with the woman who held her heart thousands of miles away.

24

The following morning, when Delta drove into her driveway, Connie was just getting out of her car. The look on her face was definately not her typical "good morning" face.

"Where in the hell have you been?" Connie demanded, ripping open Delta's truck door before she had even turned the engine off. "And if you say 'Alex's house,' I'm gonna kick your ass. No—worse than that, I'm gonna beat your butt so hard, you'll feel it in another life!"

Delta looked into the fiery eyes glaring at her and knew Connie meant every word she said. "Hold on, Chief, I can explain."

Connie crossed her arms and stepped back to let Delta out of the truck. "This had better be the explanation of a lifetime, sister, or I'll crawl all over your case like a catfish cleaning an aquarium."

Stepping from the truck, Delta held her hands out, posturing her innocence. "Nothing happened. I swear."

Connie stepped forward and got right in Delta's face. "Right. You roll home in the a.m. after spending all night at a drop-dead good-looking woman's house, and I'm supposed to believe nothing happened? What happened? Did you check your brains at the door?"

"Con—"

"What happened?" Connie pressed, leaning against Delta now. In all the years they'd been friends, Delta had never seen Connie angry like this.

"Nothing happened."

Both women stood locked in defiant postures. "I swear to God, Delta Stevens, if you went over there and did something foolish, you'd better come clean now, or—"

"Nothing happened, Connie!"

Connie held her gaze to Delta's for a short while longer before finally backing off. "Nothing?"

"Not a damn thing."

Connie studied Delta for a moment before sighing heavily. Visibly relieved, she threw her arms around Delta and hugged her. "I called and called all morning, and when you didn't answer, I thought...well..."

"You thought I'd fallen into bed with her." Delta pulled away, stung by Connie's implications. "How could you?"

Connie bowed her head. "I don't know. Maybe you were lonely, or—"

"Well it's a damn good thing we're not together, then, isn't it? I can't believe how suspicious you are."

Connie shrugged. "What would *you* have thought?"

"I don't know, but I can't believe you thought I'd cheat on Megan. You know better than that. I tho—"

"Okay, okay, I jumped the gun. I'm sorry."

Delta's scowl slowly turned into a half-grin. "Comes with the territory, I suppose."

"What if it had been *me* out all night?"

Delta grinned. "I'd have reacted the same way if I thought you were messing around on Gina."

"But you're not? Messing around, I mean."

"Not even remotely."

Connie sighed loudly. "Thank God."

"Have you been waiting out here long? Why didn't you just use your key?"

"Fear. I was afraid Megan would call and there I'd be...trying to find a way to tell her you hadn't come home. No thanks."

Delta smiled as she unlocked the front door. "Well, you could have kept my private rent-a-pig company." Walking into the house, Delta waved to the uniformed officer sitting on the couch. "If you ask me where I was all night, I'm going to poison your lunch."

The officer smiled back, yawned, and strode past Delta to the bathroom.

"He's a barrel of laughs, huh?" Delta whispered to Connie as they walked into the kitchen.

"I'll say."

"What were you calling me about, anyway?"

Connie hoisted herself onto a barstool that was too tall for her. "I have a friend who owns a pet store a few blocks from Van Clees' Arpels. She has a macaw and is willing to give us a deal."

Delta stopped and turned to Connie. "You called and called just to tell me that?"

Grinning slyly, Connie shook her head. "Not really. I just wanted to make sure you came home."

Opening a bag of day-old bagels, Delta offered one to Connie. "Look, I got there, she was hammered, scared about losing the election, and on the verge of a very big cry. I held her while she slept. End of story."

"What did she say when she woke up and found you laying in her bed?"

Delta checked her phone messages and mail before starting out the door. "She opened her eyes, took one look at me, and then buried her face in the pillow."

"You look that bad in the morning?"

"Only if you've forgotten I was there the night before."

Connie bit into her bagel as she opened her car door for Delta. "How awkward."

"No kidding." Delta leaned over and unlocked Connie's door. "When she put her head in the pillow, I walked over and whispered that nothing happened. She didn't believe me, so I said, 'Look.' When she peeked out from the pillow, she saw that I still had my clothes on. The look of relief on her face was worth a thousand bucks."

"I'll bet. What a crappy way to ruin a really good friendship."

"Not to mention my relationship."

"How did she take it after you told her what happened?"

"She was relieved and, I think, a little disappointed."

"Disappointed? Is there a little piece you're leaving out?"

Delta grinned. "Okay, so she put a few moves on, so wh—"

"Ah-ha! I suspected she had a thing for you."

"Her thing, Inspector Clueless, is friendship. Period."

"Uh-huh." Connie shifted and stared straight ahead. "You had her vulnerable, drunk, and in bed, yet you passed on a golden opportunity. Don't you think she may be feeling even lower than before?"

"Not at all. I told her this morning that I found her beautiful, strong, talented, and a great friend. She would have done the same thing for me if the roles were reversed, and she agreed."

"So, there's absolutely no attraction there?"

Delta turned and looked out the window. "I never said that. I think we're both aware of the energy between us, but I also told her I am in love with Megan and would never do anything to jeopardize that. In the end, Alex hugged me and thanked me for not letting her indiscretion ruin our friendship."

"Sometimes, you amaze me."

Delta returned her gaze to Connie. "Why is that?"

"I'm just really proud of you, that's all."

Delta suddenly warmed all over. "You know, Alex asked me if I ever got tired of doing the right thing."

"And do you?"

"Not yet. I'm sure I will someday, but not quite yet."

"Thank the goddess. I really would have hated to kick your butt."

"Would you have?"

Connie grinned wickedly. "What do you think?"

25

Just as Connie had predicted, the trip to Van Clees' Arpels yielded nothing.

"Let's walk to the pet store," Connie said, linking her arm through Delta's.

"It's too damned cold."

"Stop your whining. The exercise will be good for us."

A few blocks down, Delta saw the red and blue sign flashing in neon lights. "Your friend is going to cut us a deal?"

Connie stopped at the door and turned to Delta. "Del, have you any idea how much these birds cost?"

Delta shrugged. "How much can a bird cost?"

Grabbing Delta's hand, Connie led her into the store. "Come with me, Pilgrim, and see."

Walking past the guinea pigs, snakes, iguanas, and tarantulas, Delta spied a huge wrought iron cage standing in the corner, with a large, blue and gold macaw sitting majestically on a large piece of manzanita.

"Wow." Delta murmured, carefully approaching the cage. "He's beautiful." Delta studied the gold chest running the length of the underside of the tail. When the bird stopped preening, he looked up at her with his eyes dilated and said very clearly, "Hi there."

Delta's eyes popped open. "Did you hear that?"

"Clear as a bell."

Delta inched closer. The bird bobbed his head at her. "I didn't know they were so big."

"So is the price tag."

Carefully putting her forearm up to the macaw's chest, Delta watched as it took a tentative step onto her arm. "He's heavy, too." Delta studied the large hooked beak with the soft, wrinkly skin around it. The bird continually cocked its head from side to side while making little clicking noises with his tongue.

"Hi there," he said. "Pretty girl."

Delta laughed. "It must be a girl."

"I think she's in love," Connie said, reaching out to touch the bird's back feathers.

"So am I. I can see why Megan's in love with them, too. Look how smart she is."

Connie stepped up next to Delta as she thumbed through a book on macaws. "Says here that the ones Megan is trying to protect are the scarlet ones. This one is a blue and gold. They're not indigenous to Costa Rica."

"Wherever they're from, they're beautiful."

Connie continued reading. "Don't get too close to that beak, Del. This says they have seventy pounds of crushing power per square inch of their beaks."

Delta pulled her face away from the large, black beak. "Per square inch?"

"Uh-huh. She could rearrange your face in a heartbeat."

The clerk finally appeared from behind the counter and scratched the bird's chest. "Not Rikki. He's very gentle for a macaw."

Connie and Delta exchanged looks. "He?"

The clerk laughed. "Rikki used to be caged next to an African Gray who used to whistle and say pretty girl as women walked by. Rikki just happened to pick up the catchy phrase."

"Can he say anything else?"

"Can and will. He says his name, any variation of hello, and he can also wave, roll over, and bow. That's why he's sort of on the expensive side. We do have some in the back who—"

"How much?" Delta interrupted.

The freckled clerk grinned. She couldn't have been older than eighteen. "Two grand."

Delta stared, slack-jawed. "As in thousands?"

Connie snickered.

"But, since you're a friend of Consuela's, my boss told me to give him to you for fifteen hundred."

Delta put Rikki back on his perch, immediately causing him to shriek loudly. "Do people really pay that much for a pet?"

Freckles nodded. Her fiery hair didn't move. "For exotics, you bet. You'll pay less for an import, but I don't touch imports. Dirty business. No thanks."

Taking a peanut from the bowl in the cage, Delta handed it to Rikki, who swiftly cracked it and began turning the meat of the peanut over in his beak. "Imports? Are those the ones smuggled in?"

Freckles winced. "Makes me sick even thinking about it. Those jerks should be shot. Or worse."

Delta nodded, watching Rikki deftly shave the meat off the peanut. She was beginning to understand Megan's passion for the birds. "He is incredible."

Freckles agreed. "You're getting a healthy, happy, domestically bred bird with this one." She picked a peanut up and told Rikki to wave. He responded by lifting a foot in the air and waving. "He has the IQ of a five-year-old child."

"Like my partner," Delta quipped.

"Rikki will live anywhere from forty to eighty years. You'll have to will him to a younger family member."

Delta turned to Connie, who vehemently shook her head. "No way."

"You can be such a hard ass, sometimes. Come on, Con, Junior would love a pet."

"Junior?"

Delta grinned. "Juniorette?" Nodding to Freckles, "I'll take him."

Connie appeared surprised. "You, the woman who pinches the nickel so tightly that the Indian is riding the buffalo?"

"Very funny."

"Delta, think about it. Fifteen hundred dollars is a lot of money."

"Connie, how much did it cost you to visit your friendly neighborhood sperm bank?"

"That's different."

"Like hell. You and Gina want an addition to your family. Well, so do I. Just not one I have to put braces on, worry about driving in the dark, or pay for college. This is an investment in our future."

"Not to mention, Megan will flip when she sees him."

Delta nodded and scratched Rikki on the head. "Exactly. I want to show her that I do care about the causes that interest her. I don't see why they can't be something we both share."

"That's sweet," Freckles said.

Studying Rikki, Delta sighed. "I've said all the words and talked the talk about being supportive. Now, it's time I *showed* her I can walk the walk. Rikki will be my way of saying to her 'Welcome back. Please stay.'"

"Then I say go for it, Storm. He'll make her very happy. And, my friend, so will you."

Turning to Freckles, Delta reached into her back pocket for her wallet. "Can you hold him until she gets back from Costa Rica?"

"Sure. If she's in Costa Rica, you couldn't get her a better gift."

After signing for Rikki, Delta took one more extended look at him before leaving the pet store. "He's something, isn't he? You really think Megan will love him?"

"Of course she will. And she'll probably love you even more for caring as much as you do. Money and jokes aside, Del, I think what you've done is really sweet."

Delta stopped walking so she could face Connie. "I miss her so much."

"I know. I can see it in your eyes."

"When Megan gets home, I'm going to take a few days off and go to a bed-and-breakfast somewhere up north. Maybe to Monterey or Carmel. Someplace romantic."

"Speaking of romance," Connie said, leaning over to look inside a window displaying jewelry. "Look at that ring. Gene's been wanting a pear-shaped stone forever."

Delta looked up at the small sign that read, "Echavia's Jewelry" before peering in the window at the diamond anniversary band.

"Wouldn't you love to put one of those babies on Megan's finger?"

Delta hesitated a moment before pulling Connie into the store. "What the hell, right? I just spent fifteen hundred on a bird." Staring into the glass cases, Delta couldn't find any ring prettier than the simple band displayed in the window "See anything, Con?"

"I love this amethyst with the diamond," Connie answered, tapping her finger on the case. The saleswoman, wearing a name tag that said Judy on it, leaned over the case. "That's a very lovely ring you're wearing," she said, pointing to Connie's turquoise ring on her index finger.

Connie held her hand up so Judy could see the ring better. "It's an heirloom from my grandmother."

"It's unique in both design and color. The turquoise must be from the southwestern tip of Mexico."

Connie nodded. "I'm impressed."

"And she doesn't impress easily," Delta added, moving on to the next case.

"Have you ever had it cleaned?"

Connie pulled her hand back and examined the stone. "Not since I've had it, and that's been more than ten years."

"If you don't mind me saying so, you do a disservice to a ring like that. We have a laser cleaner here especially for softer stones and gems. If you'd like, I can have it cleaned for you in a jiffy."

Delta turned her attention from the case to the front window. The words "Free Jewelry Cleaning with the Latest Technology" were painted on the window. Then, below the store's moniker, the cleaning ad continued: "Don't let other jewelers put chemicals on your precious gems; clean them with ULTRA SHINE."

Delta moved over to the window and peered out of it. Sitting down the street from the store was Van Clees' Arpels. Delta wondered if the smaller jewelry store had a hard time being competitive. "Must be tough having Van Clees' Arpels down the street," Delta mused, returning to the counter in time to see Connie pull her ring off and hand it to the clerk.

"It was at first, but we have on-site services that Van Clees' Arpels either sends out for or doesn't have."

"Such as?"

"Watch repair while you wait, setting repair, necklace clasps, batteries, polishing, replacement gems, and cleaning are all done on-site. We do estimates and—"

"You clean the rings right here?"

Judy looked up and smiled. "Of course. We use the very latest in technology; not even Van Clee—"

"Do you keep the jewelry overnight?"

"Sometimes. Why?"

Jamming her ring back on her finger, Connie caught the tone in Delta's voice and turned her attention to the clerk. "And you keep them in a safe."

Judy frowned and stood up straight. "Of course. Many customers prefer to drop their jewelry off and pick it up later. Everything goes in the safe."

Delta and Connie looked at each other, comparing notes without uttering a word. Connie turned from their silent conversation and picked up the ball. "I have a wonderful collection of jewelry from my grandmother, but I must be able to ensure their safety. I'd just die if anything happened to any of it."

Delta nodded. "You just can't trust anyone these days."

"I can assure you, ma'am, that in more than twenty years in business we have never been robbed. We may appear small, but we have invested in the finest technology money can buy."

"Do you service a lot of Van Clees' Arpels' jewelry?"

Judy nodded. "We service jewelry from all over the world. Because we personalize our business, people feel safer leaving such sentimental items with us. We take exceptional care of both the jewelry and the customer wearing it. Your grandmother's heirlooms would be perfectly safe here."

Connie shook her head. "I don't know—"

Delta shrugged. "Forget it, Gladys. It doesn't feel right."

"I assure you, they would be in the safe if you chose to leave them overnight."

"Maybe if you could show Gladys where you keep them, she might consider it."

The clerk nodded. "Why, of course. Would that make you feel better?"

Connie nodded. "Much."

Following Judy through the back, Connie and Delta were escorted into an office about twenty by twenty feet. There were two overflowing desks and a three-foot-high floor safe tucked in the corner. On the two opposing walls, camera-like devices protruded. There was one window, and it led to the interior hallway of the small shop. Delta's keen eye picked out the fine line of an alarm system hiding in the glass. The door, made of reinforced steel, closed into a steel frame set securely in cement. Scanning the ceiling, Delta's attention was drawn to the tiles on the ceiling surrounding a small heating duct.

"What are those for?" Delta asked, pointing to the cameras.

"Infrared detection system. Once activated, there's beams of light invisible to the naked eye. If someone interrupts one of the beams, the alarm goes off immediately."

Delta had seen this type of system before. "I see."

"As you can tell, we've taken every precaution to ward off—"

"May I use the phone?" Delta asked abruptly.

"If it's local, sure."

"It is." Eyeing Connie, Delta picked up the phone and punched a number. The phone was answered on the third ring.

"Christian here."

"It's Delta."

"Hey there. To what do I owe this honor?"

"I'm downtown, Christian, and I was wondering if you had photos of those items we were discussing the other day."

Connie immediately engaged Judy in a conversation to steer her away from Delta's discussion with Christian.

"You mean the jewels your thief's been taking?"

"That would be them." Delta could hear paper shuffling on the other end of the line.

"I have two."

"Great. Can you messenger copies over to 910 Fitzgerald?"

"Right now?"

"Right now."

"You're onto something, eh? Did she slip up someplace I don't know about?"

"I hope so. Tell the messenger to look for Connie and me out front. I'll pick the pictures up there. I'm wearing a red sweatshirt."

"You got it. Anything else I can do for you on this beautiful day?"

Delta grinned. "Why are you so up, today? You been smelling too much formaldehyde?"

Christian laughed. "Close. I'm in love. But that's all the dirt you get from me. You know how rumors fly around this place."

"Gotcha. Your secret is safe with me."

"Good. And when you return the pics, be sure to let me in on your little secret, okay?"

"Will do. See ya." Hanging up the phone, Delta waited for Connie to finish distracting the clerk. "Would you mind if we stepped outside to discuss it?"

Judy looked perplexed. "Of...course not."

Delta and Connie briskly stepped through the store and closed the door behind them.

"You thinking what I'm thinking?" Delta asked Connie as they stood on the sidewalk.

"Say no more. Is Christian sending the pics?"

"They're on their way as we speak."

"So, you want to show them and ask her if she remembers seeing them? How do you want to handle this?"

"Well, she isn't Taylor, that's for sure. I don't think she's in on it, or she wouldn't have shown us the room and the safe."

"Okay."

"But did you take a look at the ceiling panels? It's possible Taylor moved through the heating duct. These older buildings have all sorts of weird nooks and crannies."

Connie rubbed her chin. "She's better than I gave her credit for."

"I think she comes here, decides which pieces she wants to steal, gets the address, and then steals them from the houses. If these pictures pan out, and this place has cleaned these jewels in the last month or so—"

"Then we've got her."

Delta grinned. "Almost. It'll just be a matter of setting Taylor up."

Connie looked down the street for the messenger. "I hate that, you know."

"What?"

"That you call her by name."

Delta laughed. "What do you want me to call her? That dreaded, awful jewelry thief? That horrible woman? That big bi—"

"No. You could just call her the suspect, or perp, or thief. Do you insist on calling her Taylor?"

Delta nodded. "Yes."

Connie snarled at Delta. "You can be infuriating. You know that, don't you?"

"That's what they say, Gladys."

Before Connie could shoot out a retort, the messenger pulled up and handed a packet to Delta, who signed for it and nodded for Connie to tip him.

"Why do I always have to tip them?"

Delta smiled. "You make more money than I do."

After removing the pictures, Delta looked at them and handed them to Connie. "You think she is capable of beating that security system in there?"

Connie looked at the pictures and nodded. "Yep. She knows exactly what she's doing. It would be a mistake to think she doesn't."

"Well, I, for one, am done making mistakes."

Connie turned to Delta and grinned. "Can I quote you on that?"

Delta grinned right back. "You betcha, Gladys."

"Next time, I want a new name, a cool one."

Delta's grin grew as she walked back in the store. "Next time, I have just the perfect one."

26

When Delta and Connie stepped onto Sal's porch, two very bright security lights flashed on, illuminating the porch, the front yard, and half the street.

"Sheesh. I left my sunglasses in the car."

Reaching for the doorbell, Connie stopped her hand in midair, when a computer-generated voice said, "Stop right there. Stand away from the door and look into the camera directly to your left." The voice was followed by a click and a buzz as the camera focused on them.

Delta laughed. "I don't believe this."

"Stand away from the door, or the gate will automatically open, releasing two killer Rottweiler attack weapons."

Delta stopped laughing and immediately stepped back. "Is she serious?"

Connie shrugged. "Let's not test her, okay?"

"If someone is home," the mechanical voice continued without emotion, "the door will be answered in one minute. If the door is not opened at that time, you have one minute to leave a message on the camera. If you do not leave within two minutes, the gates will open and the attack weapons will escort you out."

Delta checked her watch. She did not relish the idea of her legs being used for chewbones.

"Forty seconds," the voice informed.

Suddenly, the front door flew open to reveal a tiny woman wearing army fatigues and a baseball cap jammed on top of her head. Short blonde hair stuck out from underneath the cap like pieces of straw, and freckles dotted her nose and cheeks. In her right hand she held a ratchet wrench, in her left, a piece of wire.

"Hey! If it isn't my two favorite cops! Come on in!"

Delta looked at Connie and then at Sal. Nobody moved.

"Don't worry," Sal said, waving the wrench in the air. "The system shuts off as soon as my hand touches the knob." Sal stepped out onto the porch and hugged both of them at once. "Come on in." Sal pulled away and smiled widely at them. Her diminutive stature belied her greatness. Sal's electronic wizardry equaled Connie's mental prowess.

Following Sal through the door, Delta stopped when a buzzer sounded. "What's that?"

"You packin', Delta?" Sal asked.

Delta nodded as she reached for her nine millimeter in her ankle holster.

"It's okay. Don't bother." Walking over to a huge console protruding from the wall, Sal flipped a switch to silence the buzzer. "Metal detector," she tersely explained. "It's so good to see you guys again." Sal hugged Connie once more, this time, getting both her tiny arms around Connie's neck. Not only was Sal an invaluable resource, an old friend of Connie's, and an army brat, to boot, she was also responsible for Delta still being alive. In the time it takes most people to button a shirt, Sal had once disposed of a man who would, most assuredly, have brutally tortured and killed Delta in the desert.

Connie pulled away and pointed to the console. "Speaking of business, what are you up to that requires such an elaborate system?"

Sal smiled and her freckles danced across her face. "You know me. I hang out with some pretty bizarre characters. I'm just protecting my...investments, that's all. You like?"

"I'm impressed."

Delta looked out the side window. "You really got two Rotts out there?"

"Ten grand worth and meaner than bears caught in a bear trap. Can I get you guys something to drink?"

"No thanks," they answered in unison. Connie pulled a chair out from under a table laden with electronic equipment.

"I take it this isn't a pleasure call," Sal said, pulling herself up to the counter. She looked like a little girl wearing her dad's uniform. But then, that's just what she was doing.

Delta had been previously introduced to Sal when she and Carducci were hunting down child pornographers. At first, Delta thought the little waif in camouflage clothing was a little strange with her electronic gadgets and questionable allies. But Connie had explained that Sal's father had saved his buddies' lives over in Vietnam at the cost of his own. When they returned, the pack of young men took Sal under their collective wing and made sure she never wanted for anything. With her father's insurance policy and her skill at electronics, Sal managed several patents and built a mini empire for herself and "the boys." What had become of her mother, Delta never knew.

Picking up a microchip, Delta examined it closely. "How's business, Sal?"

"Great. A company in Silicon Valley wants to market my latest gadget."

"You ought to sell security systems, pal," Delta offered.

"Boooooring. I'd hate mingling with the snooty, rich yuckies; it gives me the chills just thinking about it."

Delta grinned. She was such an odd little woman, preferring the company of beer-bellied bikers and vets to anyone else.

"You guys didn't come here to talk shop. You need my help again? I had a blast the last time we got together."

Blast? Delta thought. She guessed blowing someone's heart out the back of their body could be considered a "blast."

Connie nodded and explained Taylor's case.

"So," Sal began when Connie finished. "She hasn't stolen an amethyst yet."

Connie nodded again. "And, according to the records at the jewelry store, they haven't cleaned an amethyst in two months."

"So," Delta finished, "we send in a couple pieces of jewelry, including an amethyst, to be cleaned, and we use your house as the address on record."

"Why not either of yours?"

"She knows where we live. Hell, we've been running cross patterns just in case she's tailing us."

Sal leapt off her chair and paced the floor. "She couldn't possibly beat this system."

"Don't doubt her, Sal. This woman is exceptional."

Sal took her cap off and ran her hand through her hair. "I can turn the system off."

Connie shook her head. "No. If she even suspects this is a trap, that will tip her off. There's no way she's going to pass up the opportunity to beat your system. My guess is that she cases the houses prior to hitting them. She'll case this place, Sal, and will really find it challenging. She lives for that challenge."

Delta agreed. "I think she'd dig it. She might even see it as her *coup de grâce*."

Sal set the wrench on the table. "I seriously don't think she can do it."

"Getting her here is all we really need, Sal. Do you have a safe upstairs?"

Sal jammed her hands on her hips. "Now, what kind of question is that?"

Delta grinned. Sal was truly a kindred spirit who was passionate about anything of intrigue. "Then, we'll go over the specifics of the plan and let you shoot any holes in it."

Sal nodded. "I'm telling you, the biggest hole is that she won't be able to beat my system to even get to the safe."

"Maybe. But if it were too easy, she'd bolt. We don't want that. Making it hard on Taylor will convince her it's for real."

Sal flipped her collar up and lowered her head. "Okay, super-sleuths. Where do we go from here?"

27

When Delta's head finally hit the pillow, the muscles in her body melted into the bed. She hated to admit it, but a good night's rest was exactly what she needed to escape the loneliness she'd felt more acutely since she'd laid with Alex. Delta didn't regret being the shoulder for Alex to lean on; what she regretted was that Alex wasn't Megan laying in her arms. Delta never imagined she could miss anyone as much as she missed Megan. She longed to have Megan's hair hang in her face like it did whenever Megan lay on top of her. She missed the chats over morning coffee, the evenings in front of the fire, and the nights of cuddling in the warm, flannel sheets Megan had bought just for Delta's cold feet. She missed phoning Megan "just because" and looking forward to a romantic dinner together.

Had Delta just discovered what being in love was all about, only to find it was too late? Delta shuddered at the words she had hurled at her other lovers. "I'll want you, I'll love you, I want to be with you, but I'll never need you."

Boy, had she been wrong.

Delta needed. She needed Megan's balance in her life. She needed her calm outlook, her sharp wit, and that beautiful, beautiful smile. For two months, Delta had traveled on autopilot, going to work, working too long, visiting Connie, and filling her downtime with anything that came along, and still, she could not stop that ache. The highlight of her day came at the end of her shift, when she crossed off that day on the calendar. One day down, one million to go.

As Delta's mind and body settled into a series of small twitches and Polaroid images, she heard a knock on the door. Shaking remnants of exhaustion from her mind, Delta sat up on her elbows and listened. With the uniformed man posted out front, whoever it was must have been recognized.

Dragging her tired limbs from bed, Delta reached for her robe on the chair and cinched it around her waist. Again, she heard a knock.

"Coming," she said, peering through the brass peephole. Standing on the porch was Alexandria.

"Alex?" Delta said, unlocking the door and swinging it open.

"Delta, I'm so sorry to bother you at this time of night, but—"

"Come in, come in," Delta said, pulling Alexandria in the house. "Don't be silly. Are you okay?"

Her hands resting in the pockets of her London Fog raincoat, Alexandria shrugged. "I'm not sure."

"Please, sit down. Want some coffee or something?" Delta took Alexandria's coat and hung it on the coat rack standing next to the door.

"No, thank you. I don't want to be more of a bother than I already am."

Delta studied Alexandria's face before replying. Alexandria looked exhausted; crow's feet appeared where once there were none. Her gray eyes were dull and lifeless. The fight was oozing out of Alexandria like a broken pipeline oozes oil. "What's going on, Alex?"

Alexandria sighed heavily. "I didn't want to put you in a more compromising position than I already have, but I don't know where else to turn."

Delta sat across from Alexandria. "Go on."

"I was hoping you could tell me what to do with this." Alexandria extracted a black videotape. "It arrived in the mail this morning."

Delta took the tape and turned it over in her hands. It was a regular VCR tape housed in a black sleeve. "I'm afraid to ask. What is it?"

"Play it and see."

Delta rose and pushed the tape into the VCR sitting on top of the television. Then, she picked up the remote and sat next to Alexandria on the couch. The first image that appeared on the screen was a campaign promo for Wainwright, apparently sponsored by the Citizens Against Repeat Offenders. After a little blurb flashed across the bottom of the screen, footage of Alexandria's shooting played. Apparently taken by a home video camera, the footage came from behind the shooter, as if someone were taping Alexandria's exit from the building. As the shots were fired, one of Alexandria's secretaries pulled her to the ground, while photographers snapped pictures and the crowd started running. The tape zoomed in on Alexandria laying across the steps, while a female body shielded her. As the camera focused on the two women, a deep voice came over the tape.

"If she can't defend herself, how can she protect you and your loved ones?"

Delta watched the tape end and then clicked it on rewind. When the VCR shut off, Delta plucked the tape from the VCR and handed it back to Alexandria.

"I am so sorry."

Alexandria nodded. "Me, too. But I didn't come here for sympathy, Del. The implication of this tape is clear. Either we find out in the next seventy-two hours who is behind this assassination campaign, or I'll be ruined. If I let myself get blown away in the polls, it could ruin my career forever. The only way to save face would be to drop out saying I needed to regroup after the shooting."

Delta stared down at her own hands wishing they were around Wainwright's neck.

"Delta, if this tape airs, I won't be able to get a job in River Valley as a dog catcher, let alone DA. It would do more than ruin my chances at DA. I'd have to leave River Valley."

"Leave? To where? No, don't even answer. I won't hear of it."

Alexandria reached out and took Delta's hand. "Delta, it's over."

Delta pulled her hand away and stood abruptly. "The hell it is. Before you toss in the towel, you give

Connie and me a chance. If we come up empty-handed
at the end of seventy-two hours, then you can pull out.
You've got to give us a fighting chance."
"To do what, exactly?"
"To catch the blackmailer. Whoever shot at you just
made a big mistake. Blackmailers are easier to catch
than murderers. This tape is just what we need."
"How so? It doesn't implicate anybody."
Delta grinned slyly. "Maybe not to you, but to me
it does."
"Yeah, well, don't get your hopes up."
"You just hang in there, Counselor—the cavalry is
on its way."
Alexandria smiled, and for the first time in days,
Delta saw a ray of hope in her eyes. "You never give
up, do you?"
"Never."

28

Connie walked out of her house wearing a three-piece suit with a skirt. Delta did a double take. "Was it hanging with the mothballs, or did you buy it at Goodwill?"

"Such a card. Enjoy my beautiful stubby legs while you can. Did you get the badge?"

Reaching in her pocket, Delta withdrew a black leather wallet and flipped it open to reveal a badge imprinted with Federal Bureau of Investigation on it. Connie took the wallet and examined the badge. "We're history with a capital *H* if I get caught impersonating a FBI agent."

"Then don't get caught. Don't worry, Con, he'll be too paranoid to know whether or not the badge is bogus. You'll be fine."

They climbed into the Delta's truck, and Connie examined the badge before looking up and glaring at Delta. "Prudence? Excuse me, but I specifically asked you to give me—"

"Who would you rather have been?"

"Try Martina, Billy Jean, Jodie, Lily, anyone but Prudence."

"Oh, right, like Lily is a better choice?"

Connie harrumphed as she pulled the visor down and looked at herself in the mirror. "How about Bright Star or Running Bear?"

Delta shook her head. "Or maybe Crazy One or Coco Loco. Man, Con, you go any deeper into this Native American phase of yours and you and Gina will soon be living in a teepee.

"We'd prefer a wigwam."

"See what I mean? Regardless of your name, you have to come out of there with something solid. Otherwise we'll be calling Alex something other than DA."

"Did you and Sal leave the amethyst?"

"10-4. It was a big, fat amethyst, too. Taylor won't pass up a beauty like that."

"And you left Sal's address?"

"No, we left the address to the White House. Relax, will you?"

"Relax? Delta, we're breaking the law."

"Won't be the first time."

Connie just shook her head.

"You wired okay?" Delta asked.

Connie nodded and lifted her skirt to show the taping device. "Wired and ready for action."

"Just don't do what you did to me last time. Either you stay wired and on the air, or I'm coming in after you."

"History does repeat itself, doesn't it?"

Delta cut a glance at her. "Only this time, I won't have to pull myself ten stories up a ladder."

Connie laughed. "I wished I could have seen it."

"You're a sadist."

"What can I say?"

They drove in silence for the remainder of the trip until Delta reached over and pointed to a large house set back away from the road. "That's his house."

Connie peered in the direction Delta was pointing. "House? You call that a house? That creepo lives in a fucking mansion!"

"Easy, tiger."

"Easy, shmeasy, Del. The guy is swimming in green. If money and power are what he's about—"

"Then he's in good company with 2.5 billion other men."

Connie snorted. "Makes me sick."

Pulling up about six houses from Wainwright's long, brick mansion, Delta turned the ignition off. "Don't do anything stupid like last time, or I'll come in there and kick your butt."

"Not even on your best day."

Delta grinned. "Honey, if I can't beat a woman with a name like Prudence, then I don't deserve this badge."

Allowing her grin to show, Connie patted Delta's hand. "Good point. See you in the funnies."

"You mean, we aren't there yet?"

Connie smiled as she slammed the truck door. "Almost."

Delta adjusted the rearview mirror and watched as Connie walked toward a house that looked like it was straight out of *Architectural Digest*.

"Okay, Storm, here we go."

Pushing her earplug further into her ear, Delta adjusted the volume. As much as she hated having to send Connie in, she couldn't risk being recognized by Wainwright. Reclining the seat, Delta heard the tremendous gonging sound of the four-pipe doorbell.

"Mrs. Wainwright?" Connie's voice was clear and strong over the tap.

"Yes?"

"I'm sorry to bother you at this hour, but I'm Agent Rivers from the FBI, and I'd like to speak with your husband."

"Oh...my. Why...uh...sure. Yes, please...do come in."

Delta checked the tape recorder to make sure it was on. Then, she picked up a walkie-talkie and pressed the orange button. "She's in, Sal. Are you two ready?" Delta released the button and waited.

"That's a big 10-4 good buddy. We're ready."

Delta smiled at Sal's enthusiasm.

"I'm freezing my titties off up here," Sal said.

Delta's smile broadened. "Won't be long, Sal."

"I hope not. A pigeon has found me attractive. I think he wants me to be his mate."

Delta chuckled as she set the radio next to the recorder. She hoped they had all their bases covered.

"Mr. Wainwright, I'm Agent Rivers with the FBI, and I need just a moment of your time."

Delta heard Connie flip her wallet open.

"The FBI? I've given all my information regarding the Pendleton shooting to the police. I have nothing more to add." Wainwright's voice was a baritone.

"Would it be possible to speak privately, sir? In your study, perhaps?"

"Why, yes...of course. How did you know I have a study?"

"It's our job to know these things, sir."

Delta grinned. Connie was very good.

"I see. Of course. Follow me."

Delta picked her nails while she waited.

"Terribly frightening to have villains out shooting at candidates, don't you think?" Wainwright said.

"Yes, the DA was fortunate. However..." Connie lowered her voice to a conspiratorial tone. "We, at the Bureau believe the shooter intended to miss her. This is confidential, of course."

"Of course."

"Mr. Wainwright, let me be perfectly frank. My office has been investigating the attempt, and we are under the opinion that your people—"

"Now wait just a minute, Ms.—"

"Rivers. And that's *Agent* Rivers."

"Well, *Agent* Rivers, my people have spent the last two weeks jumping through hoops for umpteen detectives and investigators. Any suspicions about this awful act being a grotesque campaign strategy have been dropped. I suggest you do the same."

"And I suggest you calm down, sir."

"Who's in charge of this insipid investigation anyway?"

"I am."

"Then I want the name of your superior. This is ridiculous. The FBI. Don't you people have better things to do than harass taxpaying citizens? Well, I will not be harassed, Agent Rivers. Not by the police, not by the media, and not by the FBI. I know my rights."

Delta rubbed her hands together to keep warm.

"In an attempted murder investigation, Counselor, the only 'rights' suspects have are those given to them. Do you understand?"

"Suspects? Are you calling me a suspect? I'll have your badge. No, better yet, I'll have your job. Who is your supervisor? I demand to know who sent you and under what authority."

"Here's my card, sir. Be my guest."

Delta leaned forward, hearing Wainwright punch the numbers on the phone.

"Agent Duncan's office, came Sal's tiny voice. How may I direct your call?"

"I would like to speak with Agent Duncan, please. Tell him it's Cole Wainwright from River Valley."

"Mr. Wainwright?" the radio sputtered as Sal's voice tripped across the line. "I'll see if he's taking any calls."

The silence hanging in the air was as eerie and as fake as this ruse. The quiet was broken by a male voice which had replaced Sal's. "Mr. Wainwright, this is Agent Duncan."

Delta could only imagine what they must have looked like atop the telephone pole; Sal in her black fatigues, and Josh with his woolly beard and huge body hanging on like a brown bear.

"This is Cole Wainwright—"

"Counselor, what can I do for you?" came Josh's voice over the air.

"I have one of your agents here in my home, telling me I am a suspect under investigation for the attempted shooting of DA Pendleton. Is this true?"

"Yes, it is. Is there a problem?"

"A problem?" Wainwright's voice boomed. "A problem? This idiotic investigation has already been dropped for lack of evidence. Of course there's a problem."

"I fail to see one, sir. You have a motive. We are checking out everyone with a motive. That's all."

"Mr. Duncan, I am a very busy man in the middle of a very important election. My people and I have already been cleared of any implications in—"

"Cleared, locally, sir, but federally is another matter. With all due respect, we don't really care whether a local agency opens or closes an investigation. If we feel there is sufficient evidence to warrant a continued investigation, then we shall proceed with that investigation."

"I resent—"

"I'm sure you do, sir, and I fully understand your resentment. But we believe someone in your organization, sir, not necessarily you, is connected with this crime. Agent Rivers needs your cooperation to help expedite the matter."

"I have been exceptionally cooperative."

"Again, we appreciate that, Mr. Wainwright, and we hope you continue to be as we conclude our investigation."

There was a slight hesitation before Wainwright spoke. "Does this mean you have a suspect?"

"I am not at liberty to divulge that information, but I can assure you we are very close to making an arrest. I have another incoming call, Mr. Wainwright, so if you wouldn't mind, I'd appreciate your cooperation for a little longer. Goodbye."

"Well?" came Connie's voice.

Wainwright's sigh was so loud, Delta heard it over the wire.

"So, what exactly is it you want Agent Rivers?"

"We believe the shooter is still in town, either awaiting payment, or preparing to blackmail the DA into checking out of the race early."

"That's ridiculous."

"There is nothing ridiculous about attempted murder, Mr. Wainwright, and you, of all people, should know that."

"I didn't mean—"

"What we need for you to do is keep your people within the county lines until the end of the election. Can you do this without rousing suspicion?"

"Of course."

"Are you aware that someone in your office is threatening to blackmail Pendleton?"

"No, I am not. And if I were, I'd—"

"Well, *we* are very aware, and whoever it is, sent her a tape of the shooting. Prints are going through the computer as we speak."

"A tape, you say? Someone from my office sent her a tape?"

"Of the shooting, yes. Someone believes you can't beat her fairly, so they're trying to take her out unfairly."

"That's preposterous! Pure speculation."

"Well, sir, what is speculation to you is fact to us. I would appreciate it if you could have your people fingerprinted. I'll send a messenger by to pick the cards up in twenty-four hours."

Delta heard the click of Connie's briefcase as she opened it to take the fingerprint cards out. "Please include yourself and members of your household staff."

Wainwright grunted. "I'm running for election, Agent Rivers. I'm not some Mafioso crime lord."

"Well, thank you for your time. I'll see myself out."

With that, Delta heard the doors close and Connie's heels clicking down the driveway.

"He knows something," Connie announced, sliding into the passenger seat. "His eyes were all over the place."

"Did you drop one?"

Connie grinned. "Like a hot potato. Geez, he's loaded. Everything was teak. Dark teak, light teak, teak paneling. Teak ain't cheap."

"Nice house, huh?"

"Incredible is more like it. But it's his wife's dough. Did you know her daddy is Vince Tognotti."

Delta turned. "Of Tognotti's clothes?"

"One and the same."

Delta whistled as they drove off. "Megabucks. Why would he need so many other backers?"

Connie shook her head and sighed in mock frustration. "When will you ever learn the importance of doing your homework?"

"Why should I? That's what you're here for."

"Humph. Okay, Pilgrim, Tognotti may have bucks, but he doesn't spread it to his son-in-law. The house was a wedding gift to the daughter."

Delta sat up. "Oh?"

"Daddy wanted the son-in-law to inherit the business, but Wainwright snubbed him in favor of law and politics."

"Because he's into power more than money."

"It looks that way. He could be living on Easy Street, but he wants the power of politics."

"What about the Mrs.? What's your take on her?"

"You know, I did a quick file on her, and she's an interesting lady. She appears to stay very much in the background of his campaign, but she's actually the one who gets all his financial endorsements."

"Because of the good old Tognotti name."

"Exactly."

"What's in it for her? Daddy's acceptance if Wainwright makes it big in politics?"

Connie shrugged. "Who knows. But Tognotti doesn't give the Wainwright campaign any financial support at all."

Delta cocked her head in question. "Why not?"

"I think it's because Wainwright has some supporters with very deep pockets that are connected to the mob. Tognotti washes his hands of anything mob related. He's definitely a self-made man."

Delta said nothing as she pulled alongside a van parked beneath a lamppost. When she and Connie got out, Delta knocked three times on the van door, which slowly opened electronically. Inside was an electronics factory which reminded Delta of the cockpit of an airplane. There was a TV, VCR, and brightly lit console with red, blue, green, and yellow lights. There were headphones, microphones, reel-to-reel tapes, and hundreds of other gadgets only a spy could appreciate.

Beeps, buzzes, hums, and clicks created an eerie electronic symphony that seemed to energize the pulsing lights.

Sitting on a milk stool with a set of headphones on was Sal, still wearing her trademark fatigues and black SOX cap. Next to her sat a very large man sporting a bright red ZZ Top beard and wearing fatigues. Josh rose and gave Delta a big bear hug before setting her down and shaking Connie's hand.

"Good to see you again, Josh."

Josh nodded. "You're better off than the last time I saw you."

Delta grinned. Josh was one of Sal's father's buddies who watched as the Cong decapitated him. For all the violence and gore Josh must have seen during the war, he was a very quiet, somber man; he was gentle unless threatened or unless those he cared about were in danger. He had slit a man's throat to save Delta's life in the desert, and yet, he never talked about it.

"How's the bug picking up?"

Sal put the headphones back on before answering. "Excellent." Then, she removed them and set them on her lap.

"Then why aren't you listening?"

Sal grinned. "It's voice-activated. See this green light? It goes on as soon as someone near the bug speaks. I don't even need the headphones, but Josh's ears are sensitive, so I do it for him."

Delta nodded in understanding as she stared at the console. "This is a little complex for my tiny brain."

"Not really. Bugs have drastically improved since Watergate. We have a prototype in the works right now that can tune out all existing sound except human voices. Josh and I are planning to use it when we open our PI business."

Delta and Connie both turned and stared at the little woman. "You want to be a private detective?"

Sal nodded. "You bet. There isn't anybody out there right now who can match our technology. After hang-

ing with you guys for a case or two, we've got a hanker-
ing to get out there and see if we can solve some cases
ourselves."

"Well, with all this stuff, you'd certainly be in
demand."

Josh nodded. "Why not put it to use, you know?"

Sal grinned at Josh, and for a second, Delta wondered if there wasn't something else going on between
them.

"Is Mac coming soon?" Sal asked Josh, who only
nodded. "Good. Try to keep each other out of trouble."

"Yeah, yeah. Be careful, Salamander. Hanging
with these two seems to be more trouble than anyone
I hang with."

Delta and Connie looked at each other with feigned
hurt. "Hey," Connie said, wrapping her arms around
Josh, "we resemble that remark."

"You resemble trouble, man." Josh said, rising and
stepping out of the van. "And as much as I like you both,
I'll still have to come after you if anything happens to
Sal."

Delta looked into a pair of eyes that meant what he
said. Sal was a connection to a man, a past, a lifetime
that had changed the lives of these men forever. Sal
was more than just the daughter of an army buddy;
she was the glue that bound them together. She was
the reason Josh didn't blow his head off when he
returned to a hostile and insensitive country. She was
the reason Mac was able to get off drugs once he settled
into the reality of a warless nation. Delta looked into
the eyes of a man who had killed in cold blood, and she
knew he would, indeed, come after them if anything
happened to Sal.

"Well, we won't let that happen, now will we, Con?"

"Go on, Josh. You know I can take care of myself."
Sal grinned at him, and he seemed to melt there on the
spot. As Josh lumbered away, Sal whispered, "He's
slightly overprotective."

"Slightly," Connie and Delta said in unison.

"Well, ladies, all we have to do is wait for Wainwright to hang himself."

Delta nodded as she stepped away from the van. As Connie exited the van and stood at Delta's side, Delta could have sworn she heard the springs of a trap being set.

29

Taylor checked her watch before pulling her cap over her ears. It was getting colder now—unusually so, from what she gathered in the news. She was beginning to look forward to her trip back to Brazil, where the air was fresher and the nights warmer. Taylor smiled to herself, remembering fondly her last few nights in Rio. The weather had been balmy, the drinks were to die for, and the women were little slices of heaven. Yes, Brazil was one of the most incredible countries she'd ever been to, and though she often returned to the little town of San Dumont after her crime sprees, she'd never stolen a thing from the Brazilian people. They were so loving and so incredibly beautiful with their golden skin that she could never bring herself to violate their trust. The people of San Dumont adored her, and not just because she had donated a great deal of money to the local school, or because she had a full basketball court and soccer field installed. They adored her because she was one of them. She missed their hospitality after being in the cold, impersonal United States, but it was time. She had played with Delta Stevens and had even beaten her. The joy of the challenge no longer existed for her. She would go back to Brazil and play in the sun until she got bored once more. Now, this game was coming to an end.

Delta had proven a worthy opponent, even if she'd never really come close to catching her. Well, it appeared close on the rooftop, but then, that, too, had been engineered by Taylor. Delta Stevens was good, but she had only come as close to Taylor as Taylor wanted. Actually, the best part of the caper was at the bar. Being so close to Delta, touching her, rubbing against her, watching her neck turn pink, gave Taylor the goosebumps. But where, she wondered, was the woman in Delta's life? How many nights had Taylor watched Delta go home to a dark and empty house? What woman would be foolish enough to leave that gorgeous hunk of woman alone for too long? Delta's powerful frame, proud stature, and bedroom eyes surely drew women to her like a magnet. Whoever held Delta's heart needed to wake up before someone else came along and stole her away.

The thought of stealing Delta someday made Taylor smile. Ah, to have those eyes gaze down into hers would be her life's *fait accompli*. Delta Stevens was an easy woman to fall for, and Taylor wished there was some way that she and Delta could have met under different circumstances. Maybe they would have been lovers. Better yet, maybe they could have even been friends. Wouldn't that have been fun? To have someone in her life who liked riding the edge as much as she did. Oh, the trouble she imagined she and Delta could cause together was delicious.

More than once, Taylor had been tempted to break into Delta's place just to look through her things. She was dying to know what Delta Stevens read. Mysteries? Biographies? Cartoons? Was she sloppy, or compulsively clean? Did she put the toilet paper over or under? What kind of underwear did she wear? And what did she eat? Taylor had lain awake at night wondering about the idiosyncrasies that made up Delta's personality. What was in her refrigerator? What kind of music did she listen to? And whose picture was in the frame on the top of her desk?

Ah, yes, Taylor had given into the urge to peek into Delta's world, but she had far too much respect for Delta to invade her private space. Besides, after what she'd read about Delta, messing around in her private life or with her loved ones was a good way to end up splattered all over the pavement or with a bullet in your head. Neither scenario appealed to Taylor.

So, she was forced to keep their relationship strictly professional and would only allow herself to dream about what it would be like to lie on the beautiful beaches of Rio, drinking mai tais with the ever irascible Delta Stevens by her side.

They were late, Taylor realized, Delta and that Italian sausage of a partner. But then, Taylor was aware that this house actually sat on the border of Delta's beat. This meant they would cruise by less often than if it were somewhere closer to the middle. Taylor was glad for this. It would make the final snatch cleaner and her getaway easier. She had worried about the ease of this job, since no amethyst had been brought in for a cleaning for quite some time. She was almost forced to steal an aquamarine gemstone. That would have been a drag, since Delta's birthday is February 10 and her birthstone is amethyst. Fortunately, her diligence paid off, and a beautiful amethyst arrived for cleaning. And boy, was it a beaut. Not worth much money, but it was the final letter and her final snatch.

Unzipping one of her pouches, Taylor pulled out the letter she planned to leave for Delta and read it for the fourteenth time.

Dearest Delta—

I regretfully inform you that this has been my last job here in River Valley, and I will no longer plague you with my presents (ha). You've truly been a good sport, and though I expected more competition from you, I am not the least bit disappointed. You've been a most enjoyable and pleasurable experience. Matching wits with you has been just as exciting as I knew it would be. However, due to the confining limitations of space and time, I must be off to new adventures and foreign lands.

You're great fun, Delta Stevens, and I sincerely hope the universe is kind to you. And

though I know you won't keep it, the piece
I'm sending you should show you how
deeply I respect you and your abilities. You
are one of a kind—

Thanks for the memories,

Love, Taylor.

Taylor grinned. It had taken her six drafts and
almost an hour to get just the right words. She had
agonized over a paragraph which spoke of their evening together at the bar, but opted to omit it, since the
words wouldn't come out right. Being with Delta that
night had been more than fun. There was an energy
between them that both surprised and delighted Taylor. Delta Stevens, the woman, proved to be far more
interesting than Delta Stevens, the cop. All around this
woman were other remarkable women whose roles
magnified Delta's own greatness. There was that red-
headed DA who did everything except dance naked on
a table to get Delta's attention, and still, Delta didn't
bite; at least, not that Taylor could tell. Taylor had
tailed Delta enough to know that this Pendleton
woman was somehow very special to her; almost too
special. And if Delta couldn't see the infatuation
Pendleton held for her, Taylor most certainly had. Of
course, that was because she was coming from the very
same place. There was definitely something between
Delta and Pendleton, and this was all the security
Taylor needed in the event she ever got caught. That
was one lesson her brother's incarceration had taught
her; always have a backup plan. Fortunately for Taylor, Delta and Connie had delivered one.
   Glancing at her watch one last time, Taylor
strained to see through the darkness. If Delta was to
respond to the incredible alarm system in this house,
Taylor had to time her entry perfectly. She had to make
sure Delta's patrol car was in the neighborhood before
setting it off; otherwise, some other cop would respond.

Getting into this house was a thrill with its incredibly complex alarm system. Whoever this paranoid individual was, she had certainly protected herself with a system few thieves would even attempt to get past. Still, Taylor was no rookie, and getting in and out would be no more difficult than any other house she'd been to.

Seeing a pair of headlights turn the corner, Taylor crouched lower behind the bushes, her leather outfit creaking as she moved. She knew even before she saw the sleek black and white that it was a cop car; the slow, deliberate movement, the way both heads turned from side to side, told her all she needed to know. She envisioned Delta laughing at something stupid her partner said as her eyes probed through the darkness. Was Delta thinking about Taylor now?

As the patrol car cruised by, Taylor barely saw the side of Delta's head as she gazed out the window. She looked preoccupied. Maybe she wasn't feeling well; she didn't appear as alert as she normally did in that car.

Taylor frowned.

This was it, then. When the tiny, red taillights shone like pinheads in the distance, Taylor slid out from behind the bushes and made her way to the back fence. Within seconds, she climbed up the chimney, cut a hole through the window, and was in the master bedroom before the second counter on her watch ran past the zero. Timing was everything now.

Scanning the room, Taylor grinned. Having already done her homework on this house, she pulled from her pocket a special pair of glasses that would enable her to clearly see the laser lights crisscrossing the hall. But she didn't need to go into the hall. Her prize was right here in the master bedroom. Seeing the jewelry box, Taylor opened it, pawed through it, and when she didn't find the amethyst, she opened the closet door and found the wall safe tucked neatly behind a stack of army jackets. She had planned a side trip like this. Seeing all the security equipment upon her initial recon, she figured that someone this insecure would have a safe. Taking her leather gloves off, she adjusted the surgical ones she wore beneath them before attempting to crack the safe.

Cracking this one would not be difficult. The tumbling mechanism had been made in Europe; she'd cut her teeth as a child on devices like this one. Grinning, Taylor cracked her knuckles. When she stopped, she thought she heard another crack.

Suddenly, before she could move, blink, or even finish her thought, the unthinkable happened.

Someone turned on the lights.

The goddamned lights.

"Looking for this?"

Taylor spun around to find Delta leaning against the door frame holding the large amethyst in the palm of her hand. "This *is* what you came for, isn't it?"

Taylor stepped outside the closet and back into the bedroom, her disbelief written clearly on her face. Instantly, she gauged the distance between Delta and the window.

"Don't even think about it Taylor. The fall would break your neck."

"How did...it's not possible. I saw—"

"You saw what I wanted you to see." Delta smiled. The sweet aroma of success tingled her taste buds.

Dropping the amethyst in her pocket, Delta stopped leaning against the door frame and stood straight up. She didn't think Taylor would try to get by her, but she knew that desperate people often broke all the rules.

"You seem surprised," Delta said flatly.

"Shocked is more like it. I didn't think you had a clue." Taylor shrugged. "Guess I underestimated you, huh?"

This made Delta grin. "Guess so."

Taylor's grin matched Delta's. For someone going to jail for a long, long time, she was exceptionally calm. "I'm glad you didn't let me down, Delta. For a minute there, I thought you were going to go down without a fight. I'm happy to say you proved me wrong."

"I almost didn't. You're very good."

Taylor shrugged again. "So are you. So, now what?"

"Unfortunately, I'm going to have to bring you in."

Folding her arms across her chest, Taylor continued grinning. "You know I can't let you do that. I'm deathly allergic to bars, cells, and prison food. I'm also incapable of eating salad and pancakes with a spoon. So, you'll have to excuse me if I beg off."

Delta admired Taylor's wit under pressure. "You should have thought of that before."

"Before what? Before I became stinking rich? Before I starved to death at the age of six? Tell me, when should the orphan have thought about not stealing?"

The smile faded from Delta's face. She hadn't expected this flare of passion from Taylor. Her glibness, yes, but her tenacity, no.

"Maybe before you chose to take me on."

"Take you on? I would have thought you'd be flattered. No one, Delta, no one has even come close to catching me. I gave you the chance to play. I thought you'd enjoy it."

Delta's lip twitched, betraying her true feelings. "I did...I mean...I have...I—"

"You and I are not so unalike, Delta Stevens. We both strive for perfection—we live life completely on the edge. We're immensely passionate about the people and things we care for. And...we're viciously competitive. That's why I came here. You know how to gamble it all and win. You gambled in that warehouse, you gambled against Elson Zuckerman, and you gambled in that inferno of a house. And each time, you came out on top. And you know why? Because what rules you can't bend, you break. Hell, you even make up new rules as you go along. That's one of the things I admire most about you. It's what sets us both apart from the rest. And we are set apart, you know. We don't settle for the mundane. We deviate, we challenge, and we dare the world to give us something more than average. We don't just live life, Delta. You and I *make* life happen."

Delta just stood there, enraptured by Taylor's words, caught by her demeanor, and her candid appraisal of Delta's very essence. It was as if Taylor could see right into Delta's heart; as if she knew things about Delta that Delta had never shared with anyone.

The odd thing about all of this was that Taylor did not appear to be a woman facing imprisonment. She was far too calm, far too controlled. This was a woman who had to be holding a trump card, and Delta wondered just how long it would be before she played it.

"I know what you're thinking, Delta. You're wondering how I can be so cool when it appears as if I'm getting ready to go make license plates. Right?"

Delta shrugged. "Maybe."

Taylor's grin turned into a wide smile. "Maybe? Come on. You can do better than that."

Delta's lips curled up slightly. "I'm wondering what card you've got up your sleeve. I'm wondering if I've missed something along the way."

"Perhaps you realize that I have no intention of spending one day, let alone the rest of my life in a six by six cell."

"Oh, is that it? You have some fancy, high-priced lawyer to get you off?"

"Not even remotely."

"Then what?"

Taylor took a step toward the window. "Draw your gun, Delta."

"What?"

Taylor took another step. "I said, pull your gun. You see, you have one of two choices; you're either going to have to shoot me or let me go. There are no other options."

"You're crazy."

"Maybe. But you and I know you can kill men. You have before and you will again, if you need to. I'm willing to bet that shooting another woman would not be as easy." Taylor was standing in front of the open window now. "I'd say the chance of you shooting me in the back is one in a million."

Delta stepped further into the room, calculating the odds of her reaching Taylor before Taylor could scoot out the window. The chances of that were slim. Taylor was only a foot from the window. Delta was clear across the room.

"Believe me, Delta, I've jumped from much higher than this and lived to tell about it."

Delta laid her hand on the butt of her gun. "So, this is it, then? I either shoot you or let you go?"

Taylor nodded. "There will be no jail time for this bird, Delta. I either fly or die. The decision is yours."

Slowly unhooking her holster, Delta withdrew her silver revolver. "I can't just let you go, Taylor."

"I'm disappointed," Taylor purred. "I'd have bet my millions that you respected me enough not to try and bluff me."

"Sorry."

"Don't be. But you are bluffing, Delta. That much I know."

Delta pointed the .357 at Taylor. She might as well have been pointing a water pistol at her for all Taylor cared.

"Explain one thing to me, Taylor. You have more than enough money to live the rest of your days in luxury. It's the thrill, then, isn't it?"

Taylor put one leg over the windowsill. "I could ask the same of you, Delta. If I gave you one of my millions, would you still choose to stay in uniform and risk your life for people who don't give a shit if you live or die?"

Delta nodded imperceptibly. "You know I would."

"Right. And for what? For the thrill, the excitement? For the satisfaction that you're the best there is? Come on, Delta, in another life, you and I were soul mates. We were on the same side riding the same wave of adventure. And now, here we are, in this life, still riding it, but this time, we're on opposite teams."

Delta wrapped her finger around the trigger and raised the gun. "Yes, we are. And my side just won."

"Have you? I'm afraid the only thing you've won is the dubious honor of deciding whether to let me go."

"You really believe those are the only two choices open to me?"

Taylor nodded. "Yes. I'm going out this window, and I'll wager all I own that you won't shoot me. And not just because of the fleeing felon rule and all that rot, but because it's not your style; and Delta Stevens, you have some kind of style."

Delta raised the revolver just a touch. "You're really willing to bet that I won't shoot you?"

Taylor nodded.

"How can you be so sure?"

Taylor ducked her head back inside and smiled warmly at Delta. "Another day, another life, and you and I really could have had some fun. You're an incredible woman, Delta, with ethics of steel. You could no more shoot me in the back than you could shoot yourself in the head. You've an honorable soul, and it would be beneath you to hurt someone who wasn't a threat to you. If we ever meet again, and I know that we will, I do hope it's under more pleasurable circumstances. But I really must go. If I stay much longer, I'm afraid I'd fall in love with you, and that simply wouldn't do. *Ciao*." With that, Taylor slid out the window, leaving Delta staring at the spot where Taylor had been.

"Honorable?" Delta queried aloud, hearing Taylor's soft soles hit the ground below. "Perhaps." Maybe deep down, Delta wanted her to escape. Maybe she felt the same way about incarcerating Taylor as she'd felt when she saw the caged panthers in the San Diego Zoo. Some creatures simply weren't meant to be locked up. Maybe Taylor was one of them.

Then again, maybe not.

Hearing scuffling sounds below, Delta holstered her gun, ran down the stairs, and into the backyard. Flipping on the outside light, Delta saw Connie holding Taylor in a wristlock.

"Her! How in the hell did I forget about *her*?" Taylor yelled, shaking her now uncapped head, revealing her tousled, short black hair.

Connie tossed a wink to Delta. "Gee, I don't know. Women have been telling me for years how unforgettable I am. Right, Del?"

Delta grinned. "I wouldn't know."

"Damn, damn, damn," Taylor groaned. "I was hoping I wouldn't have to go to Plan B."

Connie and Delta exchanged curious glances and said in unison, "Plan B?"

Taylor nodded, her arm still pinned behind her back. "Of course. Every great player has a contingency plan. Right, Delta?"

Delta folded her arms across her chest. "This, I gotta hear."

Taylor half-turned to Connie. "Uh, would you mind? It's not like I'm going to outrun you."

Connie looked over at Delta, who nodded.

"Thanks." Rubbing her wrist, Taylor grinned at Connie. "Nice leg sweep. Took me down before I even knew you were there."

Connie shrugged. "Delta said not to hurt you."

Taylor looked over at Delta and grinned like a puppy. "Aw, isn't she just the sweetest?"

"Plan B." Delta said without emotion. If ever a woman could charm a snake, Taylor was definitely the one, especially now that Delta had seen the true sky blue color of her eyes.

"Right. Mind if we go inside? It's a little chilly out here."

Delta shook her head, but stepped aside to let Taylor in. "You're something else, you know that?"

"Indeed, I am."

As the three women walked back inside and situated themselves in the kitchen, Delta couldn't help but admire Taylor's strength and resilience. Perhaps she was right about them being friends in another life. They really were kindred spirits, even if one of their souls lived on the wrong side of the law. "So, what have you got up your sleeve this time?"

A thin smile played on Taylor's lips. "I've been in town a couple of months, Delta, and I've spent endless hours watching you and your life."

"*T,*" Connie muttered, shaking her head. She asked Delta, "When you were in the hospital, someone sent you flowers and just signed the card *T*, remember?" She asked Taylor, "They were from you, weren't they?"

The thin smile grew. "A nice bouquet, I hope."

Connie nodded. "The prettiest of the bunch."

"Uh, ladies, could we move along, here?" Delta prodded, uncomfortable at the prospect of having someone study her life so closely without her knowledge.

Taylor nodded. "Sure. I've been watching you both, seeing what's important in your lives."

"And?"

"And, quite frankly, you need me and don't even know how much. Yet."

"What in the hell are you talking about?"

"Well, it's not you who need me as much as your friend the DA does." Taylor paused here for dramatic affect. "Because if someone doesn't rescue her soon, she'll be standing in the unemployment line. Isn't that correct?"

Delta shrugged, feigning disinterest. "What does she have to do with your Plan B?"

"Everything. You two have been busting your humps trying to find out who to pin the so-called assassination attempt on, and so far, you've come up with nothing."

"Go on."

"The key to successful gambling, Delta, is to have all of your bases covered. I studied your lives to determine what was important enough to you to make you break the rules in the unfortunate event that you caught up with me."

"And what rules do you think I've broken?"

Taylor laughed. "It's obvious to even the least astute that Alexandria Pendleton is important to you as both a DA and as a friend. Important enough, my friends, that you would pose as federal agents to back Wainwright into a corner."

Connie shot Delta a look, but Delta said nothing. "Go on."

"I may have what you need to prosecute Wainwright on conspiracy charges."

Connie took a step forward. "How would you know anything about conspiracy charges? Or, for that matter, the law?"

Taylor sighed. "I managed a year in law school before nearly dying of boredom. I'm familiar enough with the law to know that the transmitting device you left in Wainwright's office won't do you any good. Anything you get on tape is inadmissible in court. You'd have a pretty tough time explaining just how that bug got in there in the first place."

Delta almost fell off the stool. "What do you know about that?"

"As soon as the shooting occurred, I saw my home plate being covered."

"How?"

"She's your Achilles' heel. You care deeply for the women in your life, Delta, whether they're lovers or not. You care about her so much, both of you are willing to break the law by getting into Wainwright's house under false pretenses and leaving him a nasty little bug. I'd say that was a pretty big heel, wouldn't you?"

Delta and Connie looked helplessly at each other. "How do you know this?"

"After discovering your weakness, I looked for Wainwright's. It was fascinating, really. Usually, I just lay by the pool during the days, but since it is winter—"

"What did you find out?"

"I'm getting there. I found out a great deal, really, and when I'm done, you'll be glad I did."

Delta slid off the stool and towered over Taylor. "Spit it out, Taylor. I'm losing my patience."

"Patience isn't one of your virtues, is it, Delta? Fine. In a word, I think I have what you need to nail the person behind the shooting."

Delta was speechless. She looked to Connie, but Connie's mouth hung open as well.

"Cat got your tongue?"

"What do you have?"

"Not so fast. I simply used my unequaled abilities to break into his house and plant three tiny cameras— one in his study, one in the bedroom, and one in the kitchen— and waited for him to hang himself."

Connie came to her feet. "You did what?"

Taylor beamed proudly. "I planted cameras."

"In the man's house?"

"Yep."

"But I was there. His security system—"

"Sucks. This house has a far better system. Beating it was a cinch. I was in and out in no time."

Delta rubbed her tired eyes. "Let me get this straight. You broke into his house and planted three cameras, hoping to incriminate him, just in case we caught you?"

Taylor nodded. "I planted three more in Alexandria's headquarters and four in Wainwright's campaign headquarters."

Connie whistled. "Impressive."

"Not really. I knew that if I could get the information you needed I would become more valuable to you free than in jail."

"What do you mean 'valuable?'"

Taylor hopped off the counter and walked over to Delta. The air seemed to sizzle as they stared at each other. "I have what you want."

"Which is what?"

"Tapes of Wainwright. In exchange for my freedom, I will hand the tapes over to you."

"No way."

"Hear me out, Delta."

"Look, Taylor, there's no way I'm going to let you blackmail me into letting you go."

"Blackmail? Interesting choice of words. Delta, I never said anything about blackmail. But since you brought it up..."

Connie came over to Delta and stood beside her. "Describe his study."

Taylor did, right down to the teak and brass paperweight on his desk. Then Taylor turned to Connie and grinned. "You remember it, too, don't you, *Agent* Rivers?"

Delta's mouth moved up and down, but the words were nowhere to be heard.

"That's right. I have Connie Rivera on tape impersonating a federal agent. That's a felony, I believe."

"Why you little shi—"

"Now, now, Delta. I'm not going to play hardball with you, yet. If you bust me, I'll have no other choice but to mention the tapes and the cameras to the authorities, who will show a definite interest in a certain Latina officer fraudulently passing herself off as an FBI agent."

Delta bowed her head at what appeared to be a greater blow than she was prepared for. If her superiors or any other agency got Connie on tape, she wouldn't just lose her job. She would probably face jail time, and that was something Delta wasn't going to allow.

"She's got us, Del. If I really am on tape, I'm screwed."

Delta paced across the room. She needed time to think—she needed fresh air. She needed to figure out how to get back in control of this situation.

Suddenly, Taylor was at her side. "Hey, no need to be so bummed. If you let me go back in and get the cameras, you can have the tapes, I can have my freedom, and we'll call it even."

"Even?" Delta said, shaking her head.

"Hey, it could be worse. I could have gotten away, and your lawyer friend would find herself with Ms. in front of her name instead of DA."

"That could still happen."

"Not if you don't let it. Right now, Delta, two careers are in your hands." Taylor took one of Delta's hands in hers. "Think about it. I haven't really hurt anybody.

Alex, however, puts away those who do. Connie, on the other hand, may be sitting in a cell next to mine. Our lives are literally in your hands."

Delta pulled her hand from Taylor's grasp and walked over to Connie. "Chief?"

Connie shrugged. "It's your call, Storm."

There it was again. The decision of doing what was right versus what was best. Time and time again, she'd been forced into deciding between the two. It was that gray area of her life that had threatened her relationship with Megan, put her life on the line more times than she dared count, and caused her more pain and anguish than any other single element in her life.

Like at this moment.

She was painfully aware that the right decision was to arrest Taylor and hope that Alexandria and Connie survived their own professional potboilers.

Right.

Wrong. The best decision, on the other hand, was that which hurt the least people even though it meant breaking their own codes of conduct. The best decision was to ignore what was right.

Again.

"You really haven't left me much of a choice, have you? Tossing aside two careers to arrest an international jewel thief would really be a waste."

"Quite."

Delta looked at Connie with apologetic eyes. "How do we know you won't just take off?"

Connie spoke up. "I know. We'll tape her confession to all the crimes she's committed. If she bolts, we'll have her picture sent to so many agencies that she won't be able to board a bus."

Taylor looked up into Delta's green eyes. "That works for me. At the end, we'll trade a tape for a tape."

"That presupposes we trust you."

Taylor grinned. "Have you any other choice?"

Delta shook her head.

"No copies?"

"None. You'll have to trust us as well."

"Then I guess we've made a deal." Taylor stuck her hand out and took Delta's. "After I come out with Wainwright's stuff, you make no calls, no tips, no nothing for twenty-four hours. You have to give me a head start of some sort. Deal?"

Delta looked over at Connie. She was wearing a poker face that even Delta couldn't read. She hated this; she hated being backed into a corner. Still...how could she justify it to herself? Letting an international criminal blackmail her into submission left an unpleasant taste in Delta's mouth, yet there seemed to be no way out.

Inhaling a bitter breath, Delta nodded. Sticking her hand out to Taylor, Delta forced a grin. For the first time since she could remember, Delta had been had. She had been outmaneuvered by someone more cunning than she. The weird part was, she didn't quite know how to feel about that.

Taking Taylor's hand, Delta shook it. Well, if she were going to be beaten by someone, at least it was by another woman.

A beautiful woman at that.

"Deal."

30

Holding the newly-made videotape up to Taylor's face, Delta shook her head. "Burn us, Taylor, and I swear that you'll be locked up faster than you can say three Hail Mary's."

Taylor grinned. "Didn't know you were Catholic."

"I'm not."

"Look, Delta, there's no need to threaten me. I may be a thief, but I'm a woman of my word. We made a deal and I intend to abide by it." Taylor hooked her arm through Delta's and led her to the kitchen. "You know, you really do need to lighten up. You take yourself way too seriously. In the overall scheme of the universe, my arrest would mean nothing."

"Not to me."

"How sweet. You'd worry. But trust me—"

Delta laughed as she shook her head. "You keep saying that, Taylor, yet you must know it would be impossible for me to trust you. You're a criminal!"

"Are you trying to hurt my feelings? Try not to look at me in that dark light, Delta. Look at me as a woman who would do anything to meet the great Delta Stevens."

Delta couldn't stop the grin from spreading across her face.

"See?" Taylor said, pointing to Delta's smile, "There really *is* a human being beneath that uniform. Oh...and a very shapely one at that."

Connie shook her head as they walked toward the front door. "You're going to give her a big head."

Taylor cuddled up to Delta's arm. "Not my Delta. She's as humble as they come." Checking her watch, Taylor sighed. "Well, I'd love to hang around and party with you animals, but the sooner I get my equipment out of his house, the sooner I can fly off to some exotic place. Jamaica sounds intriguing. Ever been, Delta?"

Delta shook her head.

"Want to come?"

"I'm taken."

Taylor's eyes suddenly lit up. "That means you'd think about it if you weren't already committed! Now isn't that just about the best news a girl could have?"

"I meant—"

Connie laughed. "Forget it, Del. You'll only get in deeper."

Taking Taylor's arm, Connie escorted her to the van, and Delta followed, wondering how it was that this woman seemed to get to her every time.

"Here they come," Connie said, pointing to a car slowly coming up the street.

Delta walked over to the patrol car and leaned in the window when it stopped.

"How'd it go?" Tony asked across Sal, who was wearing a wig like Delta's curly brown hair.

"Uh...better than expected. But there have been some...uh...complications."

"Complications? Did you catch her or not?"

"Well..sort of."

Tony and Sal looked at each other like one might be able to explain or interpret Delta's ambiguities. "You 'sort of' caught her?"

It took Delta ten minutes of explaining before they finally had the whole picture.

"Need anything else from me?" Sal asked, opening the passenger side door.

"Not really, Sal. You were great. Thanks."

"You sure? Sounds to me like you could use one of my Ladybugs."

Delta grinned. "Ladybugs?"

"Sure. Just like the transmitters we used in the Camaros for the porn case, only smaller. That way, you can be sure she won't bug out on you."

"Sal, you're a genius."

Sal blushed and ran her hands over her hair. "Not me. But the Ladybugs are. Wait here, and I'll throw one together for you. Shouldn't take a minute."

Delta could only shake her head as Sal headed for the door of the house. "She's something, isn't she?"

Tony nodded. "I'll say. Man, have you heard the story about her dad saving those guys in 'Nam?

"Pretty incredible story. They take great care of each other, too."

"Sounds to me like she's set for life. You know, if she didn't look like a little boy..."

"Yes?"

Tony turned from Delta, but she could still see his blush. "Nothing. Forget it."

"What were you going to say, Carducci?"

"Look, I made the mistake once. I'm not about to hit on another lesbian."

"Why, Carducci, I think you have a little crush."

"Do not."

"If you say so."

"Besides," he continued, lowering his voice some, "I don't know if I could go out with a woman who could kick my ass."

"Why not? You're partnered with one."

Tony rolled his eyes. "That's not what I mean. Isn't she..." He lowered his voice and whispered, "One of you?"

Delta busted out laughing. "I haven't a clue."

Tony looked like he'd just been slapped. "You don't? But I thought you could tell."

"I could in the old days, but we come in all shapes and sizes, Carducci. I honestly wouldn't know."

Tony eyed her suspiciously. "You wouldn't play the same gag on me twice now, would you?"

"Yes, I would. But I'm not. I really don't know. Ask her out and see what she says."

"What who says?" Sal asked, approaching the car. Delta turned and appraised her new friend once more. Sal really did look like a little boy, but she could keep up with any man. She could talk about guns, cars,

motorcycles, boats, and weapons for days. She knew
every major league baseball player's average off the top
of her head on any given day, and she loved hockey and
football. Delta could see how a man would be attracted
to her. She spoke their language.

But Carducci? Master of the superficial?

Delta wondered if maybe she had really rubbed off
on him. There was only one way to find out. "Sal, Tony
was wondering—"

"Delta!"

"...If you're gay."

Sal grinned. "Sort of."

Tony sighed. "That seems to be the answer of the
month."

"Not really. I'm an omnivore."

"A what?"

"She goes both ways, Carducci. She's bisexual."

Sal snickered as she handed the Ladybug to Delta.
"Lately, it's been more like asexual. Here you go, Delta.
She's set and ready."

Taking the device from Sal, Delta winked at Tony.
"Be careful, Carducci. I hear she wears fatigue undies
as well." Turning on her heels, Delta walked back to
the van.

Omnivore? Indeed.

31

Half an hour later, Delta, Connie, and Taylor pulled into the road before Wainwright's estate. The street was well-lit, and the quarter moon assisted the newly-installed street lights. When Tony pulled in behind them, Delta got out.

"Okay, Carducci, one more time. You hear any calls to this address for alarms, prowler, etcetera, you call dispatch and tell them you're on it. If Henry wants to know why we're so far from our beat, just tell him you were returning a lost kid."

Tony nodded. "Gotcha."

"Just remember—if Taylor is busted, Connie's job goes with her."

Saluting, Tony put the car in reverse and backed down the street with his headlights off.

Stepping back on the sidewalk, Delta opened the van door. "Everybody ready?"

Connie leaned out the window, her face a mask of seriousness. "It looks like Wainwright is home."

Shrugging at this news, Taylor walked over to Delta and fingered her clip-on tie. "No problemo. I've done it before in a pinch."

Delta looked over at Connie. "We're in a pinch."

As Taylor stood closer to her, Delta could smell the black leather outfit and sweet spice of men's cologne waft through the air. "Luckily for you guys, pinch happens to be a forte of mine." Putting her arm around Delta, Taylor squeezed her. "And if you just spoke tenderly to me, Delta, I'd love to pin—"

Palming the Ladybug, Delta patted Taylor on the back, leaving the tiny device square between Taylor's shoulders. "This is business, Taylor."

Taylor's eyes seemed to glitter. "Oh? And if it weren't?"

Delta pulled away and shook her head. "Just don't get caught."

"For you, anything." Standing on her tiptoes, Taylor planted a kiss on Delta's cheek before reaching her hand out to Connie. "Thank you, Connie, for not kicking my butt back there. I know how much Delta means to you, and...well...I've kinda been driving her crazy."

Connie smiled warmly at Taylor. "She needed the diversion, Taylor."

With that, Taylor disappeared between two houses.

"You trust her?" Connie asked after Taylor vanished into the hands of the night.

Delta chuckled. "Hell no. She's a loose cannon with a short fuse. There's no telling what she's liable to do in there."

Connie reached out and touched Delta's arm. "It bothers you, doesn't it?"

"What?"

"The fact that you like her so much."

"Bite your tongue."

"Hello? It's me, Chief. You haven't fooled me for one second, Delta Stevens. I see the way you look at her— how you vainly try to hide your admiring smiles. I see how you two look at each other. It's so damn obvious."

Delta did not respond.

"And if I didn't know how crazy you are about Megan, I'd almost be worried."

"Almost?"

"Okay, I get it. You're trying to drive *me* crazy, aren't you? Is that it?"

Delta looked into Connie's eyes and smirked. "You're being ridiculous."

Connie took Delta's face in her hands and gazed deeply into her green eyes. A sound from Connie's mouth—a language Delta had never heard before, whispered passed her lips as she read the truth in Delta's eyes that no woman but Connie could ever decipher. "Uh-huh. Just as I thought. You may never admit it, Delta, not even to yourself, but I can see the truth in your eyes."

Delta tried to shrug noncommittally. "So I admire her work—the way she's perfected her craft, so to speak."

"So to speak. And now," Connie continued, reaching into her purse, "we have..." Stopping suddenly, Connie pulled her purse into her lap and furiously began digging through it.

"Con?"

"Where's the tape? Goddamn her, she stole the tape." Jumping from the van, Connie looked under the seat and in the back. "It's not here."

Delta ripped open the passenger door and started pawing through the cassettes and books scattered about the floor of the van.

After frantically searching for a minute, Connie threw her hands up in exasperation. "I don't know how, and I don't know when, but that bitch copped the confession tape."

Delta pushed the seat back and sighed. "Like we said—"

"I'm sorry, Del. I had it in my purse. I don't know—"

Delta retrieved a small black box the size of a television remote from her pocket. "Ladybug, Ladybug, fly away home..."

Connie sighed with relief. "I'd forgotten about that."

"Maybe because you were too concerned with my love life."

Connie chuckled. "Maybe. I can't believe that little shit tried to burn us."

Delta nodded and flipped a button. "It's all just one big game to her."

"But if she's got our tape, why would she need to go to Wainwright's house now?"

Delta looked down at the blinking green light on the receiver. "Shit. Stay here." Jamming the receiver back in her pocket, Delta took off toward Wainwright's house, leaping over the hedges. When she landed near the porch, she pulled the receiver out and saw the green light was flashing faster. Only then did Delta notice the large dogs barking at the chainlink fence. As she carefully approached the fence, the receiver's light went wild.

Delta didn't need to look at the receiver to know what had happened. Somehow, Taylor had managed to find the transmitter and, as per her own strange sense of humor, put the receiver on one of the dogs. How Taylor had gotten close enough, how she even knew it was on her back, Delta did not know. What she did know was that Taylor, the international jewel thief, had outplayed them to the very end.

Trudging back to the van, Delta shook her head.

"Don't tell me—"

"I won't."

"She burned us?"

"Like french fries."

Connie looked up at the sky. "What now?"

Delta closed her eyes and rubbed her pounding temples. She'd let Taylor's game playing get out of control, and now, it cost them.

"Think she'll burn me?"

Delta shook her head. "No way. All Taylor wanted was to get away. Wainwright will never find the bug."

"Maybe not, but what if he finds the cameras?"

"So what? If he's guilty of any wrong doing, he'll simply destroy them and any evidence along with them."

"But Alex—"

"Hey, Con, we tried. I gambled more than I should have and lost. I'm sorry."

Connie put her arm around Delta's shoulder. "You gave it your best, Storm."

"Bullshit. I let her get to me. We should never have made a deal with her. We had her right here, Con, right in the palm of our hands, and I let her—"

"Snuffy-Smith us?"

Delta paused and barely grinned. "Yeah. That's exactly what I let her do."

Connie got in the van and motioned for Delta to get in. "Let it go, Del. This time, we weren't anybody's heroines, that's all."

Delta sighed like a deflating balloon.

"Hey, we win our fair share of fights."

"But Alex—"

"Is on her own. She's a big girl, and you don't owe her anymore. You're not responsible for Alex and her career. Hell, for all we know, Taylor could have been lying about the cameras just to buy some time."

"Buy? Hell, Con, I gave it to her for free."

"You're being too hard on yourself."

"She suckered me, Connie."

"Yes, she did. But what's done is done. You finish your shift, go home, and call your woman. You'll feel a lot better after you talk to Megan."

Slowly getting out of the van as it rolled to a stop in front of her patrol car, Delta sighed once more. "Let's just hope I don't let Megan slip through my fingers as easily as I let Taylor."

"You won't. Now, pick your bottom lip off the ground. Forget about it. We've won our share of games, and this just wasn't one of them."

Closing the door, Delta shook her head. "I hate losing."

Connie grinned. "I know. Me, too. Try to have a good night."

"You, too, Chief. Good night."

32

After three unsuccessful attempts at connecting with Megan, Delta pulled her uniform off and flopped on the bed. Pulling the flannel sheets up to her neck, she closed her eyes and tried to forget how awful she felt. All she could see was Taylor's face smiling at her—how she must be enjoying her victory. Delta hated that.

When one of the cats jumped on the bed, Delta opened her eyes, grateful for the company. For some strange reason, the house felt quieter than usual. Maybe it merely echoed the emptiness Delta was feeling.

She missed Megan more than she thought possible. She'd blown it tonight and had nobody to blame but herself. At least, if Megan were here, she would hold her and tell her everything would be all right. That's what she missed most. Not the sex, not the laughter, but Megan's consistency.

Enjoying the warmth of her cat's body against hers, Delta relaxed enough to try to sleep. Reaching over to turn out the light, she gazed at Megan's picture on the night stand. Before Megan left for Costa Rica, Delta had asked her to marry her. It was a huge step for a woman who was afraid of any commitment not involving a badge and gun; but she had asked her nonetheless, and Megan promised her an answer when she returned from Central America. Wouldn't that be something, Delta mused as sleep curled itself around her. Marriage...settling down...

She didn't know how long she'd been asleep when she heard it, but Delta knew it meant trouble. Without opening her eyes, Delta listened for the exact location of the growling noise coming from the cat's throat. She'd only heard him make that sound a few times—

always when a stray cat tried to enter the house. Focusing on the low, guttural noise he projected, Delta guessed his location to be atop her chest of drawers, which was not someplace he usually hung out. As Delta became more fully awake, she felt it—she was not alone.

Delta continued breathing as if she were asleep. Someone was in her house—maybe even in the same room, frightening the cat enough to send him scurrying for higher ground. If she could get her left hand out of the covers, she could reach her nine millimeter hanging in her ankle holster on the bedpost.

Cracking one eye open, Delta saw the silhouette of someone standing at the foot of her bed. Instantly, her left hand shot out from under the covers and grasped for the holster, which, to her surprise, was empty.

"Tsk, tsk," came Taylor's voice as she flipped on the light. In her left hand, she held the Beretta, in her right, a brown paper bag.

"You?"

Taylor grinned. "Miss me?"

Tossing the covers from the bed, Delta's feet hit the floor. "I ought to strangle you."

Still grinning, Taylor turned the Beretta around and tossed it on the bed. "Nasty things, guns. I had to make sure you wouldn't shoot me."

Perplexed, Delta looked at the Beretta laying on the bed. "I should have shot you back at the house."

"And ruined my beautiful jumpsuit? I hardly think so."

Delta picked the Beretta up and jammed it back in the holster. "Are you trying to drive me nuts, or what?"

Taylor looked Delta up and down. "Pretty sexy lingerie you wear to bed, Storm. Sweats? Very attractive. Someone hold me back."

Delta looked down at her sweats and suddenly felt vulnerable. "You didn't break into my house to discuss my nightwear, Taylor."

"True. But I had so hoped that you slept in the buff."
Taylor's eyes flitted over Delta flirtatiously. "Maybe in
the summer, eh?"

"Maybe. What do you want, Taylor?"

Taylor stepped closer, bridging the distance between them. "Aren't you just a teeny bit curious about
what I have in this little bag?"

"Actually, I'm more curious about how the hell you
got in here past the guard."

Taylor, still smiling, shook her head. "Sorry, trade
secret." Taylor tossed the bag on the bed. "Don't worry,
I won't tell anyone how sexy you look when you sleep.
You're one of the few women I've ever seen who look
beautiful even when you're drooling."

Heat rose in Delta's cheeks. If she'd missed it
before, she wasn't now. Taylor was indiscriminately
flirting with her, and for the first time, Delta noticed
the shapely curves and mounds of flesh tucked neatly
inside the skintight leathers. God, where had she seen
that jumpsuit before?

Taylor's grin stretched into a smile as she noticed
Delta's appraising look. "Well?"

"Well, what?"

"Aren't you going to look in the bag?"

Delta slowly reached for it and peered inside. Three
black videocassettes lay on the bottom. "Are these what
I think they are?"

"I don't know. What do you think they are?"

Delta pulled three VCR cases from the bag and
looked at them.

"I told you, Delta. I'm a woman of my word. I told
you I'd get you the tapes, and there they are."

Delta slowly looked up from the tapes. "Are these
Wainwright's tapes?"

Taylor nodded. "Yep."

"Then, why'd you take off?"

"Because it pissed me off that you didn't trust me."
Stepping right up to Delta, Taylor reached out and took
one of Delta's hands. "Delta, we're mirror images, me
and you. You gave me your word, and I believed you.

You insulted and hurt me by placing that stupid bug on my back."

"I'm sorry. Trusting a criminal isn't something that comes naturally to me." Delta gently pulled her hand out of Taylor's. Connie was right. There *was* some strange kind of energy flowing between them, and Delta could no longer deny her attraction to Taylor. "I apologize for insulting you."

"Luckily for you, I have a very forgiving soul. I forgive you."

"You put me through the ringer, you know. I thought I'd never see you again."

Taylor stepped so close that they were touching. "Oh, really? Was that important? Seeing me again?"

Delta swallowed and took a step back. "Sure. I...thought I'd never see those tapes. I thought you—"

"I know what you thought, Delta Stevens. You thought I'd take the tapes and laugh at you on my way out of town."

"Why didn't you? You were free."

"I still am."

Delta's left eyebrow rose. "Are you sure of that?"

Taylor nodded. "We made a deal. I stuck with my end of the bargain, and you're going to keep your end. It's that easy."

Delta gazed down into Taylor's eyes. She doubted anything involving Taylor was 'easy.' "Well, I'm glad you came back."

"Because of the tapes?" There was a slight hint of hope in Taylor's voice.

"Because..." The heat on Delta's cheeks spread down her neck, through her arms, and landed somewhere in the pit of her stomach. Only her mind kept it from spreading any lower. "...of the tapes. Yeah."

Turning away to hide her disappointment, Taylor sighed. "I suppose I should be going."

Delta swallowed. Why was this so hard? "Going? Where will you go?"

Taylor stopped at the bedroom door. "Somewhere warm and sunny. I think I'm going to retire after this."

Delta grinned and joined her at the door. "I'd like that."

"Would you?"

"The idea of you being in jail doesn't sit right with me. You are a free spirit, Taylor, that much I know."

Taylor started through the house, flipping lights on as she went. "You have a nice place here, Storm."

"Thanks."

Taylor stopped at the front door and leaned against it. "If you were my lover, you better believe I'd never let you sleep alone."

The fire in Delta's stomach raged out of control and spread down her groin and thighs like molten lava. Somewhere in her, the flicker of desire ignited and Taylor's cool touch seemed to fan the flames.

"She's...uh...out of town."

Taylor's eyes smiled as she reached out to finger the Excalibur sword necklace hanging around Delta's neck. "I know, and it might make all the difference in the world."

Delta swallowed hard, but found no verbal response.

Gently tugging on the pendant, Taylor pulled Delta to her. "But then," Taylor breathed huskily into Delta's mouth, "leaving would be that much more difficult, wouldn't it?"

Their mouths inches apart, Delta allowed the fire to burn beneath her skin. "Would it?"

Inching closer, Taylor slid her arms around Delta's neck. "Another time, another place, and I could make you love me..." Slowly moving her face up to Delta's, Taylor brought her mouth to Delta's lips and kissed her very lightly, very tenderly, at first. Bracing herself with both hands against the door, Delta returned the kiss. As Taylor's lips caressed hers, they slowly transformed the gentle, tender kiss into one of eager passion. Searching Delta's mouth with her tongue, Taylor pulled Delta to her and locked her hands behind Delta's neck. For a long moment, their lips moved in the unison of two lovers who had known each other's pleasures for a lifetime. Locked in an embrace which neither fully understood, their lips slid over each other's, tongues meeting and departing, teasing, yet stretching for more. And as Taylor slowed her mouth and retracted her tongue, she took Delta's face in her hands and gazed longingly into it.

"You are one hell of a woman, Delta Stevens. You were way worth the risk of getting caught."

Delta took Taylor's hands in hers and kissed each palm. "And you, my friend, are one hell of a thief."

Gently pulling away, Taylor reached one finger up to touch the small scar on Delta's left eyebrow. "Good enough to steal your heart?" Moving her finger from the scar to Delta's lips, Taylor grinned. "Rhetorical question. I'd rather leave with my hope of the answer." Turning, Taylor ducked under Delta's arm and grabbed the knob. "We'll meet again, you know."

Delta nodded and smiled. "I sure hope so."

"And when we do, Delta, your girlfriend had better be ready to put up a fight for you." Opening the door, Taylor stood on her tiptoes and kissed Delta's cheek. "And you know what a formidable opponent I can be."

Delta held the door open for Taylor and took in her jumpsuit one last time. "Take care of yourself, Taylor. The world wouldn't be the same without you."

Winking at her, Taylor nodded. "You, too, Storm." With that, Taylor disappeared quickly into the night, leaving a faint scent of leather, her warm touch, and her passion on Delta's lips.

33

Wrapping her robe around her, Alexandria stood in front of the door. "This is a nice surprise," she said, waiting for Delta to enter. "You okay?"

Pushing quickly past Alexandria, Delta tossed her new bomber jacket on the couch. "Hang on to your hat, Counselor. The cavalry has just arrived."

Alexandria's eyes opened wide. "At five in the morning? Does the cavalry ever sleep?"

Delta grinned. "Let's just say I get by with a little help from my friends."

"Well, while you're singing old Beatle tunes, mind if I get some coffee?"

Delta followed Alexandria into the kitchen. "Please. Cream and Sweet and Low if you have it."

"Preservatives. Yuck. Do any police officers eat right?"

"Sure we do. Denny's, Winchells, The Happy Hound Dog; three balanced meals a day."

"All that cholesterol will kill you."

Delta snickered. "I seriously doubt that's what's going to take me out."

Handing Delta a steaming cup of coffee, Alexandria poured herself a cup. "Okay, what's got you all fired up?"

Delta reached over and pulled a tape from the inner pocket of her jacket. "I've got something here that is really of interest."

Cocking her head, Alexandria followed Delta into the sunken living room.

Snatching the controls, Delta popped the tape in the VCR. "First off, I'm here as one friend to another. I'm not Officer Stevens, and you're not the district attorney."

"Uh-oh."

"I can't answer any questions unless you agree that's the way we play it."

"I don't know—" Alexandria paced across the room, her robe belt flapping behind her like a tail. "You make me nervous when you cut deals like that."

Delta crossed her arms. "That's the way it has to be. Any other way won't work."

Alexandria frowned. "Fine."

"Friend to friend?"

Alexandria nodded, wrapping both hands around her mug. "Friend to friend."

Delta studied the control device for a moment before figuring out how to work the VCR.

"Is there an introduction, or is this subterfuge from beginning to end?"

"Patience. Believe me, it's well worth the wait."

Suddenly, the television screen came to life with a still picture of a very large, very white kitchen.

"Home videos?"

"Hardly. Shh," Delta admonished, turning the volume up.

"Whose house? Can you tell me that much?"

"Look."

The back of a female figure walked past the camera and opened the refrigerator before turning to face the camera. As her face came into focus, Delta paused the video. "Recognize her?"

Alexandria nodded. "That's Teresa Wainwright. Delta, what's going on?"

"You'll see. Trust me. You have to see this to believe it." Hitting the play button, Delta glanced over at Alexandria, who was staring fixedly at the TV. She watched Teresa Wainwright pace back and forth across the kitchen floor checking her watch every now and again.

"Nervous woman," Alexandria surmised.

"She has a lot to be nervous about."

Suddenly, the phone rang and Mrs. Wainwright snatched the receiver before it could complete one ring. "Yes?" she said curtly. "I received your notes and I do

not appreciate—" Mrs. Wainwright stopped suddenly
and listened to the caller. "But we had a deal. You said
twenty thousand," her voice lowered a bit. "That's what
you asked for, that's what I paid. How dare you come
back and—"

Delta paused the tape and turned to Alex, who
didn't move. "Alex?"

Slowly removing her eyes from the screen, Alexandria looked at Delta. "I'm not sure I should see the rest
of this."

"Of course you should. It's fascinating, really."
Delta clicked the button and Teresa Wainwright continued.

"...demand more! Do you know who you're dealing
with? Twenty thousand is a great deal of money..."
Again, she lowered her voice. "...to pull a trigger a few
times." Listening, she tapped a pencil on the counter.
"Look, everyone knows she saw your face, you idiot.
What were you thinking?" Pause to listen. "No, *you're*
the one in trouble, mister! She saw you, not me. So, if
you know what's good for you, you'll take the money
and get the hell out of town."

"Delta stop." Alexandria stood up and reached for
the controls. "I can't hear any more. Please." Adjusting
her robe, Alexandria paced over to the huge picture
window overlooking her garden. It was still pretty dark
outside, but the moonlight cast an eerie glow upon the
plants.

"Alex," Delta said, pausing the TV, "I'm really
sorry. I didn't mean to upset you."

"Upset me? Good God, Delta, that's an under-
statement and a half."

Taking Alexandria's hands in hers, Delta gazed
steadily into her eyes. "She planned this whole thing,
Alex. She paid that guy to shoot at you with daddy's
money. She knew your schedule, she knew the press
would be there, and she knew that getting you out of
the picture meant a victory for her husband."

"But why? Why would she do such a thing?"

"Connie gave me some background on her life, and
it appears that her daddy didn't care much for Wainwright. Connie thinks that she was willing to set you
up because her daddy would have approved of Wainwright becoming the DA."

"I feel like vomiting."

Taking Alexandria in her arms, Delta lightly caressed her back. "I won't show you the rest if you don't
want to see it."

Holding Delta tightly, Alexandria sighed. "I need
to see it. I need to get angry enough to prosecute her
ass."

Gently pulling away, Delta smiled warmly into
Alexandria's face. "That's more like it. If you need me
to pause it again, just let me know." Delta grabbed the
remote and and the video resumed.

"Look, you son of a bitch," Teresa hissed. "You're
not threatening some dumb little girl. One call to your
parole officer and you'll spend the next five years
behind bars." Mrs. Wainwright listened a little more.
"No. What you have is twenty thousand dollars. No
proof, no nothing. So stop trying to squeeze me. You
got all you're going to get, so I suggest you spend it
wisely. If you even try to snitch on me, I'll take you
down with me, you understand?" With that, Teresa
slammed down the phone, pulled out a cigarette, and
lit it with trembling hands.

"Blackmail me, you stupid fuck, and I'll see that
you rot in hell." Drawing deeply on the cigarette, Teresa stared out the window. "Should have finished her
off myself," she growled, tapping her ashes into the
sink. Puffing once more, she checked her hair in the
mirror. "Doesn't matter anymore anyway. Pendleton's
ruined." A cold grin curled up on her face. "Simply
ruined."

Delta clicked the VCR off and leaned back. For a
long, suspended minute, Alexandria stared at the
blank television set, neither blinking nor moving. Only
the gurgling sounds from an aquarium filter disturbed

the early morning silence. Then, ever so slowly, she turned. "So... what now Officer Stevens?"

"That's up to you. We can't go public with this tape because it would—"

Alexandria held her hand up. "I don't want to know how you obtained this incredible piece of filth. The less I know, the better."

Alexandria blew out a heavy breath. "What a sick woman. She's even more power hungry than her husband."

"Connie said she's done everything to get Wainwright in her daddy's favor. It seems this is the only thing that could do it."

"Daddy would be horrified if he knew his little daughter was a conspirator to commit murder." Alex slowly stirred her coffee. "Okay, we can't take this to the authorities, we can't take it to the press, so..."

Delta had a peculiar glint in her eye that did not go unnoticed. "I do have a plan."

Alexandria smiled. "Why am I not surprised. What do you want me to do?"

Delta leaned forward. She loved it when plans came together. "I want you to hold a press conference this afternoon at three. Tell them you have a suspect in the shooting and that an arrest will be made shortly."

Alexandria's eyes grew wide. "An arrest? You want me to arrest her?"

Delta shook her head, but her smile never wavered. "As a civilian at this moment, I think it best if you don't know all of the details, but trust me when I say we should have the shooter by nightfall. If worse comes to worse, and he slips through our hands, we'll settle on Mrs. Wainwright and take our best chance with her."

"Delta, blackmail is out of the—"

"For you, of course. But this isn't your operation Ms. Pendleton. It's ours."

"I won't hear of it—"

"Don't worry. Blackmail is only the backup plan, and you have nothing to do with it. There are other people I have to protect."

"What others?"

"Can't say. But this is important to others as well."

Alex nodded, smiling at Delta. "What now?"

"Now, I want you to get in the shower, make yourself more beautiful, and dress in the most powerful suit you've got. We have an election to win."

Suddenly, Alexandria's eyes glazed over as she took both of Delta's hands in hers. "I can't thank you enough."

"Don't thank me yet, Alex. Give me twenty-four hours, and I'll be eating a lobster dinner with you in the back room of Pauline's."

Alexandria grinned. "Pauline doesn't serve lobster."

"She will if you bring it in." Delta winked at her.

"You pull this off, and I'll buy the damned restaurant."

Gently retrieving her hand, Delta wiped away a single tear clinging to the corner of Alexandria's eye. "The lobster will suffice. I won't let you down, Alex."

Smiling weakly and pulling her robe closed, Alexandria nodded. "You never have, Delta Stevens. Never."

34

It was almost 7:30 in the morning when Delta arrived at Connie's. Connie answered the door dressed from cap to boot in a chauffeur's uniform.

"You rang?" Connie said in a deep voice.

"Lurch was a butler, not a chauffeur. You give me the willies wearing that thing."

Connie held her hands up for Delta to see. "But at least I still have all my digits."

"Digits, maybe; marbles, I'm not so sure. Where's all your hair?"

Connie doffed her cap to reveal a short-cropped black head. "A wig from one of our Halloween parties. You like?"

Delta shook her head. "Nope. I love you just the way you are, Chief."

"Aw, shucks."

"What time does she expect you?"

"About 8:15."

"What about him?"

"Appointments all day. He won't be a problem."

Hopping in the cab of Delta's truck, Connie set her cap in her lap and adjusted the wig. "Alex okay?"

"It shook her up, but she handled it. She's a pro."

For the next few minutes, they rode in silence until Delta turned up the street toward Sal's house. Out in front sat a shiny, black limousine. Sal was leaning against it, reading a magazine.

"She's ready to roll," Sal said, rolling up a copy of *Today's Weapons* magazine and putting it in her back pocket.

"You're incredible, Sal," Connie said, hugging the little woman. "You finished her so soon?"

Sal shrugged. "I called in a few favors and Josh was able to get me one with almost everything we need."

"She's a beaut," Delta said, caressing the chrome bumper.

"She's okay for a limo."

"We should have her back to you in a few hours, Sal, and then we'll set a date for that dinner we owe you."

"Owe, shmoe. When Josh and I go into the PI business, you can pay me back with all sorts of favors."

Checking her watch, Delta nudged Connie. "We should be off."

"Go get 'em, gals. Oh, and Con, just flip the little red switch on the door and it will activate the locks on all four doors. The button on the console will bring up the glass, and the knob will adjust the speaker volume. Let's see...anything else?"

"The keys?"

"In the ignition. Good luck."

Connie smiled. "Thanks."

"You guys are an adventure. Oh, I gotta run. I'm expecting a fax from South America. Call me about dinner." After hugging Delta and Connie goodbye, Sal dashed into the house.

"I sure do like her," Delta said.

"I know. What's not to like?"

"You ready?"

Connie nodded. "And you?"

"I relish the opportunity of scaring the hell out of Mrs. Wainwright. Mess with *my* friends, will she?"

"That, my dear, was Mrs. Wainwright's greatest mistake."

35

Delta watched the limousine from a safe distance. It wouldn't be much longer before Teresa Wainwright entered it for the ride of her life. Delta hummed a seventies sitcom theme song as she popped open the lid to her Chapstick. She was confident that this would save Alexandria's career and keep Connie out of harm's way. Squeezing Teresa Wainwright would be more fun than Delta imagined, and if she had to, she'd squeeze until she couldn't squeeze anymore.

Two minutes later, Delta saw the woman who had risked Alexandria's life and career saunter past Connie and say something to her before ducking her head into the back of the limo. Connie snapped Teresa's door closed. Delta waited until the limousine pulled into the street before following them.

Inside the truck, Delta grinned.

Less than twenty-four hours ago, she'd felt defeated; she'd lost a battle. Maybe she had. But in the end, she would win the war, and that was all that mattered: the end. She remembered a conversation with Captain Henry about the ends justifying the means.

She smiled to herself as she thought about the ending to a different story in the early chapters of her life. It was the bottom of the seventh, one out, her team was down two to one, with runners on second and third, and Delta was up. Delta's coach called a time out and motioned her over.

"You know they're going to walk you," her coach had said, putting her arm around Delta and turning her back to the field. Delta had a .312 batting average for the season and surpassed that at Nationals thus far. Walking her was the wisest choice.

"I know."

"I want you to let the first three pitches go by. On the fourth, I want you to get your bat out there and lay down a squeeze."

Delta couldn't believe what she was hearing. "Suicide or safety?"

Her coach smiled. Safety had never been Lynn's style, and she wasn't about to start changing now. "Suicide. They'll never expect it. Tronvig's been in a slump the whole tournament. We need to tie this thing up right now."

Delta had looked into Lynn Eubanks' eyes at that moment and knew she could do it. Her whole life had been filled with women who believed in her. No wonder she felt the awesome responsibility of always coming through for others. It was her way of paying the universe back; her way of acknowledging that although she was born gifted, it took many, many people to mold her gifts into useful skills. Lynn Eubanks went against the grain that day; she made a call some coaches applauded and some criticized as too risky. But she wanted the game tied, and she put that responsibility in the hands of a woman she knew could come through. And come through, Delta did.

As she stepped into the batter's box, she noted the first pitch was far out of the strike zone; it was an obvious walk. Setting the bat on her shoulder to give the pretense that she was prepared to be intentionally walked, Delta watched as the second pitch was thrown just a little closer to the strike zone. If the next two pitches were anywhere close, laying down a drag would be a piece of cake.

The third ball whizzed by practically in the same spot as the second. If there was one thing Delta had learned in all her years behind the plate, it was that intentional walks were very difficult for most pitchers, since accuracy was something they spent their lives working on.

With the bat still on her shoulder, Delta watched the wind up and the delivery before dropping the bat with her left hand and starting out of the box. When the ball hit the bat, there wasn't one player on the opposing team ready to field it as it trickled down the third base line. The pitcher, in a pitiful attempt to make a play, overthrew first, allowing both runs to score and leaving a triumphant Delta standing on second as her coach rushed out to hug her. It had been one of the most exciting days of Delta's life and would forever remind her that rules and conventions were made for others, but not for Delta Stevens.

So, here she was once more. Pulling a baseball cap over her head and putting on clear, wire-framed glasses, Delta followed the limo for about a mile before seeing Connie steer over to the side of the road.

Pulling onto a side street and then walking up to the limo, Delta ripped the door open and sat next to Teresa before the shaken woman could utter a sound.

"Hi there," Delta said, closing the door. As she did, an ominous click reverberated throughout the car.

"Driver!" Teresa said, tapping the glass. "Get this person out of here this instant!"

Connie pulled her cap over her eyes and pretended to sleep. Teresa simply stared at Delta before raising her hands in the air. "I...I don't have any money with me."

"Neither do I," Delta quipped, tapping the glass. Without looking, Connie adjusted her cap and continued driving.

"Oh...my...goodness..." Mrs. Wainwright said, grabbing her chest.

"You wouldn't know goodness if it bit you on the ass."

Teresa went pale and backed as far away from Delta as she could. "Please, don't hurt me. My husband—"

"Is a jackass, Mrs. Wainwright. And you needn't worry that we're going to harm you." Delta pulled the videotape from her inner jacket pocket and popped it in the VCR tucked in the far corner of the limo. "I have something here that I think you'll be quite interested in. I want you to watch it in complete silence, and when we're through, then we can talk. Do you understand?"

Teresa Wainwright nodded and started for her purse. "I need a cigarette."

"And give me your secondhand smoke? I think not. Just watch the video." Pressing play, Delta leaned back into the soft, black leather. As the tape flickered on the screen, Delta watched Mrs. Wainwright go completely white as she saw herself walk into the camera view.

"What is this?"

"I said without a word, Mrs. Wainwright. Don't make me have to gag you."

Ball one.

When the video came to the part where she was speaking to the shooter, she raised one hand to her mouth to stifle an anguished yelp. "Turn it off."

"Nope. No can do. The best part is yet to come."

Teresa Wainwright watched the remainder of the tape in complete silence. When it was over, she cleared her throat and said in a voice indistinguishable from her own, "How much?"

Ejecting the tape and placing it back in her pocket, Delta crossed her legs. "How much what?"

"Please. Let's not play games, Ms—"

Delta smiled. "No, that would be Agent," Delta replied, pulling Connie's fake FBI badge out and showing it to Teresa. The cool, haughty arrogance in her eyes went out like a light.

Ball two.

"I see," she said coldly, ineffectively trying to hide her fear.

"I don't think you do." Putting the badge away, Delta turned and faced Teresa Wainwright. "Have you any idea what the sentence is for conspiracy to commit murder?"

"I'm married to a lawyer, Agent—"

"Storm. Agent Storm."

"Well, Agent Storm, I am aware of many things concer—"

"Then you must know that this tape is going to send you to the Big House and destroy your husband's career. You're going to jail, Teresa, and if we can prove it, so will your husband."

"No! He had nothing to do with this. I swear! He would die if he knew...if..."

"I'm afraid you won't really enjoy the prison cuisine, Teresa, and the weekly strip-searches—"

Teresa narrowed her gaze at Delta. "Please, that's enough. What is it you want from me?"

Ball three.

Delta's grin spread. "Want? What makes you think I want anything?"

"It's pretty clear you aren't arresting me."

"Not at this moment. There may be something else you can do for us."

Teresa Wainwright looked down at her hands and nodded. "Anything. I'll do anything, just don't tell my husband."

"We want an arrest, Mrs. Wainwright, but not necessarily yours. Someone is going to jail, and it's up to you who that person is going to be. Are you picking up what I'm putting down?"

Teresa Wainwright looked up at Delta with tears in her eyes and nodded.

"I want the trigger man, Teresa. I don't care how you do it or what it costs you, but turning him over to us is the only way you'll maintain your freedom."

"But he'll implicate me."

Delta shrugged. "What does he have on you? He's an ex-con, Teresa. It would be your word, your family's word over that of a convicted felon."

Teresa stared out the window. "I suppose."

"Take your chances, Teresa, but I guarantee someone is going to jail."

"But I have no idea where to locate him."

"Don't be stupid. Of course you do. He's still in town. He's still trying to bleed you dry. Right now, you're his own personal bank. He'll stay in town until he's certain you won't pay him any more. If you nail him for us, I'll destroy the tapes. Understand?"

Teresa nodded. "He goes by the name Derek Conroy, but I don't think that's his real name. Maybe his probation officer will know."

"Do you know his name?"

"No, but I can tell you Derek was let out of Folsom eleven days before the shooting, if that helps."

"That helps." Delta flipped open the cellular phone that was laying in the console. "Tony? Check out all parolees with release dates eleven days before the shooting. He currently goes by Derek Conroy." Delta moved her mouth from the phone. "With a C?" she asked Teresa, who nodded. "Yes. Dig up an address, his parole officer, any living relatives in the area, and all visitors while he was locked up. Thanks." To Teresa she said, "the driver is going to drop you off at a friend's house for a while."

"But I have an appointment."

"No, you don't. You'll stay in our custody until Mr. Conroy is apprehended. At which time, you will receive the tape and be free to go home."

"Why can't I go now? You have everything I know."

Leaning forward, Delta sneered at her. "Because I don't trust you, Teresa. You're a snake, and I'd rather not have you slithering around fucking things up for us. I need you to keep your mouth shut and stay out of our way."

Teresa Wainwright sighed loudly and stifled a sob.

"Driver," Delta said, tapping the window. "We're ready."

As the limo sliced its way to Sal's house, Delta leaned back and smiled.

She had just laid down the perfect suicide squeeze.

36

For the remainder of the morning, Delta and Connie called in every favor owed them. It wouldn't be enough to just haul Conroy in, Alexandria's office needed to get the credit for the collar. About twenty calls later, it was just before 2:00 p.m. when Derek Conroy, a k a David Seltser, was brought in for questioning. Delta and Connie were so far removed from the scene that no one but those who owed them favors knew they had a hand in the arrest, and none of them was about to say anything to anybody.

Shortly after five, Alexandria called a press conference to announce that her office had a suspect in custody. Delta, meanwhile, sat on her couch with a cat in her lap, a Diet Pepsi in her hand, and her eyes glued to the TV. She couldn't help but grin when Alexandria began her speech.

"My office is very proud of the work done by our investigating teams to bring in a suspect." Alexandria paused for affect. "The public should know that we will work even harder to prosecute criminals who victimize our citizens, whether a public figure, a merchant, a househusband, or anyone else who wants to walk our streets unafraid. We will do everything in our power to keep our neighborhoods and our communities safe."

Flashbulbs popped, reporters thrust microphones toward her face, and Delta smiled, knowing that she had done the right thing. Alexandria was good. Exceptionally so. Wainwright would need a miracle to beat her now.

Delta hit one of the pre-programmed buttons on her phone, then pressedthe receiver to her ear.

"Isn't this great?" Connie said, without benefit of a hello.

"Fantastic. Looks like we can rest easy until the next time."

"Who got the collar?"

"One of Leonard's guys was on loan. Their team found the weapon in Conroy's apartment. They're waiting for a ballistics match."

"Think he'll go down alone?"

"I doubt it. He'll squeal like a stuck piggy, but I don't think they'll be able to get anything on the Mrs."

"Hey, thank Sal for me next time you see her, okay? We couldn't have done this without her."

"Will do."

Delta started to reply when there was a knock on her door. "Someone's at the door. Do me a favor, will you, and call Alex's office. Leave a message that says Pauline's at 8:00 and bring the claws."

"Claws? Never mind. I don't want to know."

Hanging up the phone and dumping a disgruntled furball onto the floor, Delta peered through the peephole before opening the door. A messenger in a blue jumpsuit stood at the door with a package in one hand and a clipboard in the other.

"Yes?"

"Ace delivery, ma'am. Package for an Officer Stevens."

Delta signed the clipboard and took the package. For a moment, she thought it might be from Megan, but the writing on the envelope told her otherwise. Opening the lavender envelope, Delta grinned. On the front of the card was a picture of Mrs. Emma Peele from *The Avengers* old television show. She was poised to strike and wore a drop-dead, black leather jumpsuit similar to the one Taylor wore. On the inside of the card, it read:

To my favorite cop—

If you're ever in Rio–

Look me up–

You're the best–

In crime and passion—

T

Opening the small package, Delta stared down at one of the most incredibly beautiful bracelets she'd ever seen. It was her name spelled out with diamonds for the *D*, emeralds for the *E*, lapis for the *L*, topaz for the *T* and amethysts for the *A*. The stones were so perfectly cut that they sparkled like a kaleidoscope.

"Geez," Delta uttered, gently lifting the bracelet from the velvet box. Underneath was a tiny note that read: "Please keep. This one I paid for."

Staring down at the colorful bracelet, Delta didn't know whether to laugh or cry. It was too beautiful for words.

"Damn you, Taylor," Delta said to herself as she lightly ran her fingertips over the gems. As if that kiss wasn't already burned into her memory forever.

Setting the card on her roll-top desk, Delta started for the bedroom. She had a dinner date with a soon-to-be-re-elected DA, who was sure to notice the beautiful bracelet Delta would be wearing.

Rio? Delta smiled. If only.

37

When Delta arrived at Pauline's, she poked her head into the kitchen and nodded at the owner, who waved and jerked her head toward the back room. "Your new lady friend is in the back," Pauline said in a conspiratorial tone. "Don't worry, sweety. It's our little secret."

Delta started to reply, but thought better of it. Let Pauline enjoy a little intrigue. "Is that for me?" Delta asked, pointing to the large bubbling pot.

"Your lady friend brought it. I think—"

"I already know what you think, Pauline, you troublemaker, you." Kissing the old woman's cheek, Delta slid into the back room.

Immediately, she came to a stop. The entire room was lit by candles, and there were dozens of different kinds of bouquets scattered about the room. Sitting regally and wearing a black, scoop-neck dress with a most dazzling smile was Alexandria.

"Well?"

Delta didn't move. "I don't know what to say."

Alexandria rose and took Delta's hands in hers. "Please, sit down. Can I get you something to drink?"

"Drink?"

"You said champagne and lobster. You delivered your end, and I'm delivering mine." Alexandria sat down and poured two flutes of bubbly. "To a friendship that apparently knows no bounds."

Delta clinked her flute to Alexandria's. They pinged together, and Delta let the bubbles tickle her nose. Lowering her glass, Delta smiled over the two fat candles flickering in Alexandria's face. She looked radiant.

"I don't know how to thank you, Delta. You've very likely saved my career, which ranks right up there with saving my life."

"Then, that makes us even. Not too long ago, you did the same for me."

Alexandria grinned. "I'm glad we're on the same side."

"Me, too."

Setting her glass down, Alexandria took a serious turn. "Delta, don't you ever find your job...monotonous?"

Delta cocked her head. "No. Why?"

Alexandria leaned forward. "I don't want an answer right now, but I have a proposition for you. It's something I've been thinking about for some time."

Delta swallowed. "A proposition?"

"I've watched you for two years now. I like the way you work, the way you think, the way you never give up. And to be honest, Delta, I think you're talents are being terribly wasted pounding a beat."

"But I love my beat."

Alexandria flashed a patronizing grin. "*You* make your beat exciting, Delta. You go above and beyond others. But your mind and your talents could be put to better use."

"Doing what?"

"I want you to come work for me."

Delta's jaw dropped. "For you?"

"Yes. If I am re-elected, I'm going to need a special investigator. Ron Dearing is retiring, and I believe you're the perfect person for the job."

"Special investigator?" Delta looked down at the champagne glass. If it was still full, why was her head was spinning. "You want me to be a dick?"

"I want you to just consider the possibility. Toss the idea around with Connie."

"Connie?" Delta's eyebrows shot up.

"Of course. I certainly can't break up the set. You two would make excellent partners."

"Partners?"

Alexandria laughed. "You're beginning to sound like a parrot. I realize separating you two would be like trying to split an atom, so I am prepared to offer you both a position."

"Me and Chief partners?" Delta felt a rush tickle the base of her neck. "What about Carducci?"

"It's only a matter of time before SWAT takes him and you have to start all over. Why not start with Connie as your partner."

Delta leaned back and let a sigh escape her lips. "Geez."

"There would be no uniform, fewer rules, and a heck of a good boss."

Delta nodded and tossed back her champagne. She and Connie partners? Alexandria her boss? Someone pinch her and wake her up.

"I'll have to discuss this with Connie."

"I expected that you would."

Suddenly, Pauline came in carrying two steaming plates. "Enjoy," she said as she set down the plates. The lobster looked delectable. As Delta reached for her plate, her bracelet swung in the light.

"What a beautiful bracelet, Delta. Is it new?"

Delta's face reddened. "Uh...let's just say it came with the tape."

"Really?"

"Yes, and that, Counselor, is all you're going to get from me."

Alexandria grinned mischievously. "Darn. And I was hoping for so much more."

Delta lowered her fork and smiled at Alexandria. "We do make a good team, don't we?"

"You and Connie?"

Delta blushed. "Yeah. But I meant you and me."

Taking Delta's hand, Alexandria squeezed it. "Yes, Delta Stevens, we most certainly do."

38

When Delta finally got home, she was stuffed, tired, and she had a champagne headache. So much had happened in the last twenty-four hours. She needed a bath and wanted to sleep for the next two days.

When the phone rang, Delta looked at it and considered letting the machine pick it up, but she didn't want to miss it if was Megan.

"Hello?"

"Delta?" The voice was unfamiliar.

"Yes. Who is this?"

"This is Elizabeth. Megan's friend in Costa Rica."

Delta gripped the phone hard. "Is something wrong? Where's Megan?"

"Well...that's what I'm calling about."

Delta's heart picked up speed. "What? What is it?"

"I don't quite know how to tell you this, but..."

"But what?" Delta said impatiently. "Where's Megan?"

"I don't know."

"What do you mean, 'you don't know'?"

The line was quiet except for a muffled sob. "Oh, God, Delta, Megan is missing."

PARADIGM
Publishing
Company

Elevating Lesbian Voices

Books Published by Paradigm Publishing:

Taken By Storm by Linda Kay Silva
(Lesbian Fiction/Mystery)
A Delta Stevens police action novel, intertwining mystery, love, and personal insight. The first in the series.
ISBN 0-9628595-1-6 $8.95
". . . not to be missed!" — *East Bay Alternative*

Expenses by Penny S. Lorio
(Lesbian Romance)
A novel that deals with the cost of living and the price of loving. ISBN 0-9628595-0-8 $8.95
"I laughed, I cried, I wanted more!" — Marie Kuda, *Gay Chicago Magazine*

Tory's Tuesday by Linda Kay Silva (Lesbian Fiction)
Set in Bialystok, Poland during 1939 Nazi occupation. Marissa, a Pole, and Elsa, a Jew, are two lovers who struggle not only to stay together, but to stay alive in Auschwitz concentration camp during the horrors of World War II. ISBN 0-9628595-3-2 $8.95

"Obviously knowledgeable about the period, Silva builds a historical framework around her various characters, drawing in the reader with her steady prose and effective dialogue." — Terri de la Peña, *Lambda Book Report*

"*Tory's Tuesday* is a book that should be widely read — with tissues close at hand — and long remembered." — Andrea L.T. Peterson, *The Washington Blade*

Practicing Eternity by Carol Givens and L. Diane Fortier
(Nonfiction/Healing/Lesbian and Women's Studies)

The powerful, moving testament of partners in a long-term lesbian relationship in the face of Carol's diagnosis with cervical cancer. It is about women living, loving, dying together. It is about transformation of the self, relationships, and life. **Finalist for the *Lambda Literary Awards!*** ISBN 0-9628595-2-4 $10.95

"*Practicing Eternity* is one of the most personal and moving stories I have read in years." —Margaret Wheat, *We The People*

"That they . . . recorded every deed and every thought of this harrowing period of their life together is the richness and reward of this book, the essence that makes the reading of it a matter of conscious decision for all of us." — Barbara Grier, *Lambda Book Report*

"I more than recommend it . . . it should be required reading." — Shelly Roberts, *Arts, Entertainment and Travel*

Seasons of Erotic Love by Barbara Herrera
(Lesbian Erotica)

A soft and sensual collection of lesbian erotica with a social conscience. Herrera leaves us empowered with the diversity in the lesbian community.
ISBN 0-9628595-4-0 $8.95

". . . the sex is juicy and in full supply." —Nedhara Landers, *Lambda Book Report*

Evidence of the Outer World by Janet Bohac
(Women's Short Stories)

Janet Bohac brings us a powerful collection of feminist and women centered fiction that examines relationships in this symmetry of short stories.
ISBN 0-9628595-5-9 $8.95

"...compelling short stories. Bohac made me care. I was sorry that the book had to end." —Barbara Heath, Women's Studies Librarian, Wayne State University

The Dyke Detector
(How to Tell the Real Lesbians from Ordinary People)
by Shelly Roberts/Illustrated by Yani Batteau
(Lesbian Humor)

The Dyke Detector is lesbian humor at its finest: poking fun at our most intimate patterns and outrageous stereotypes with a little bit of laughter for everybody, single or coupled. This is side-splitting fun from syndicated columnist Shelly Roberts.
ISBN 0-9628595-6-7 $7.95

"What a riot! A must read for all lesbians. Brilliant!" — JoAnn Loulan

"*The Dyke Detector* is the funniest necessity since we used to wear green on Thursdays. It's the perfect handbook in the confusion of these post-modernist times." —Jewelle Gomez

Storm Shelter by Linda Kay Silva
(Lesbian Mystery)

Officer Delta Stevens is back in the second book in the series. Delta and her best friend, Connie Rivera, again join together in a deadly race against time. Only now, they must enter the complex world of computer games to solve the mystery before the murderer can strike again. ISBN 0-9628595-8-3 $10.95

"A lesbian 'Silence of the Lambs'"—Catherine McKenzie, *Queensland Pride*, Australia

EMPATH by Michael Holloway
(Gay Fiction/Sci-fi)

This is a story of industrial politics, and how one man with supernatural abilities is thrust into this vortex to single-handedly eliminate the AIDS epidemic. This is a book about AIDS that has a **happy** ending and it will keep you on the edge of your seat!
ISBN 0-9628595-7-5 $10.95

"...brilliantly written, fast paced and highly entertaining..."—Catherine McKenzie, *Queensland Pride*, Australia

". . . read[s] at a breakneck pace." —Robert Starner, *Lambda Book Report*

Hey Mom, Guess What! (*150 Ways to Tell Your Mother*) by Shelly Roberts/Illustrated by Melissa Sweeney
(Lesbian/Gay Humor)

The Dyke Detector does it again! This time best-selling humor author, Shelly Roberts, trains her razor-sharp wit on another favorite pastime for all gays and lesbians: coming out to Mom. Whether. When. Where. What. And how! When Roberts writes, we all laugh at ourselves. ISBN 0-9628595-9-1 $8.95

"Don't call home without *Hey Mom, Guess What!* A fabulously funny book." —Karen Williams, Comic

---

A Ship in the Harbor by Mary Heron Dyer
(Lesbian Romance/Mystery)

A murder mystery unfolds within Oregon's recent climate of increasing homophobia and anti-choice fervor. It is the story of a woman discovering how to live on her own, how to fight for herself and what she believes in, and how to release the past and love again. ISBN 1-882587-00-6 $8.95

"...tender, moving, interesting and intriguing..."
—Catherine McKenzie, *Queensland Pride*, Australia

Golden Shores by Helynn Hoffa
(Lesbian Romance)

An oceanographer, an artist, and an actress are soon caught up in an emotion-charged triangle. Romance is set against the backdrop of international intrigue involving top-secret charts of potentially valuable marine mineral deposits. ISBN 1-882587-01-4 $9.95

Weathering the Storm by Linda Kay Silva
(Lesbian Mystery)

In the third of this renowned mystery series, Officer Delta Stevens again joins with Connie Rivera and hastens to save children abducted by a child pornography ring. With Silva's name on it, you know it's a thriller. ISBN 1-882587-02-2

"...well written, absorbing...I thoroughly recommend..."—R. Lynne Watson, *Megascene*

Make News! Make Noise! (How to Get Publicity for Your Book) by Shelly Roberts
(Author How-to in Book Marketing)

Shelly Roberts shares her book marketing tips! This is a road map of what any author can do on a limited budget to spur book sales. ISBN 1-882587-03-0 $5.95

"If you want to get on TV or radio, this is the book for you!"—Meg Porter, Producer, Special Projects, WSVN TV

Storm Front by Linda Kay Silva
(Lesbian Mystery)

New release! Fourth in the Delta Stevens series! An assassin is after District Attorney Alexandria Pendleton and an international jewel thief is plaguing Delta's beat. The thief is a woman attracted to more than jewels—she's doing everything she can to steal Delta's heart. ISBN 1-882587-07-3 $10.95

Rites of First Blood by Karen Dale Wolman
(Lesbian Adventure)

New release! Sara Hansen, a NY lesbian and doctor, journeys to the Amazon jungle to research a plant that helps boost the immune system. While hiking up the bank of an Amazon tributary one morning, she is wounded in a hunting accident and a matriarchal hunting and gathering tribe encounter their first Westerner. This is an adventure you will not want to miss! ISBN 1-882587-08-1 $10.95

"...a novel of contemporary issues, intrigue, romance, and humor."—Terri de la Peña

Paradigm Publishing appreciates your support. Our books are available at your local bookstore or can be ordered directly from the publisher. We would like to remind you that we support independent—especially women owned—bookstores, and we urge you to support those in your area.

You may correspond with any of our authors by sending letters to them in care of Paradigm Publishing at the address below.

Ordering Information

California residents add appropriate sales tax for your area.

Postage and Handling—Domestic Orders: $2.50 for the first book/$1 for each additional book. Foreign Orders: $3.50 for the first book/$2 for each additional book (surface mail).

Make check or money order, in U.S. currency, payable to: **Paradigm Publishing Company, 2323 Broadway, Studio 202, San Diego, CA 92102.**